Praise for Unfurling the Sails

"*Unfurling the Sails* propels readers on an exhilarating voyage across untamed oceans and through uncharted territories. In this captivating young adult adventure, Branson masterfully constructs a vibrant world that is both thrilling and deeply immersive. This book unfurls a narrative as vast and unpredictable as the ocean itself, creating an epic that will pull in readers and not let go until the final page is turned."

Katlyn Duncan, award-winning author of *Soul Taken*

"I love this book! There is excitement at every page turn. Grey is relatable because she has insecurities we all feel at 14, but she has the knowledge and where-withal to take command of a challenging situation. Formidable!"

Emily Auerswald, Upper School librarian, Greenwich Country Day School

"I LOVED IT! I don't usually like books but this one really blew me away. I liked Grey as a character and I kinda wish we were friends in real life."

Lia, 14

"It's been three years since that awful summer when Grey Shima and her twin brothers were held hostage. Now, Grey is fourteen years old, and is determined to put the past behind her and show her mother (the formidable Kat Wallace) that she's a capable young woman by taking part in The Great Sea Race.

When disaster strikes her sloop, she finds herself face-to-face with the person she despises most on the planet, Ashton Abernathy. Can she work through her mistrust? Or will she find herself in even more trouble than being marooned at sea?

Unfurling the Sails is Branson's first venture into Young Adult fiction, and it is an absolute triumph. The continued story of Kat Wallace and her daughter Grey Shima is a tale that will not only tug your heart strings but fill you with joy."

Sally Altass, author of *The Witch Laws* and book
reviewer at The Indie Book Nook

"Sarah Branson's novel, *A Merry Life,* is a rousing page-turner. Her tough-as-nails heroine is relatable and genuine, and the plot is action-packed from start to end. Great for any reader ready to buckle in for a lightning fast ride of a book!"

— Andrea Vanryken, author

"Swashbuckling, vengeance and heart - all wrapped up in one heck of a strong woman."

— Sally Altass, author of *The Witch Laws* and Reedsy.com reviewer

"Readers who enjoy a rollicking adventure firmly rooted in family interactions ... will find that *Navigating the Storm* comes steeped in a battle between love and loyalty in which Kat reconsiders her ultimate goals."

—Diane Donovan, Senior Reviewer, *Midwest Book Review*

"I absolutely adored *A Merry Life*.... If possible, *Navigating the Storm* is even better than the first instalment in Kat's tale. Branson isn't afraid to rip your heart out or to make you laugh."

—Sally Altass, author of *The Witch Laws* and reviewer, Reedsy.com

"This is an incredibly impactful, emotional, entertaining, funny, heart-tugging book."

—Martha Bullen, author and owner, Bullen Publishing Services

"*Navigating the Storm* is not your typical pirate book. Rather, it is a blend of science fiction with steampunk and cyberpunk interlaced with realistic human emotions and experiences set in the twenty-fourth century. Action is high paced and riveting. Kat matures as the book progresses; hitting rock-bottom makes her stronger and savvier, and puts her on firmer ground to face whatever lies in the future."

—Cindy Vallar, editor, *Pirates & Privateers*

"Kat Wallace, wife, mother, pirate. The order probably should be mother, pirate, wife. Kat's a strong woman who knows her priorities. Her marriage is faltering, her attempts at destroying the man who kept her in captivity for many years keep falling short, and now she has someone living with her family to watch her children thanks to threats. Even then … well, you know something has to happen. The anticipation kept me turning the pages.

Burn the Ship is as action-packed and entertaining as the first two books in the series, but in the third novel we see Kat growing as a person, actually feeling her feelings—yikes—and this deepens her personality and increases the stakes in her relationships. *The Pirates of New Earth* novels are fast-paced, engaging, other world creative, and leave you cheering for Kat at every turn."

– Jacqueline Boulden, Author of *Her Past Can't Wait*

"This is Kat's third outing, and each book has gotten better and better. Branson writes her heart and soul into these astonishing novels, bringing the reader joy and heartbreak in equal measure. [Kat is] the most imperfect heroine that I've ever had the pleasure to read, and it's what makes her so compelling. It's a brilliant narrative on how you can never really know who someone is behind closed doors. I only hope Kat's story is to continue. The snippets that were revealed about her past life were so heart wrenching – and with enough left unsaid that leaves you thirsting for more. Bravo, Sarah."

– Sally Altass, The Indie Book Nook and Author of *The Witch Laws*

"*Blow the Man Down* caps Sarah Branson's wonderful, exciting *Pirates of New Earth* series perfectly. The deeply dimensioned characters leap off the page, the action is nonstop, and the thrilling ending more than satisfies. A real crowd-pleaser. I'm sorry the series had to end!"

– Andrea Vanryken, author and editor

"Don't mess with Kat Wallace! *Blow the Man Down* is the thrilling fourth installment in the *Pirates of New Earth* series. This action-packed novel will keep you on the edge of your seat with suspense and adventure as Kat strikes back when her family is threatened. Branson's writing is engaging and concise, making *Blow the Man Down* a fast and captivating read. You won't be able to put this book down until the very last page. It is a must-read for fans of action, adventure, and romance."

— Brittany Coffman, Kat aficionado and midwife,
Aglow Midwifery

"Sweet New Earth—the Pirates series culminates in spectacular fashion! Rob Abernathy is one of the most hateable villains in modern literature, and now he seeks the flesh of Kat's precious loved ones. Even if you're a peace-loving pacifist, you will pray for Abernathy to suffer ultimate pain when…or if…Kat gets her vengeful hands on him. This story is more riveting than anything you can watch on Netflix tonight."

— David Aretha, award-winning author

"Kat Wallace has come a long way since the day she climbed as a stowaway into Teddy Bosch's vessel. But the shadow of her past is always looming. Strap yourself in for a rip-roaring, riveting ride through New Earth as Kat, Matty and the Bosch Pirate Force charge through the skies with vengeance in their hearts."

– Sally Altass, The Indie Book Nook and author of
The Witch Laws

"*Blow The Man Down* dishes out the divine retribution and karmic justice that we've been patiently waiting for. Accentuated with signature Branson shock value, it's impossible to step away from this book once the first pages are opened. The only remaining question is 'what does Kat do next?'"

– Iris Hermann, wordsmithing farmer

"Kat Wallace, Bosch pirate, is at it again, swashbuckling her way through an art heist and doing her bit to stymie those trading in slaves and freeing those in bondage. Mum of three kids, she can instantly switch from doting mother to knife wielding, gun toting pirate who doesn't hesitate to wallop those who seek to profit from human suffering. Come on board for a rollercoaster, page-turning ride! Kat Wallace, you have done the Bosch pirate guild proud, and I will certainly miss you."

– Steven Savanna, author of the *Hotel Exotica* future
crime series

"[In] *Blow the Man Down*, Sarah Branson builds a story that centers not just on Kat's strength, but the emotional currents and forces that buffet those around her. As Kat begins to realize the real impact of past, present, and future decisions, readers absorb a powerful crescendo of events that challenge her and solidify her life purpose. Sarah Branson creates just the right special blend of action and discovery that keeps Kat growing, evolving, and challenged to do and be more.

Women who look for characters that can serve as role models for adaptation and courage will find Kat's dilemmas emotionally compelling. Libraries that choose *Blow the Man Down* should consider the series as a whole. Each book builds another piece of Kat's character and world. Together, the books create a world both realistic and thoroughly absorbing. Book clubs will find many discussion points sparked by the series."

— D. Donovan, Senior Reviewer, *Midwest Book Review*

"This is the ending we've been waiting for! The first book in the *Pirates of New Earth* series starts off with a breathtaking chase and the last book ends up with another one. In between we watch Kat Wallace struggle with her past as a thrall and her burning passion for preventing others from the same fate. And of course, she wants to make the man who imprisoned her pay— with his life.

Kat goes through loves, losses, and redemption, and matures from a young woman to a mother with three children. Three children that her former owner decides are now his. I hate to see this series end because I've enjoyed all four books so much. Branson's creative mind dreams up details, settings, characters, and challenges that vividly bring this series to life. It's been five stars from me all the way."

— Jacqueline Boulden, author of *Her Past Can't Wait*

UNFURLING THE SAILS

A Grey Shima Adventure

SARAH BRANSON

SOONER STARTED PRESS

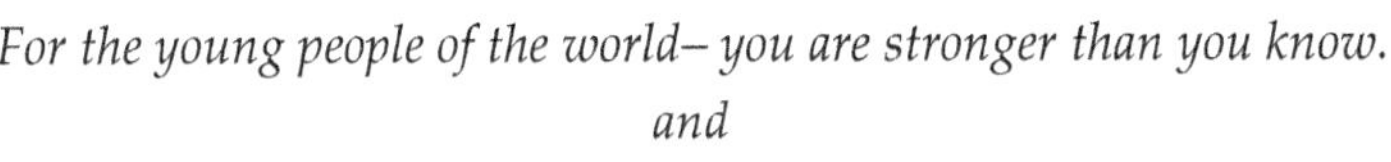

For the young people of the world– you are stronger than you know.
and
For Rick, who makes even the stormiest sea seem like an adventure.

A sailor is an artist whose medium is the wind.

Webb Chiles

Author's Note

Unfurling the Sails takes place on New Earth, three hundred years in the future, after decades of fires, floods, famine, and pandemics remade Old Earth. New Earth, and specifically Bosch, were first introduced to readers in my award-winning debut novel, *A Merry Life*, the first book in the *Pirates of New Earth* series. *Pirates* is a rollicking action-adventure series that follows Kat Wallace from her days as an enslaved person through her rise to leadership in the Bosch Pirate Force. Throughout the series, her former enslaver, Rob Abernathy, seeks to regain control over Kat.

Bosch is a fictional mid-sized island off the coast of the Central Continent of New Earth, or what is today's North America. It was settled by a group of pirates who traded their expertise as seafaring marauders for a homeland. As the technology allowed, they became expert pilots of the airships of the twenty-fourth century, which enabled them to deliver Glitter, a mind-altering substance found only on Bosch, to an ever-increasing customer base throughout New Earth.

Grey Shima, the protagonist of *Unfurling the Sails*, is the eldest daughter of Kat Wallace. She appears as an infant in *A*

Merry Life and grows throughout the series. *Unfurling the Sails* begins three years after the close of the final book in the *Pirates of New Earth* series.

If you enjoyed meeting Grey and would like to know more about Bosch and Kat Wallace, I encourage you to read the series. But be aware, the series was written with adult readers in mind and as such deals with adult issues including grooming, sexual assault, suicide, and violent death, all heavily peppered with a pirate's vocabulary of swearing.

In the series you will meet Grey's papa, Takai Shima, her brothers Kik and Mac Shima, the monstrous Rob Abernathy, and very briefly, his son, Ashton Abernathy, along with a delightful ensemble of supporting characters who, along with Kat, will take you on a multi-year journey of action and adventure, revenge, and romance as you explore this exciting place called New Earth.

But you don't have to read the series first to enjoy *Unfurling the Sails*. So, for now, happy reading and be sure to drop me a line at author.sarah.branson@gmail.com and let me know your reaction to the first adventure of Grey Shima.

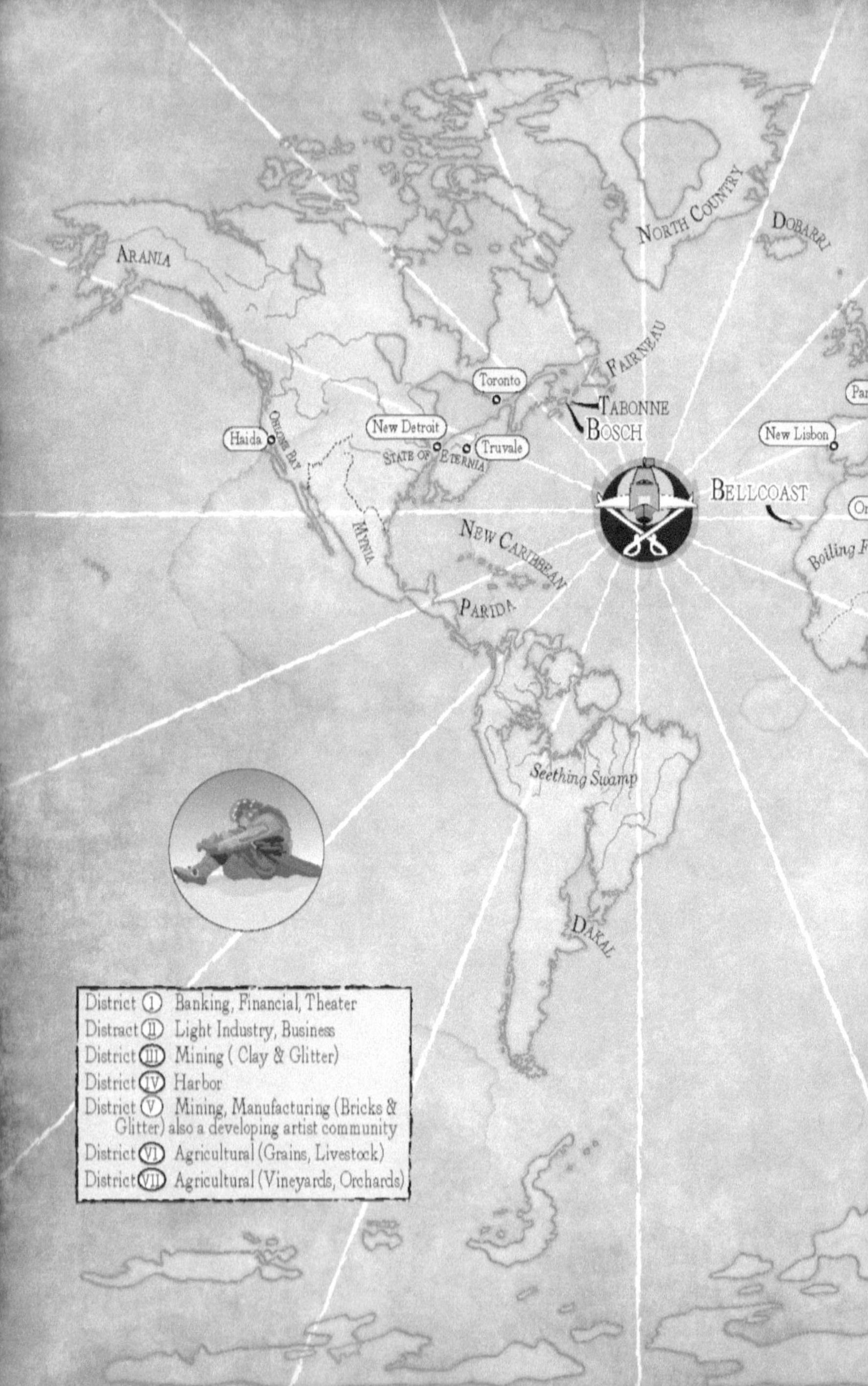

ARANIA
NORTH COUNTRY
DOBARRI
FAIRNEAU
Toronto
TABONNE
BOSCH
Par
New Lisbon
Haida
New Detroit
ORLONE BAY
Truvale
BELLCOAST
STATE OF ETERNIA
Or
MYNIA
Boiling F
NEW CARIBBEAN
PARIDA
Seething Swamp
DAKAL
District ① Banking, Financial, Theater
Distract ② Light Industry, Business
District ③ Mining (Clay & Glitter)
District ④ Harbor
District ⑤ Mining, Manufacturing (Bricks &
Glitter) also a developing artist community
District ⑥ Agricultural (Grains, Livestock)
District ⑦ Agricultural (Vineyards, Orchards)

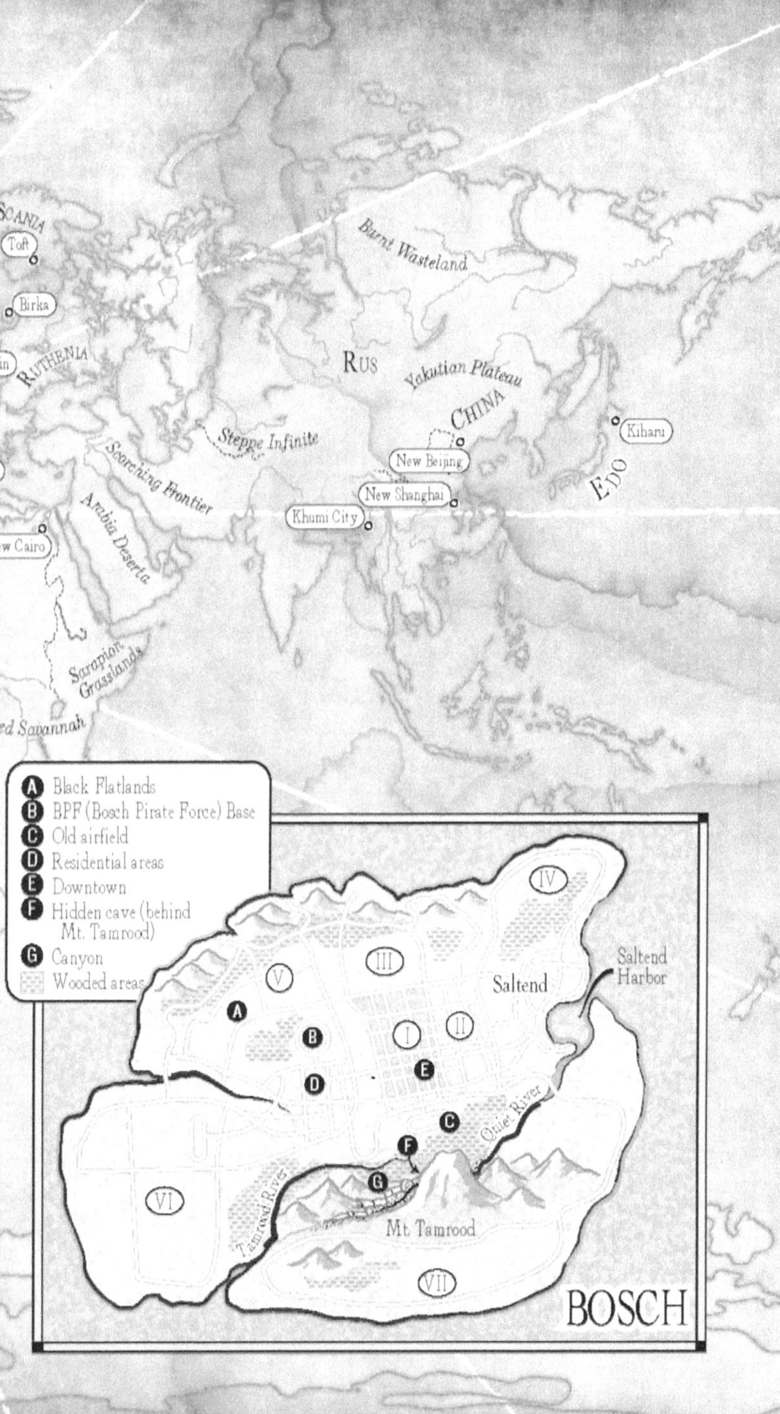

SCANIA
Toft
Birka
Berlin
RUTHENIA
Rus
Burnt Wasteland
Yakutian Plateau
CHINA
Steppe Infinite
New Beijing
Kiharu
EDO
Scorching Frontier
New Shanghai
Khumi City
Arabia Deserta
New Cairo
Sarapion Grasslands
Scorched Savannah
A Black Flatlands
B BPF (Bosch Pirate Force) Base
C Old airfield
D Residential areas
E Downtown
F Hidden cave (behind Mt. Tamrood)
G Canyon
Wooded areas
IV
III
V
Saltend
Saltend Harbor
A
B
I
II
E
D
C
Quiet River
F
G
Tamrood River
VI
Mt. Tamrood
VII
BOSCH

Burnt Wasteland
Rus
Yakutian Plateau
China
Kiharu
Steppe Infinite
New Beijing
Edo
Scorching Frontier
New Shanghai
Khumi City

Arania
Fairneau
Toronto
Tabonne
New Detroit
Bosch
Haida
Truvale
Ohlone Bay
State of Eternia
Mynia
New Caribbean
Parida
Haunted Islands
Seething Swamp
Maui
Moku-o-keawe

Contents

PART I

Sailing In Bosch, Lesson One

Ahoy there, young pirates. Welcome to your first lesson in sailing!

History of Sailing in Bosch

The Bosch come from a strong sailing heritage. When New Earth was born—after the great fires, floods, pandemics, and famine destroyed Old Earth in the late twenty-first and early twenty-second centuries (please review pages 213–217 of Vazquez's *History of the Seventy-Year Horror*)—there was a shortage of workers. Thus, as New Earth rose, so, too, did the practice of keeping people as thralls to be worked as their owners saw fit.

People from all lands who had survived The Horror were now captured and sold into thralldom. Our ancestors were forced to work aboard fishing and cargo ships under terrible circumstances.

Our forebearers were stronger and smarter than their

captors, and they arose from their bondage, taking over the very ships that had been their prisons and using them to feed themselves and their families, and later, to free other thralls both on the sea and on land. The first recorded thrall revolt at sea took place in 2168. In 2184, Dr. Ahmed Qusay, in his book *This is New Earth,* made the first mention of a pirate fleet marauding on what had been known on Old Earth as the Atlantic Ocean, now referred to as the Eastern Sea.

Over time, more ships joined the fleet of freed thralls, and in the early part of the twenty-third century, this impressive armada ruled the Eastern Sea from the North Country to the Horn of Africa and the Horn of the Southern Lands. However, around 2263, the powerful traders on both sides of the sea grew determined to strike back, and together, raised a navy to attack the pirates.

However, the ten-ship fleet was led by the great Hizir Bosch, its commander over the last ten years, and it was through his leadership and cunning that the fleet was able to both win in battle and escape to peace. By consolidating his people on five ships, which he sailed north while sending the remaining five empty ships south as decoys, Hizir Bosch reached freedom, settling his people on this island we now call Bosch.

Though the Bosch Pirate Force now conducts its business in elite flying vessels, we have not forgotten our past. It is in honor of the brave sailors who ruled the seas that all Bosch young people learn to sail. Be proud of who you are and get ready to join part of the history of Bosch.

Glossary

There are many terms specific to sailing. Please study these words and their definitions carefully as they will be part of the first exam in two weeks.

- <u>Bow</u> – the front of the boat
- <u>Stern</u> – the back of the boat
- <u>Port</u> – the left side of the boat as you look to the bow from the stern
- <u>Starboard</u> – the right side of the boat as you look to the bow from the stern
- *Note: Always use "port" and "starboard" aboard your boats and not "left" or "right" as the latter terms change depending on your position.*
- <u>Aft</u> – toward the stern
- <u>Astern</u> – behind the boat
- <u>Bilge</u> – the bottom of the boat where water accumulates; should be cleared regularly, either manually or automatically
- <u>Boom</u> – the pole that runs perpendicular to the mast and is used to control the mainsail
- <u>Cleat</u> – a device for securing lines (rope)

- <u>Forestay</u> – a piece of rigging that runs from the top of the mast to the bow
- <u>Forward</u> – toward the bow
- <u>Head</u> – toilet on board the boat; also, the uppermost corner of a sail
- <u>Headsail</u> – any sail that sits forward of the mast, giving more control to the bow
- <u>Heave to</u> – the technique of parking the boat at sea when anchoring is impossible; typically used in heavy weather
- <u>Hull</u> – the body of a boat
- <u>Jib</u> – a triangular headsail—and the one you use in this class
- <u>Lines</u> – ropes used on a boat
- <u>Mainsail</u> – a large, triangular sail—the largest and most important one, which extends astern from the mast and controls the stern
- <u>Mast</u> – the tall pole the sails attach to
- <u>Puff</u> – a gust of wind that can be harnessed to sail quickly
- <u>Reef</u> – reducing the size of sails in strong winds for safety, usually done by tying the sail in a roll to the boom or forestay
- <u>Regatta</u> – a sailing race; you will participate in your first one at the end of your sailing unit
- <u>Savvy</u> – a pirate term meaning, "Do you understand?"
- <u>Sheets</u> – lines used to control the sails
- <u>Sloop</u> – a sailboat having one mast with one mainsail and one head sail, typically a jib
- <u>Sole</u> – bottom of the boat
- <u>Squall</u> – a sudden storm

- <u>Starboard rights</u> – a boating rule to avoid collisions; the vessel with the wind on its starboard side has the right of way
- <u>Stays</u> – wires or ropes that run from bow and stern to the top of the mast to stabilize the mast
- <u>Storm sails</u> – small, strong sails used in heavy weather
- <u>Thwart</u> – the seats that lie perpendicular across the hull of a boat
- <u>Tiller</u> – the handle that attaches to the rudder to steer a boat

More terms will be added as we progress through the lessons. Now, strap on your life vests and climb aboard your waiting sailboat. Adventure awaits. Savvy?

ONE

The Storm

"Shima! Grey Shima! Get your skinny butt up here and man the tiller. The waves are getting big, and the air's getting heavy. We need to get farther away from the shore."

Shocked at hearing Darvin use my actual name, I toss my reader on the shelf in the *Fascination*'s tiny cabin and watch it slide as the boat rolls. I lean and make a quick grab before it falls and tuck it beneath one of the storm straps, where it sits securely. Scrambling up and out from below, where I was using the small head—really just a bucket with a seat and a curtain—I appear on deck; sea spray slaps my face, and I give my head a quick shake in response. The salty water blown up by the wind stings my squinting eyes as they try to adjust to the dim lights on deck and the intense dark of the sea at night.

The sky is squally, with clouds roiling and folding like some giant's clay on a table. The waves are cresting and turbulent in deep shades of purple and black. The ocean winds sing that magic that makes my skin tingle and my heart swell. There are so many voices and songs that swirl over the waters —sometimes they sing gentle, whispering lullabies; sometimes crashing symphonies; and other times, a raucous blending of tympany and horns so that a sailor has to listen closely to even find the hint of a melody. It is this tune that catches my long, dark ponytail now and whips it into my face. I take a moment to tie it into a quick knot.

"Skinny butt" indeed, my mind grumbles. While he technically isn't wrong—my butt's not big; in fact, nothing about me is—it annoys me that Darvin takes every moment, even in a storm, to remind me that I am small and look like a kid, which I am not. I turned fourteen in April; so, hardly a kid, even though I am minus much of the bumps and curves other girls my age sport. But I do as my captain has ordered and direct my skinny butt to my place at the tiller as the boat rocks and bucks in the waves. Apparently, Captain Darvin's critique of me doesn't extend to my arms since I have managed to navigate the *Fascination*, our blue, twelve-meter sloop, across the Great Sea from Ohlone Bay to the Drowned Islands for the past two weeks.

The next wave threatens to topple me as it smashes over the stern, where I stand attempting to hold the tiller steady. The air is August warm, but the sea is chilly as the water soaks my leggings and hair. The jacket that Matt, my bonus dad, gave me before the start of the race is working its own brand of magic, so my chest is dry and fairly warm. I look forward.

Darvin stands on the bow, chest out, the wind blowing his dark, straight hair back from his face. He looks how I envision the stuck-up hero from my newest book, *Pheidon Duan and The Sword of Transformation*, does. Pheidon, the crown prince of Brinada, is on a journey to restore magical power to the kingdom. Darvin, on the other hand, is apparently on a journey to be the most annoying person from the Central Continent. I had hoped the race would transform him into someone less irritating, the way I hope the sword will for Pheidon, but as of this moment, it hasn't happened for either of them.

I swear, Darvin is using the storm to strike a pose. He fancies himself quite the sailor and ladies' man. Just like Pheidon, he is always bragging about all the girls who fall in love with him. I snort to myself. Darvin doesn't need a magic sword to make that happen; he needs a magic toothbrush. He is nineteen and, while not completely hideous, has such foul-smelling breath, it rivals the damage the dragons from *The Obsidian Shore* can create with their fire. I try to stay upwind of him at all times.

Still, nasty breath and improbable tales aside, the Great Sea Cup folk decided that his five extra years on the planet was sufficient reason to make him captain once they paired us. At first, it seemed like a reasonable call; after all, Darvin spends four days a week on the sea in his regular life, crabbing for his uncle's fleet. But there's a catch. His uncle's boats are motored, not sailed. Clearly, Darvin over-inflates the stories he tells about, well, everything. I mean, sure, he's a decent sailor, but he has crappy judgment.

For example, we would have come close to being first in our division two days ago if he had listened to me. We had a nice puff and were heading for the mark. But then the *Blue Whisper* came up tight on port. We should have headed up to go behind and maintained our course and speed. Instead, he just had to get into drama with the *Whisper*'s crew, insisting on his starboard rights. Darvin and the *Whisper*'s captain got into a tangle, with words and gestures exchanged; so, we lost the time we had made over the four days previous, and that cost us the Cup in my estimation. Sure, third place is decent, but it sure ain't first.

I yell forward, hoping some of my voice won't be carried away by the wind. "Darvin, we should heave to and get the storm sails up."

"Nope. You worry too much, Little Edo. We can just reef the jib and the main," he hollers back.

He's an idiot. And not just because he has called me "Little Edo" since the race began. I mean, I'm proud to be half-Edoan, but he could have just as easily called me "Little Bosch." But his brain is not large, and he couldn't see beyond the shape of my eyes and my face, the shade of my skin, or my slight frame. So, "Little Edo" it was, and the more I protested, the more he laughed and called me it. But his idiocy extends beyond his vague skin-bigot comments to his sailing judgment. These winds are picking up fast. We need to heave to, get a sea anchor out, and put the storm sails up. And we needed to do it an hour ago.

While I won't say it to Darvin, I'm actually a bit surprised that the storm developed as quickly as it did. If I had known it would blow in with such intensity and speed, I would have stayed on deck. But I wanted to finish the chapter I had begun last night at bedtime, and I really had to pee. Another swell strikes the boat, and water rushes over the deck. I reposition the tiller, trying to keep the bow pointed toward the waves, but we are moving too fast with both sails up.

I mutter to myself, my words slipping into the wind, unheard, "I'd have been ready for this storm. The sky was red this morning, and the pressure's been dropping." It's not the first squall I've managed on the *Fascination* in the past two weeks, and it won't be the last before we make port back in Haida—that's just part of sailing the ocean.

Lots of people like to take a boat out on a nice day when there's just enough breeze for a pleasant sail. Those folk never lose sight of the shore. And that's fine–for them. Me, I like the wildness of the open ocean, its unpredictable character, the way it spreads in every direction as if there is nothing else on the planet except for blue water and you on your little boat. To be sure, the sea is unforgiving, but it is fair. If you respect it and have the skills and understanding of how it functions in all its moods, you'll do fine. But there are no guarantees and that's the thrilling part. To sail the open ocean, you have to be prepared for storms, for rogue waves, even for sea life, like whales. All those things can upend your ship and drop you into the depths.

Of course, during the race there were always watchers sailing near–especially for the under-twenty crews. Now, the watchers are gone, and we are on our own. Adrenaline pulses through my body making me vigilant and somewhat anxious. I glance up. The mast stands firm. The storm will likely only last a couple of hours. Maybe Darvin will be proven right, and we can sail out of it sooner. Maybe.

Darvin reefs the sails, and I find the tiller a bit easier to handle as the boat slows a bit. He turns and points a *See? I was right* finger at me and grins. He starts to say something, then turns his head toward starboard, his face wrinkling and his mouth dropping open to yell, but I don't hear whatever he is going to say. Instead, there is a groaning and crunching that fills my ears, and the huge hull of a yacht slides in front of my face. The smooth, white side looms at me like some behemoth of the deep, and I know for certain I am going to be crushed and killed until I feel my feet come up, and I am tossed backward off the stern into the churning, foaming waters of the Great Sea.

The darkness envelops me as I plunge backward into the chill and choppy saltwater. At first, there is the noise of the crash, then the sudden silence as water fills my ears, eyes, nose, and mouth. Everything is so dark, I don't know which way is up, and I am so scared. All I can think is *Mama*. And somehow, this thought calms me a little, and I open my eyes ever so slightly and blow out a tiny bit, like I used to do in the tub when I was little and would stick my head under for fun, knowing all was well because Mama was sitting nearby, saying, "Follow the bubbles, Baby." So, now, I follow the bubbles, pushing with my hands and kicking with my feet to chase them until my face breaks the surface. I pull in a huge breath of sea air with an audible gasp before I start to go under again. I liberate myself of my boat shoes and start rotating my legs like an eggbeater while sculling my arms forward and back to stay afloat. I turn my head and raise my chin from the breaking foam to catch some breaths. The rain from the deep, gray clouds spatters on my face, and the waves have lost their musicality and now sound angry as they roar. I am lifted with a swell and then down again, over and over. While I can tread calm water for quite a while, I won't be able to for long here.

My thoughts are coming fast and none of them are good: It's so dark. The watchers from the race are docked. I can't see land. How will anyone know what happened? Am I going to die? At this thought a voice in my head says, *Probably*, and I feel my stomach drop with fear. Will I drown? Will a shark get me? Will it hurt? Panic starts to tighten my chest and it's getting hard to breathe. Mama's voice comes to me– "When you get scared, let go of the *What ifs* and stay in the present. Find a mantra to keep you focused and work the problem. *Oh, Mama–this is a really big problem, but I'll try.*

My mantra is *I will live*. I say it over and over and as I do, I start to believe it. I will stay calm. I need a plan.

I decide to roll onto my back to float, and almost immediately, I am hit in the face with a mouthful of seawater. *Roll over.* I take a deep breath, roll onto my belly, and bob face down, consciously making my arms and legs relax. When I need a breath, I lift my chin up, pull my arms in, and give a kick, taking a breath and then settling back. This is how I pass… I don't know—minutes? Hours? I develop a pattern, which keeps me focused so that the part of my brain that is freaking out and scared can't be heard: I tread water for a count of five hundred and then float for fifty breaths. I repeat this at least four times.

While part of my brain is engaged in counting, I keep the rest of it entertained and distracted by imagining and remembering. I imagine I am Beverlee, the hero of one of my favorite books, *The Queen of the Marsh*. Beverlee's mother had been a mermaid, and though Beverlee was born with legs and was cruelly bullied for it, she could swim almost as fast as her merfolk kin. Next, I remember when I first met Darvin, ten days before the start, when I was eager to get onto the water and practice, and we selected the *Fascination* as our racer. Then, I imagine that I was captain, and we won the Great Sea Cup, and everyone I know is cheering for me. "Hooray for Grey!" they all say, and, "Her mama never did that!" I see Mama's face, and it is glowing with pride.

I doubt she would look proud if she knew what had just happened. She'd be in a panic and mobilizing the Force to rescue me. It'd be "No more sailboat racing for you, young lady. You stay on land where it's safe." A bit rich for someone who pilots her own air vessels and used to go on raids with weapons. It took everything I had to convince her to let me run this race. I had to promise the moon and stars and that I'd be okay about a million times. And that was after the evening of the big fight.

TWO

Life is Easy Until it Isn't

"Hey, what time do we eat?" Nicco asked from his place on the orange lounge chair, where he lay, body relaxed, eyes closed. A glass of champagne sat on the small table next to him, half-consumed. The sun was only a couple of hours past its zenith, but a breeze eddied up from the bluff. Ashton Abernathy laughed and answered without looking up from the sketch-book, where his pencil moved in small strokes as he sat leaning forward on the edge of his deep green lounger. "Sit still. I almost have your nose right. And dinner is at the same time as yesterday and the day before and the day before that, Nick—6 p.m."

Nicco Castellanos grinned and nodded, opening his eyes for a glance at the sky before settling back and sighing with contentment. Ashton squinted his piercing-blue eyes at the man shaded by the large, brown-striped umbrella that covered them both. Nicco had a boxy face and broad cheekbones, easy enough to sketch, but his nose, though mostly straight, had a distinct shape that Ashton had been struggling to draw, erasing and redoing it several times that afternoon. Nicco was a good-looking man with deeply tanned olive skin and dark hair with a few summer highlights. He was compact, not particularly tall, but well-muscled and fit in the way that someone in their mid-twenties who had all day to work out, swim, and run on the beach would be. Ashton, on the other hand, was tall, with dark-blond hair and skin that was also tan but carried the rosy hue that developed in those who were naturally pale. He was also classically handsome, at least according to Isda, a woman he had met at a club in Haida a few weeks ago. He grinned at that memory as he smudged a pencil line with his little finger.

A shout and then a large splash came from the large, oval swimming pool to Ashton's right. He pulled his sketchbook to the side and shouted back, "Hey, you jerks, be careful. I'm drawing here."

"Don't worry, Ash. Your crayons are safe from us," Nicco's brother, Constantine, yelled back using a mocking tone. Con and his friend Brian Walsh both laughed and returned to wrestling, pushing, and hollering as they splashed and dove into the pool. They were both twenty-two but acted, in Ashton's opinion, more like young teenagers.

Ashton had known Nicco since boarding school and had offered the Castellanos brothers a place to stay for the warm season while their parents were on their luxury ship exploring the Aotearoa Islands, ostensibly leaving the boys in charge of the conglomerate they owned. Though as far as Ashton could tell, their responsibilities were limited to participating in the occasional video comm on the Obi. Obi stood for Obelisk, the Federal Alliance video station that broadcast throughout New Earth. The comms Nicco and Con had were with a group of gray-haired men in conservative, Federal Alliance-style suits. During those events, Nicco would simply listen, occasionally nodding in agreement with whichever suit was talking, while Con would typically wander off after a few minutes to get a beer and a taste of Glitter, the delectable drug that made everything feel just fine.

After a bit, the two young men in the pool quieted, and Brian, who apparently was a constant presence in the Castellanos home, hopped out and began to towel himself dry from the pile of large, soft, white towels stocked poolside, compliments of the household help. Ashton kept a cook and two cleaners on staff, paying them a skimpy salary directly from his mother's income. This issue was a source of contention and was brought up in each of Ashton's weekly comms with Sandra, including the one on the previous night.

"Things are different now, Ashton, since your father is gone. You could cook for yourself and learn to clean up," she had said pointedly. He was tempted to ask her if she did her own cooking and cleaning, but this thought was interrupted by his mother's next question.

"Are those Castellanos boys still there? And their little tag-a-long, Bobby, or Billy, or whatever?" The words dripped with displeasure.

Ashton gave a small sigh. "Brian. And, yes, they are still here. And will be for the season at least." He continued, "I like them. They are funny, and they keep me from becoming old and stuffy."

His mother gave a small, derisive laugh. "You mean, keep you from acting your age, don't you, Ashton? You do realize you'll be thirty in just over a year." Sandra paused but not long enough for him to respond before adding, "I doubt they would continue to be so entertaining if you...excuse me...*I* wasn't paying for all their fun."

Ashton was thrilled his mother was finally sober and remarried to a decent man, but she sure could be a killjoy. He had toyed with a few salty comments in response but given that his trust money did not cover all expenses, and he was asking her for an advance, he instead answered obsequiously, "Yes, Mother. I know. Thank you. I will consider what you've said."

She had closed the conversation with, "Ashton, you need to learn to live within your means. I have told you before, I won't continue to supplement your lifestyle beyond your thirtieth birthday. It's time to step up. Drawing and painting aren't jobs; they are hobbies. You were groomed for a place in business, in politics. Something that pays you your own markers. Somewhere you can be somebody."

Ashton had shrugged. Thirty was over a year from now. He'd think about that when it was closer.

Now, Brian came over, dropped the towel on the smooth stone patio, and flopped into the blue lounge chair. He was lanky, with sandy-brown hair, freckled skin, and full lips. "Are we really going to follow the race, Ash? I hear there are some gorgeous women crewing some of them. And I've never been to the Drowned Islands."

Brian reminded Ashton of a half-grown dog one of his friends had when he was about ten. It had hair about the same shade and was ever eager to explore and see what lay beyond the fence line. Ashton regarded the rough portrait of Nicco and closed his sketchbook. "Yeah, we'll go down to the start tomorrow and then take the *Abundance* to the Drowned Islands in the spectator flotilla. Should be able to see some impressive sailing." He glanced at Brian's unimpressed look and laughed. "And don't worry—some of those sailors will be in tiny little swimsuits."

Brian's face brightened, and he nodded. "Excellent. I haven't scored a sailor girl yet."

Ashton chuckled, shaking his head. Brian was indeed like a dog.

"What the...?" Ashton mumbled as he woke to the sound of the *Abundance*'s motors and the shudder and rumble as the anchor came up and the boat began to move. He rolled over, resting his face against a cool spot on his black, silk pillowcase, then slowly moved his head from side to side in an attempt to clear it of the Glitter and rum he and his friends had consumed earlier in the day.

The *Abundance* was anchored at the far edge of the natural harbor of Moku-o-keawe, the volcanic island that served as the port of celebration for the GSR finishers. Just as they had the past four days since the race concluded, the four men had taken their individual water bikes into the island's harbor village that morning to explore the tropical surroundings and, more importantly, opportunities of meeting and romancing some of the GSR sailors—women and men. While Ashton enjoyed both pursuits as much as the rest of his friends, Brian was single-minded and in his element, using his boyish good looks and puppy-like enthusiasm to pursue short-lived dalliances with several sailors.

"I like sampling, not buying," Brian had laughed and shrugged on their second night ashore when Ashton asked him where the red-haired sailor he had been buying drinks for their first night on shore had gone. "This place is a tropical banquet of beautiful, fit women and men. I intend to try a bit of everything before we leave."

"Well said!" Nicco had responded, raising his glass. Ashton and Con laughed and nodded as well, lifting their tropical drinks in approval of the plan.

Tonight, though, Ashton decided to return early and alone to the yacht, leaving the Castellanos brothers and their eager, randy friend to their own devices. Before they left Haida, he had the bar on the *Abundance* stocked with top-shelf liquors and told the crew to keep the drinks flowing. The food was exquisite as well, prepared creatively by the chef he insisted the skipper bring on. Once they reached the island, he began buying drinks on shore for everyone. Now, Ashton was broke until the next installment of his trust came in at the end of the month. So, he returned to the *Abundance* and, feeling warm and magnanimous from the late-afternoon rum drinks, dismissed the crew member who had been left to watch the yacht, allowing them to head into the village and join the skipper and his friends. *Why not? We are just anchored here*, he reasoned.

He sat up for a bit with his new sketchbook, working to get the perspective right from his seat on deck with the railing of the *Abundance* in the foreground and the tiny lights of the village and the coastline in the back. Eventually, though, the combination of the Glitter he had taken just after he had dismissed the crew member and the rumbling from clouds that had rolled made a strong case for finishing the sketch another day. The wind began to pick up, and he decided that was his signal to head to the master quarters for a full night's sleep.

Now, with the unexpected rumble of the engines in his ear, he rolled out of his expansive bed and made his way to the bathroom door. He paused at the toilet to move his right leg back and forth before getting to business. His knee was always stiff when he first got out of bed, reminding him of his old injury. He glanced at the large mirror on the wall. His long, dark-blond hair was halfway pulled out of the ponytail he had gone to sleep with. As he stood emptying his bladder, yawning, and trying to make sense of what was happening, he felt the yacht pick up speed. That was odd; they weren't scheduled to leave for two more days. He wiped his hands on his deep blue, silk night shorts, peered into the mirror to fix his hair, and saw his ice-blue eyes looking back. Rubbing a hand on the night stubble on his chin that he always shaved off carefully each morning, he considered getting dressed but quickly discarded the idea, opting instead for his black, silk robe. He headed toward the stairs via the oakwood hallway, with its elegant rugs imported from near the Mediterranean and the Casplack Seas. The gilt-framed paintings on the walls had been selected by his father years before. None of his drawings, of course, had made the cut. Father, without emotion, only selected the best, after all. Ashton paused for a moment to work his jaw and then roll his eyes at the long-ago slight, then climbed the shiny wooden stairs, carefully holding the handrail as he felt the yacht pitch just a bit to the left.

Once on the main deck, Ashton could see the choppy gray waves through the rain-streaked, wide windows surrounding the enclosed section of the lounge and feel the yacht's undulations as she rose and fell with the swells.

He turned and looked toward the wheelhouse that was the skipper's home base when they were at sea. Filled with screens, maritime apparatuses, and navigational equipment far too complicated for him, its large windows and glass door partitioned it off from the elegant saloon. That particular room held buttery-soft, buff-colored, leather sofas that formed a U-shape around a cherry wood table and faced the large-screen Obi that had provided Ashton and his friends many hours of entertainment throughout the trip.

Now, the big screen was dark, but in the wheelhouse, several screens were lit up and active, and moving among them, pushing buttons, was, oddly, Brian.

Ashton leaned on the jam of the wheelhouse door and glanced out the front windows, watching as the *Abundance* headed seaward. "Hey, Brian, what's going on? Where's the skipper?"

Brian glanced over at Ashton and then over his other shoulder. "Don't know where the skipper is. There was no time to get him." Brian paused and leaned his elbows on top of some screen that glowed with a red exclamation mark as he held his head in his hands. "I'm in trouble, Ash. Remember the redhead from night one? Her boyfriend arrived island-side today, and I guess he got wind of our little romance and came looking for me. Nic, Con, and I were in The Volcano House, having a couple drinks, and he and about six of his friends showed up." He spun around, and Ashton could see a combination of alcohol, Glitter, and panic in his eyes. His voice was frantic as he continued, slurring a little, "And they were serious. One of them flashed a knife, Ash, a really big one! We all took off. Nic told me to go back to the boat, so I grabbed my water bike and headed here—but then I saw boat lights behind me…. I knew it was them. Shit, man, I really think they want a piece of me, so…" Brian pointed toward the back of the yacht and trailed off, his hand dropping to his side.

Ashton looked at the dark sea behind them as well and, in between the rise and fall of the swells, saw a glimmer behind them a fair distance. Brian definitely did not use his brain when it came to satisfying other parts of his body. Ashton chuckled. "Maybe you need to ask more questions before you take all those ladies for a night on the beach." Then he gestured to the navigational equipment. "So, do you know what you're doing here?"

"Um, sort of. The skipper showed me a couple things, and I remembered where the autopilot button was after I started flipping all this stuff on, so I engaged that." Brian shrugged with a grin. "Smart, huh?"

Ashton preferred not to weigh in on whether any of this was *smart*, but at least Brian sounded like he knew something about the controls. "Okay, then," he concluded. "I don't want any assholes with knives on board my boat either, so you better speed up."

Brian's face relaxed, and with a laugh, he pushed on the throttle. The *Abundance* moved quickly away from the pursuing lights and into the deep darkness of a stormy sea. Ashton figured they could give it about twenty minutes. Then they would just turn around and motor over to the windward side of the island. There, they could drop anchor outside the smaller harbor and lay low until they got a hold of the crew and the Castellanos brothers on shore. After that, they would head back to Haida.

As Ashton walked toward the large picture windows at the front of the wheelhouse to peer out at the wide swath of sea ahead of the *Abundance*, his foot kicked something. The old compass the skipper kept on display had slid off its perch, and Ashton leaned down to reach for it.

Brian muttered, "Oh, shit."

A tremendous crunching sound filled the air, and Ashton almost lost his footing, grabbing onto the edge of the helm to maintain balance as the compass skidded away. Keeping a grip on the counter, he turned his head and glared at Brian, whose face had gone quite white. "Goddammit, Brian, did you hit a sandbar?"

"It was a boat," Brian whispered. "I smashed it." His eyes were big and round, and his mouth hung open a bit. He looked like a child who had misbehaved terribly and been caught.

They stared at each other for just a moment and then turned as one and ran back to the rear deck, ignoring the rain and wind, to see if there was any wreckage. Both the sky and sea were dark, and the *Abundance* was moving briskly. So, at first, nothing was apparent. Ashton turned on the floodlight that was attached to the railing and scanned the water.

"Maybe I missed it." Brian's voice held a note of hope.

"Then what was the crashing sound?" Ashton wiped his face of rainwater and glared at the man. He continued to run the light over the water and had just started hoping that maybe Brian was right when something came into view. Protruding from the sea was a T-shaped mast with its sail still up, a blue-and-green GSR flag flapping at the top. It was sinking slowly down into the rough waves. "Holy shit, Brian, it was one of the racers."

"I didn't mean to," Brian said with a slight whine.

Ashton barked, feeling his temper rise, "I sure as hell hope not, you idiot. There were people on that boat."

Brian shrugged. "The other boat will help them."

"You mean the guys with knives that you were running from? No. We have to go back." Ashton felt a slight thrill of surprise at his own vehemence as he turned and jogged toward the wheelhouse, Brian following after.

They both stood, dripping from the rain, looking at the instrumentation.

Ashton gestured at the screens and devices. "So, turn it around."

Brian hesitated, looked over at Ashton, then shook his head and shrugged, turning his palms up. "I don't know how to turn the boat around." He pointed at one screen. "Only how to turn on autopilot and go faster or slower. The wheel locks on autopilot."

"Then turn the autopilot off and stop the boat." Ashton was almost yelling.

Brian pushed one of the buttons and frowned. Then he pushed another and another. The *Abundance* continued on her path. He turned toward Ashton. "That should've worked. That's the one I pushed for autopilot." There was a note of panic in his voice.

"You've got to be kidding."

Brian shook his head. The men looked at each other, and both turned and began to push buttons and turn knobs helter-skelter across the length of the helm. But still, the *Abundance* pushed on through the water.

Ashton felt like someone had knocked the wind out of him. He no longer was worried about being pursued, the boat they had hit, or the people who might even now be in the water. He wasn't concerned with anything but his own survival. He sounded as breathless as he felt as he turned to Brian and said, "You know, there's all sorts of rocks and sandbars out here. And if we get past them, there's just open water for...well, forever."

"I know, man," Brian responded. "So, what do we do then, Ash? Comm the skipper?"

The weight of responsibility did not sit well on Ashton. He shut his eyes for a moment and took two breaths before his temper exploded. "And what? Tell him we are speeding along into the ocean, but we aren't sure what direction, and he should swim out and take over? 'Just follow the wrecked boats, Skipper.' I don't think so. But I'm sure as hell not going to be out in the middle of the Great Sea without the skipper." He took a breath and tried to think of what to do next. "Slow way down."

Brian just stood there looking at Ashton.

"You do know how to do that. Do it now!" Ashton yelled and Brian seemed to wake up. He moved to the throttle, pulling it back.

Ashton looked around, hoping some solution would present itself. "Okay, that buys us some time. If we crash into rocks, at least it won't be as bad." A voice yelled in his head, *Bullshit. Get off the boat before that happens.* "Where's your water-bike?"

Brian shook his head. "I couldn't pull it up by myself. So, I just left it next to the yacht and climbed up the ladder."

Ashton was once again aghast and annoyed by this infant's irresponsibility. "You didn't even tie it up?" he snarled and watched Brian shake his head again, looking for all the world like a scolded puppy.

He considered, for a moment, just saving himself and letting Brian suffer the consequences of his mistake. But he pushed that thought aside when he realized that was exactly what his father would have done. With an effort, he shifted his tone from angry to matter-of-fact. He grasped Brian by the arm and started to hustle him out of the wheelhouse, saying, "Okay, then, we'll take the small dinghy. Skipper and crew took the big one earlier, but the small one will work for us. We'll just drop it in, abandon ship, and motor back to the island. Maybe we can even use it to go help the wrecked boat."

THREE

The Fight

The fight had been going on since well before dinner, with my mom saying things like, "You went behind our backs to enter," and how I was "just springing this on us," and how she "had serious reservations about letting a fourteen-year-old do something so hazardous." I was really trying to keep my temper, but when she said, "Aren't there other races, closer to home and not as risky?" I lost it.

"Well, I don't care what you say. I qualified—on my own—and I'm going!" I grabbed at the sides of my sleeveless shirt. I felt my hands tighten into fists and my jaw clench. I couldn't believe she'd be so unfair as to try to keep this from me.

Mom's blue-green eyes were ablaze, and she twisted her neck from one side to the other, the way I used to see her do when she and my dad would fight. "Grey, I didn't say you couldn't go. I said I have reservations." Her voice sharpened at that last word, then she glanced over to Matt, who sat at the dining room table, hands on top of his head, his tall form leaning back in the chair with his legs extended in front of him.

Matt has lived with us for almost three years, which is a

good thing. He's like my bonus dad, and he treats me like I'm capable. Now, he was just watching this argument unfold. His scarred face was calm with his usual hint of a smile, and his dark eyes held Mom's for a few moments. She took a breath in and slowly exhaled. Turning her head back to me, her eyes were calmer. She started again. "Listen, why don't we pause this..." Her forefinger moved back and forth between us. "...conversation for now? I'll collect my thoughts. And tomorrow, we can sit down, and you can tell me more about this race."

But I saw no reason to let her have it so easy. "Mom, a conversation is when two people exchange ideas, generally in a calm and pleasant way. This..." I mimicked her finger movement. "...is a fight." I flipped my long hair back and lifted my chin. "But, fine. We can talk tomorrow. Tonight, I'm going to confirm my place in the race." I paused and let my eyes narrow just a bit, daring her to be the one to restart the dispute she was trying to set aside, then turned my back and headed to the stairs in what I believed was an exquisitely orchestrated exit.

Behind me, Mom's *I'm-the-one-in-charge-of-everything* voice started, "No, that's..." But it was interrupted by Matt saying in a low tone, "Kat, let it go. Wait until morning." By then I was up the stairs and in my room, body shaking and angry tears starting to well up in my eyes. I sat down at the captain's desk that used to be my papa's and opened my Obi. The picture of my used-to-be-best friend Leia and me at the Flying Wednesdays concert came up. *I need to change that.* I called up my mail and clicked on the one labeled GSR (Great Sea Race) Invitational.

I read it over again.

June 9, 2369

Dear Grey Shima,

Congratulations! The contestant committee of the GSR has reviewed your application to participate in the August 2369 run from Haida to Moku-o-keawe in the Drowned Islands. Based on your showings in the Fairneau and Toronto regattas, we are pleased to offer you a crew position in the under-twenty, two-person class.

You will be required to arrive on August 1, 2369, for safety training. Subsequently, you will be paired with your crewmate and, based on a random drawing, will select your racing vessel from the fleet. The GCS committee will assign crew roles predicated on experience.

The race will begin at dawn, August 11, with an expected run time to the Drowned Islands of eleven to fourteen days. All boats are to be returned to the fleet by September 15.

Please note, this is a competitive race with many more applications than we can accept. We ask that you confirm your intention to compete before June 12, 2369. If we have not received your confirmation and your consent and waiver forms by midnight of the 12th, along with the balance of the entrance fee of 300 FA markers, your invitation will be rescinded, and the position offered to the next contestant on the waitlist.

Again, congratulations on taking the first step in becoming part of the tradition of the GSR. We look forward to hearing from you soon.

Fair Winds,

Zoe Calderon

Great Sea Race Committee Chair 2369

. . .

My eyes lingered on the word *congratulations*, then flicked back to reread the confirmation deadline. I opened the attachment marked *Confirmation*. It was simple—just a checkbox and place to sign. I marked the box next to the line that read *I accept the position in the 2369 Great Sea Race*, used the Obi stylus to sign my name, and then punched the Save button. My finger moved the cursor to the other attachment labeled *Consent*. I hesitated for just a moment, then clicked it open. This one was much longer and filled with a good dozen small-print paragraphs about the race, its rules, and potential hazards. At the very bottom were two black lines, one that read *Participant Signature* and the final line that read *Parent or guardian signature for participants under seventeen.*

I glanced over my shoulder and opened my desk drawer. Pushing aside all the little pieces of wood in various stages of being whittled into simple animals, some real and some mythical, I slid a folded piece of paper out from underneath. I unfolded it and regarded all my attempts at a Kat Wallace signature. Some were pretty close. Using my finger, I traced the one that I thought was best. Another glance at the door. Maybe I should have just signed Papa's signature in Edonese. The committee probably wouldn't be able to read it and so wouldn't question it. But then Mom would have raged at him, which would have made him impatient and offended until they figured out it was all me, and that didn't seem fair. I stuffed the paper back into the drawer.

I played with the stylus and spent a few moments staring at the consent form. *No,* I decided, *I'll go back down and tell her how much this means to me and convince her.* Then she can come up and sign it. Yes, that's what I should do. Decided, I was up and out my door and to the steps in a moment. Voices drifted up from the kitchen through the air vent on the landing, and I paused, looking first down the stairs and then back at the source of so many eavesdropped conversations when I was little. I bit my lip and stepped back toward the landing, taking my childhood spot on the step just below it so I could tilt my head and catch the whole conversation.

"Matty, I don't know what to do," I heard Mama say. "It used to be so easy with her. She was my shadow, always talking about joining the Force. Right after that July, it seemed like she was dealing with it well. But since she's been in secondary school, it's like she's angry all the time—at her brothers, at her papa, but most especially at me. And she refuses to talk to Ruth anymore."

I frowned and felt the tension in my shoulders that came when Mom and I fought. I composed a comeback in my head. *I am not always angry. And Ruth is* your *therapist, Mom. I don't need to talk about that Awful July anymore. I just need to forget it happened. And maybe there's more to me than being your shadow.*

Silverware rattled and clinked in the sink as Mom washed. "Her teachers say she's pulling away from her friends at school. Even Leia. The only people she doesn't seem actively angry with are you, Flossie, and Mama. Well, and, of course, Rini."

I scoffed under my breath and rolled my eyes. *By the Boiling Flats, Mom, and you call me dramatic? I'm not "pulling away" from anybody. If anything, it's them. They are the ones changing and trying to act like they are so adult. Especially stupid Leia...*

There was a soft bang as a cupboard opened, and I heard the sound of plates being stacked. Matt answered, and his deep voice sounded a little muffled. I could picture him leaning down and talking into the plate cupboard as he put away the dishes he had dried. "It's hard to be fourteen, Kat, for anyone. And Grey feels things pretty deeply. As I recall from your stories, you used to be pretty angry with the world."

This comment evoked a scowl from me as I practically yelled in my head, *It's not the same!*

Mama's voice was sharp now. "It's hardly the same. I had reasons to be angry. What reasons does she have?"

Her echo of my thought really provoked me. *I have my reasons. I am so sorry I'm such a problem and not the perfect MC's daughter. How inconvenient for you.* I crossed my arms and stuck my hands in my armpits.

Matt's deep baritone rumbled, "I think that is something you have to ask her about, Kat." I heard my mother give a deep sigh in response. Then Matt said, "Come here, love."

Now Mama's voice was the one muffled; Matt had to have been hugging her. I could picture them standing with their arms around each other, and my anger started to recede a little. My brother, Kik, says when they hug, it looks like they are stitched together because the scar on Matt's left cheek seems to connect to the one that runs from my mom's left ear to her right collarbone. "But Matty, how is she going to be able to get along with, much less sail with, someone else for 3,800 kilometers and back? And why the hell does it have to start from there? Why Haida? Of all places, why go back there?"

As I heard the word *Haida*, I catapulted up from the vent in a flash and held my breath. After a moment, I leaned back a little to hear the response.

"It's where the race starts. And maybe she needs to go back there. Maybe we all do." Mom gave a little groan in response.

Matt started humming a little tune, and I knew they were dancing the way they do. But the word *Haida* still hummed like electricity through a wire in my ears. That was where the Awful July happened.

The tightness in my shoulders increased, and I heard a low whisper in my head. There were no words, but the tone was ugly. I tried to shake the half-sound aside. My breath was coming fast, and my hands felt clammy. I rubbed at my jaw and swallowed against the pressure that seemed to appear in my throat.

Abandoning my mission to get the consent signed tonight, I crept back up the stairs and went straight to my little sister's room. The night was warm, and Rini had kicked her covers off. She was sleeping on her stomach, hands at her sides with her knees under her and her little bottom thrust up in the air. I stood for a moment just looking at her. My breath slowed as I smiled, and the phantom pressure at my neck faded. I gathered her up in my arms, smelling her sweet toddler fragrance and feeling her wrap her chubby arms around me as she roused and whispered, "Sissy Grey bed," lisping the *s*'s in "Sissy," melting my heart. So, like most nights, I carried her to my room. We tucked in together in my big, soft bed with its soft, rose sheets and the fairy lights I have strung around the headboard. The fan on the ceiling slowly rotated, creating a pleasant breeze. Rini opened her big, brown eyes and said, "Read."

"Okay, sweetie." I kissed her deep, black curls as I pulled out *The Obsidian Shore* and opened it to its bookmarked page. "Nyra Jhone looked both left and right and up and down before she slipped from the cell where the Birdfolk had imprisoned her. She moved silently through the branches, knowing she could not call Sindress yet, for the dragon was too young to have learned the ways of stealth..."

Rini murmured, "Wanna dragon," then her eyelids sank shut, and she returned to breathing steadily on my shoulder.

I smiled at her little face, so peaceful. "Me too, Rini." I'd wanted to read more, but instead, I tucked the book back in its spot under my pillow, turned down the lights, and snuggled my sister close so she could keep the whispers away.

FOUR

I'm Not Cut Out for This

The cramped dinghy had been bobbing about for hours in the dark, lifting and rolling with the heavy waves and wind. Neither Ashton nor Brian had been able to get the small motor on the back to do more than sputter and cough, no matter how much they swore and struck it. Engines were something for the skipper or crew to take care of, not the passengers. Now, the two men lay in the boat, moving up and down in rhythm with the sea, exhausted from the events of the tumultuous night.

Upon dropping the dinghy to the sea and jumping in after it—two actions that had been pretty dicey from the moving yacht—they had watched the *Abundance* move steadily away from them.

"We need to comm the skipper and get him to come for us." Ashton was determined to get to land as fast as possible. "But I don't have my comm."

Brian reached into his pocket and pulled his comm out. It was soaked with seawater. He pushed the button, and the screen flickered on, causing both men to exclaim, and then, just as quickly, it flickered out and did not respond again.

So, they had turned to the job of staying afloat and staying alive, confident that the Castellanos brothers and the skipper and crew would be out searching for them within the hour.

At first, they had both bailed the water out of the boat that splashed in from the swells and came down from the heavy rain. Brian discovered a used jug of some sort in the bottom of the dinghy. Its base was cut off, making it prime for bailing. The men traded off, one using the jug and the other using cupped hands to keep the small boat from filling with water. It was far harder than Ashton had imagined. His knuckles were scraped and stinging, and his arms were growing more and more tired from the repetitive movements. In addition, the small boat pitched and lurched, allowing neither man to maintain balance. They finally settled on one man crouching near the front and one near the back as they bailed. Though they tossed what seemed to be a kiloliter of seawater back to its source, the ocean and sky seemed to have other plans and kept returning almost as much as the men ladled out.

After about the first hour, seasickness engulfed Brian, first brief and minor, then progressing to a literal gut-wrench as he spewed everything from his body. Ashton watched, repulsed and feeling his own stomach clench in sympathy. "There's vomit on your shirt," he pointed out after the fourth round of purging.

Brian gazed down and made a gagging sound as he pulled off his shirt, using it to wipe his face and mouth. He moved on to dry heaves every few minutes soon after, leaving Ashton to cope with the bailing alone. *At least I get to use the jug*, he thought as he rubbed his bloodied knuckles.

The rains slowed, then stopped midway through the second hour, and the strong wind subsided after what must have been three hours. Ashton finally stopped the ceaseless ladling. He rubbed first one exhausted shoulder, then the other. His arms felt like jelly. His right knee was in agony. There was still plenty of water sloshing at the bottom of the boat, but as no more was coming in, he was satisfied the dinghy was not going to sink. At least not tonight. *But what about tomorrow? You are going to die out here. You will be mine....* Ashton's exhausted mind imagined the sea was taunting him.

He growled and yelled out at the ocean, "No! I am not dying here. There will be a rescue. So shut up!"

Shaking his head after his outburst, Ashton turned his attention to rest. There was no moonlight, and the stars were just beginning to appear as the clouds scudded away. Ashton felt about for the dinghy cover they had shoved to the side before they left the *Abundance*. Brian had collapsed on the bench nearest the useless motor, head propped on one side and feet up on the other, periodically moaning and gagging. Ashton sat down on the shorter seat, straddling the protrusion that jutted toward the center of the boat, and pulled the tarp over them both, tucking the edges secure under their bodies.

Now out of the wind, Ashton realized how chilled he had become. His robe and night shorts were soaked and plastered to his body, the dampness seeping through to his very bones. Brian was moaning in his sleep, emitting vomit-scented burps every few minutes. Still, the heat of their two bodies warmed their enclosure. Even though Ashton's belly was roiling from the smell and memories of Brian's purging, and he had to work to keep panic at bay, he was exhausted and so sank into the warmth, resting his head on the lumpy backpack they had filled on their way to the dinghy, and fell asleep.

Morning sunlight streamed over Ashton's face as if someone was shining a strong, red light into his eyes. He grunted, and it took a moment for him to come to consciousness. As the fog of sleep drifted further away, he realized that his face was not pressed onto a soft, smooth pillow but instead on the side of a small boat. The events of the night before came to him in a rush, and he sat up, eyes still shut against the bright sun, body tangled in the blue tarp. He recalled that he had stuck his face out of the tarp at some point in the night to avoid the noxious odors within. Now he pulled his head back underneath to fully open his eyes. He took only one breath in, and the stench of vomit engulfed him. He breathed out and then quickly stuck his face out to take in a lungful of sea air. Ducking back under, he kicked at Brian. "Hey, wake up. We need to figure a way back to land."

Brian groaned himself awake and was slow to sit up. Once he was awake, though, he began struggling with and batting the blue tarp off him as if it were a trap. The breeze caught it, and it billowed up and over the edge of the dinghy and would have gone to sea had Ashton not been holding one edge and jerked it back at the last moment.

"I feel awful," Brian complained, his words slurring. He started to stand at the side of the dinghy, and the small boat lurched in that direction.

All the frustration Ashton felt last night flooded back. He was not a sailor by a long shot, but he did know some basic concepts. He growled, "Stay down! No standing in the boat." He glared at Brian, who complied without comment.

Ashton continued to berate the younger man. "You think you feel bad? Bet I feel worse. It was my boat that just drove off into the ocean last night. And that boat you smashed? I bet the people who were on it feel worse than you—if they are even alive to feel anything." He could feel his breathing increase. For a moment, the old anger resurfaced, and he really considered striking Brian. He took a deep breath in through his nose.

For the past three years, Ashton had struggled with flashes of anger that usually ended in him breaking something and lashing out with his fists and feet. It had peaked about eighteen months ago when he was still living in Truvale at his mother and her husband's home. He had gone out to several bars with his friends and, as usual, was looking for a fight. Since the only skills Ashton brought to a fight were reckless enthusiasm and a desperate need to drain his anger, these fights required specific parameters. The intended fightee had to be at least as drunk or, better yet, drunker than Ashton; they needed to be alone; and that other party needed to be smaller, with no indication they could defend themselves. When those three requirements were met, Ashton could swing away, and the individual on the other end of his fist would usually take off running while Ashton and his dwindling cadre of friends could move on to celebrate his battle victory.

That night, however, things turned out differently. He had gotten into an argument with the bartender, a young woman almost twenty centimeters shorter than him and twenty-plus kilos lighter. When she refused to pour him another drink as he could barely keep his seat at the bar, he took a swing at her. In a moment, two burly bouncers were on him. They dragged him through the front door and deposited him on the street, where they would have simply left him had he not charged them and leaped upon the larger of the two men's back, yelling and pounding at him with his fists.

The next thing he recalled was his mother's lawyer bailing him out of jail several hours later. She took him to a physician, who was very discreet, to have his injuries assessed. The man placed a few stitches in the cut above his left eyebrow, gave him some painkillers, and took a fat envelope from the lawyer. Ashton arrived back at his mother's, hoping to fall into his bed and not wake until his hangover disappeared. But, alas, there was one more hurdle he had to clear to get there: his mother, Sandra Abernathy Saunders.

"Enough of this," Sandra had declared. "What is wrong with you, Ashton Abernathy? This sort of brawling is not acceptable. Do you know how much I had to pay that bartender and those bouncers to keep their mouths shut? Not to mention the doctor. Why am I the only one concerned for your future, Ashton? Why do you feel the need to embarrass yourself *and* me with these outbursts? Are you intentionally trying to destroy your chances to move ahead in this town?"

The questions kept coming as if shot out of some rapid-fire weapon, leaving no time for Ashton to compose a response. His brain was fuzzy from both the pummeling it had been subject to and the remnants of last night's alcohol and Glitter, and he stared at his mother as she paced back and forth, hands in the air, gesticulating wildly, her mouth moving at a breakneck pace. He said, "Sorry, Mother. It won't happen again," as he had so many times before, trying to shift past her to head to bed.

"No, it will not," she declared. "You can get some sleep. Then you will pack your things. I have spoken to my pilot. He will fly you to Haida tonight at 8 p.m. You will stay at the Karuk estate until further notice. Am I clear?"

Ashton wanted to argue the point since the mention of Karuk caused his insides to clench, but he knew his mother's tone. This was a done deal. He was being exiled to Haida.

Now he realized it had been the right move. He had gotten his temper under control, for the most part, by throwing himself into his drawing. And he had made new friends and reconnected with some old ones like Nicco. He wished it had been Nicco he was stuck in a dinghy with instead of this man-child, Brian. But that was not how things had turned out.

Now Brian said in a quiet tone, "Sorry, Ash. I didn't mean to."

Another breath and Ashton let some of his anger go; he ran his finger along the bench he sat on, creating lines and shapes in the damp. He wished he had something to draw with. Now he opened and began to scrabble in the backpack at his side. As they had retreated to the dinghy last night, they grabbed the bag hanging over a stool and paused at the galley, filling it with two large bottles of champagne from an ice bucket, several bottles of sparkling water, and a couple of handfuls of the small cakes the chef had made to celebrate the end of the race. Ashton thought belatedly that a torch would have been good to grab, but he wasn't even sure where one was on the *Abundance*. With the many chandeliers, deck lights, and electric side lights, he had never needed one there.

Now he took out a bottle of water and began to drink. Usually, he would pause to avoid the belching that resulted when he drank the seltzer too quickly. But he hadn't realized he was so thirsty and finished the bottle in three gulps, belching loudly after. "Want one?" He held a bottle out to the younger man—a peace offering.

"Ugh, no way. My stomach is still shit. And my head hurts like hell. These little boats are awful." Brian made his way to the front of the boat. "I'm going to lie in the sun. That always makes me feel better."

"Suit yourself." Ashton shrugged and filled the empty bottle with seawater, washing the residual puke off the deck and sides to settle into the water at the bottom. He moved to the back and tried the motor again. This time, he received only silence. So, he ate three small cakes and drank another water, this one more slowly as he looked around at the blue waves that stretched as far as he could see on all sides. The sun was hot, so he fashioned the tarp into a low tent across the dinghy, fastening it on the engine seating and with the backpack and the two empty bottles that he had refilled with seawater.

Surveying his handiwork, he smiled. A sudden childhood memory of building blanket forts with his sister in the New Detroit house flooded his mind. He hadn't thought of that for years. His smile slipped. He missed his sister. They had been partners for years, allied against Father's moods and sudden violence until the day Ashton had decided the best way to fully avoid the pain his father meted out was to become exactly what his father wanted from a son—an extension, a byproduct, a vassal. He'd like to say he and his sister had grown apart but knew that wasn't accurate. With his choice to ally himself with his father and his father's causes, he started viewing his sister the way Rob Abernathy had—homely and disheveled—an unworthy embarrassment to the family name. He had actively turned away from her, and then suddenly, Farris had disappeared, and his father seemed less than unconcerned. What if he had been the one to vanish? He was sure his father would have come looking for him. He contemplated, not for the first time, just how much his father had to do with his sister's disappearance.

Looking out at the boundless stretch of the sea, he realized that as far as the world was concerned, he, too, had now disappeared. *Would anyone care about that?* Ashton frowned and shook his head to dislodge this uncomfortable thought and the others that waited near it. He slid under the tarp to nap. It would be fine. His skipper, or someone, would come for him soon. Someone always did.

He woke, hot, under the tarp, disoriented once again to time and place. The world around him was a steamy blue and rocked in a steady rhythm. He rubbed his face and murmured, "Oh, damn," as he recalled his new reality. He stuck his head out from the tarp tent and looked at the sky to get an idea of the time. He was annoyed that he hadn't put his watch on back on the boat. It was a quality Swiss watch, very expensive. One of the many personal items at the estate in Karuk that his father had left behind three years ago. Ashton considered his good fortune that his father was gone; otherwise, he would have been subjected to Rob Abernathy's personal brand of disappointment and disgust for losing the *Abundance*, for failing—again—and for creating an "unseemly" scene. So, while there was no longer a watch, there was also no one to discipline him for its loss. Ashton's hand went to the side of his face as he recalled several episodes of "discipline." He grinned to himself. No watch, but he had the sun, and it was high and so bright that Ashton had to shade his eyes with both hands.

He looked down the length of the boat and saw Brian stretched out and snoring. Brian had been wearing his vomit shirt, short pants, and the island shoes that did not cover the tops of his feet when they escaped the yacht. Now it was the tops of his feet that caught Ashton's attention. They were bright red, and the skin was looking slightly bubbly and rough. "Oh, shit," Ashton said under his breath as his eyes traveled up the lobster-red legs. Brian's shirt was tucked under his head, and his chest, arms, and face were deeply burnt as well.

It was clearly afternoon by now. How long had Brian been there? Hours. "Hey, Brian. Wake up!" Ashton crawled over and gently shook the young man.

"Ow! What the hell?" Brian shoved Ashton back.

"Damn it to Earth, Brian. You should have gotten under the

tarp. You are really burnt." Ashton pulled out a bottle of fresh water from his backpack and thrust it toward his boatmate.

Brian sat up, his movements guarded and slow, his lips pressed together. He took the bottle, twisted off the top, which he dropped to the bottom of the boat, then drank the water greedily. Only after it was all gone did he pause and say, "Thanks. Do you think it'll make me puke?"

Ashton frowned. "I sure as hell hope not. Besides, you'll die without water, especially looking like that."

Brian turned his bright-red arms in front of him, taking in the damage. Then he peered down at his chest and legs and, with two careful fingers, touched his face. "Shit." Then, to Ashton's surprise, he crouched, kicked off his island shoes, and vaulted out of the dinghy into the deep ocean with a loud splash. Ashton had just a moment of panic staring at the point in the water Brian had disappeared into before the sandy-brown head popped up, and he surfaced.

"What the hell are you doing, Brian?" Ashton demanded, reaching a hand to his companion.

"Cooling my skin off. It feels better in here." Brian tread water for a moment or two before reaching up to take Ashton's hand and climb back on board.

"You know there's sharks and stuff in the water, right?" Ashton asked, frowning.

Brian waved him off with a laugh. "I didn't see any. I'm getting under the tarp."

Ashton looked after him for a moment before he, too, took refuge from the heat of the day beneath the tarp. He wasn't sure if his fear was for Brian's safety or over the possibility of being left all alone.

The sun sank down, just hovering above the horizon, turning the sky and its clouds a tumult of purples, pinks, and oranges as a cool breeze caused both men to stir.

Brian woke and gave a groan as he stretched his arms. "My skin feels so tight and hot. I can't bear it." Ashton tossed him a bottle of water, and he quickly splashed it over his skin with a sigh.

"Let's fold up the tarp back and eat something before it's pitch black," Ashton suggested.

Brian nodded, tossing the bottle to the bottom of the boat as he took one end of the tarp and did his part to fold it. "I'll have some water and something small. I don't want to start puking again."

Ashton snorted. "Nobody wants that. But you have to eat." He tried to make it sound like an order.

Shrugging, Brian accepted one of the cakes and nibbled on it. Ashton ate three, and they each drank another bottle of water. There were five cakes left and a pile of crumbs in the bottom of the backpack that was probably equal to two more. Six bottles of water remained. Those wouldn't last long. They needed to get to land.

Brian lay back and let out his breath in a whoosh. "Sunburns make me sleepy. I'm going to cool and crash." He once more jumped into the ocean, then, after a few minutes, climbed back into the dinghy with Ashton's assistance, sighed, then lay down on the bench seat closest to the back and shut his eyes.

This second dip into the sea did not unsettle Ashton as much as the first, but he was glad Brian was back in the boat safely. "Well, I'm going to see what's in this boat while there's light." Ashton started to search the boat, turning the locks on hatch covers and exclaiming as he discovered items. The first thing he found was a set of oars and oarlocks. "Hey, look,

Brian. I guess we could paddle, but which way?" Ashton looked over at the younger man stretched out, eyes closed. Brian shrugged but stayed silent.

So, Ashton answered himself, "Yeah, no sense in working against the current. We'd just get exhausted." He sat back for a moment and inwardly cursed that they couldn't get the motor running. Though even if they did, he still had no idea where he would steer it. With something between a sigh and a groan, he looked up at the clear sky. "I wonder when it's going to rain again. I mean, I don't want a storm, but we could drink rain." He shrugged and rattled the lock on another hold. "Hey! Water! That's lucky." He pulled four large bottles from their nest in the dinghy, holding one up. Brian said nothing, so Ashton tucked the bottles safely back away. He looked again in the hold and found an empty box that had contained food bars. Some asshole had eaten them and not replaced them. He rooted about a bit more, opening a third hold: "Got a couple of buckets and a rope. Wish I had known that when we were bailing."

Brian was definitely asleep, but Ashton continued to talk. It made it less lonely. He opened the next hold. "Hey! Four life vests, and…look at this, Brian. Flares!"

At the sound of his name, Brian opened one eye and peered over to where Ashton was grinning and holding up a long, red tube. "Hey, that's cool." He pressed himself up on one elbow.

Ashton nodded. "There's three. I'm gonna set one off." He'd never used a flare, but how hard could it be? He pulled the cap off and waited, but nothing happened. He shook it. Nothing. "The damn thing is broken, Brian."

"Bummer." Brian laid his head back on the seat but kept his eyes open to watch the flare show.

Ashton tossed the first one to the bottom of the boat and picked up another one. This one had a cap on the top and bottom; when he pulled the bottom cap off, a string dropped down. "Okay, let's try this one."

He pulled the string hard, and bright red sparks began to spew from the top, scattering on the deck and tarp. "Shit!"

Brian moved off the seat and yelled as a spark hit his burnt skin. "Ow! Dammit, Ash—get it away from me!"

Ashton quickly moved his hand over the side of the dinghy. The red sparks continued to blow upward, coming down in a cascade. Several hit his hand. "Ow! Damn!" He shook his hand, and the flare arced away from the boat and plunged into the ocean, taking its red sparks with it. Ashton licked his hand and shook it slowly as he watched the flare bob, and the sparks move away from him. "These flares suck, don't they, Brian?"

"Maybe it's you who suck at using them, Ash. Guess you should've listened to the safety talks. Let's save the last one for when the rescue boat comes," Brian murmured.

Ashton scowled at the comment. It echoed his father's constant criticism and chiding. He barked a response. "Like you could do better." But he couldn't help but think, *He's not wrong, though. Probably should have listened to the skipper. Too late now.* The sun had fully set, but adrenaline still pumped through Ashton from the flare mishap, keeping rest a good distance away. So, he busied himself with dropping his hand into the water to cool it. He watched the water lap at the sides of the dinghy as the sparks slowly faded away. He nodded and said to Brian and the universe, "Yeah. We'll just wait for the rescue boat."

There was no reply from Brian who was propped at the back of the boat, feet hanging over the bench; he had slipped easily back to sleep.

~

Ashton came suddenly awake, breathing heavily. He squinted and tried to catch the thread of his dream. He had been running in the rain along a dark road. Explosions were going off around him. He tried to recall where he was trying to go, but now, as his mind awoke, the dream's details shredded and faded away. He stretched his sore arms and legs, his right knee sending a small spasm of pain through him from being tucked up against the hull of the boat for a couple of hours.

He took a deep breath. The cool night air felt good. Ashton lay back and looked up at the stars. There were so many out here. The Milky Way arched above him, with its millions of tiny lights on either side of it covering the sky. The moon had not yet appeared; night was deep and dark. It took a few minutes to orient himself, searching among the millions for the *w* of Cassiopeia. He grinned. It had always been his sister's favorite; even back in New Detroit, they could see it when the city lights were dimmed from one of the many brownouts. Now, he looked for the Hercules constellation. *Remember when you thought you were a hero?* He had spent hours as a child pretending to rescue toys for Farris and fight off many-headed snakes and other fearsome creatures. He stopped the day his father had come upon him and asked what he was doing.

"I'm the hero. I'm fighting this monster to rescue the whale," Ashton had said proudly.

His father had scoffed. "Heroes are fools. Someone smarter always comes along to take them down. Smart boys don't want to be a hero. It is far more delightful to be the one who makes them fall, especially if you get paid well for it."

Ashton had never played hero again after that. He had been ten. Now, he considered, his father likely was correct. Heroes did not get ahead. No, Rob Abernathy had taught him it was better to stay grounded in the real world. Exploit those you could. Forget make-believe; seek power. The more your power, the stronger you were, and the more control you had over others. Ashton gave a derisive snort. *How'd that all work out for you, Father?*

He pushed thoughts of his father aside and looked back at the stars. After a bit, he began to feel a bit sleepy and had just closed his eyes when a heavy thump came on the side of the dinghy.

He sat up immediately. Had they hit a sandbar? Unlikely, this far out. He had heard stories about whales crashing into boats and breaking them up. He glanced over to where Brian was still softly snoring. Maybe it was a dream. Then he saw a narrow beam of light flash at the side of the dinghy near the front, and a voice came up from the sea. "Hey, anyone there? Can you give me a hand?"

FIVE

Keep Kicking

Remembering the warmth of my bed with Rini, I am almost ready to give in to my fatigue and let myself drift to sleep in the sea when something bumps into my chin, pulling me back to the present. I was on breath number fourteen, I think—it may have actually been the fifth rep or the sixth—but either way, as I lift my chin up, something pushes into me. My hand comes up to grab it, and I feel a whole slab of something floating.

I try to scramble on top, but my arms and legs are rubbery from all the exertion and won't do as I ask. So, I flop my upper half over as far as I can and let the slab hold me so I can rest. *No falling asleep, Grey—you might drown.* I have no intention of doing that, not after following my bubbles, treading water, and floating for thousands and thousands of counts. Instead, I return to *The Queen of the Marsh*'s tale in my head. Beverlee was small and slim, but she found her strength and was brave as she searched for her place in the world. She swam to an island and discovered the Marshfolk who had been waiting for someone like her, who could bridge the world of water and land for generations.

At some point, the rain stops, and the winds die down. I make-believe a dragon is about to fly down and pick me up, and I spend quite a while visualizing how I would climb onto its back and let the wave sound become the thrum of its beating wings as it soars up and up into the sky with me. I imagine it would be like when Mama flies me in the little vessels, but I'd be out in the open with the wind blowing my hair and the big body of a warm dragon beneath me.

The sky shifts from its deep darkness to purple, then to deep blue, which slowly brightens until an orange glow appears on the horizon. I smile for two reasons—because I survived the night and because now, I know which way is east. I am so tired; I have to sleep. So, I take a deep breath, grip the slab with my hands, and kick my feet hard, pulling with my arms. Just like that, I feel solidness under my whole body. The fog of sleep starts to embrace me almost immediately, but I feel the warmth of the sun even as it is born again for the day and remember to pull my hood up and tuck my hands into my long sleeves to protect my skin from the sun. Then I grasp both sides of my little floating chunk of survival tight with my hands and spread my legs wide for balance as I allow my exhausted mind and body to drift away.

The sun is almost at its zenith when I awake, sweaty, weak, and so very, very thirsty. I want to open my mouth and lick up the water from the surface my face is on, but I remember what Matt said about saltwater being dangerous to drink. Instead, I seal my lips, sucking on my tongue to bring up spit, and then move that around in my mouth and swallow. It helps but not much.

I lift my head and shoulders up to get a look at my raft. I'm pretty sure it is a slab of hull from the *Fascination*. It's made of wood and is the same shade of blue as the sloop had been. It must have floated in the same direction I did. I scoot my arms and legs closer together in tiny movements, making sure I don't overbalance to one side or the other. It is tricky. The raft leans heavily first to one side and then the other as my weight shifts. My movements have to be very slow so I don't end up back in the sea. When I am finally up on my hands and knees enough, I unzip my bright-yellow storm jacket partway, keeping it fastened at my waist, and slide my arms out. Cool air circulates around my arms and chest, and I immediately feel better. The coat and its hood make a decent awning, and I push my sleeves up and fan the bottom of my shirt a little, enjoying the shade for a moment.

Once my temperature has evened out, I start to feel the pockets of my coat, unzipping each only if I can't tell what it contains by feel. A smile crosses my face as I remember when Matt gave it to me….

"Okay, I'm calling this your *Make-Your-Mama-Happy* jacket." Matt laid the brand-new, bright-yellow storm slicker out on my bed in the kaadanaay, or guest house, where the family was staying in Haida.

I teased my bonus dad, "Everything you do is to make Mama happy."

Matt's copper-brown face wrinkled thoughtfully as his thick, black eyebrows took turns lifting and falling atop his brow. Then he shrugged, and his big smile blossomed. "Well, you have me there, Grey. It seems to be my mission in life. I do like seeing her smile."

I laughed. Mama and I had been getting along pretty well this summer. Not only had she signed the permission form in June, but she also helped me pack and even flew me and the whole family to Haida for the start of the race. She arranged for Papa and Hayami to be there as well to see me off. She was planning to fly to Moku-o-keawe and retrieve me after the race, but I said she couldn't. "Mama, getting the boat home is part of the process."

She had dropped her head and then laughed, saying, "Okay. I've come this far, I guess I can be patient for you to sail back to Haida." She made me promise to comm her from the Islands, though. Which I did.

As Matt and I were talking, she appeared at the doorway of my room, Rini squirming in her arms, and asked, "Making who happy?"

Matt laughed. "You. Who else?" I watched as they paused and looked at each other, their eyes connecting and smiles growing.

"Oh, Earth," I moaned. "Don't go getting all lovey-dovey, you two. I have a race to run!" Mama and Matt were always snuggling and kissing, holding hands and saying, "I love you." When my friends were over, they all thought the two of them were "so romantic" and that Matt was "so handsome." I mean, he is, but it's weird for them to say that. He's old, and he's my bonus dad. And they've been together for more than three years—you'd think they could tone down their mush, at least around kids, right? Papa and his new wife, Hayami, never act like that.

Matt grinned and refocused; Mama peered at the jacket on the bed as he ran through its treasures. "Okay, you're right, Grey." He held up my favorite knife that I used for carving and tucked it into the right lower pocket. "In this pocket are your jack knife, some fishing line, and a twist of wire." He moved on to the left lower pocket. "Here, I put a waterproof torch and a first aid box your mama made up, and in here is a bag with desalination packets." He slid the pile of sealed packets into the big pocket in front and zipped it shut.

"That's too many," I complained. "I'm never going to use all of those."

He shrugged. "Fine. You can bring back the ones you don't use. Better to—"

"Have them and not need them rather than need them and not have them?" I recited and grinned.

Matt smiled sheepishly. "I suppose I have said that once or twice. But that doesn't make it wrong." He showed me the compass that he'd placed in my right shoulder pocket. Then he pointed to the small pocket on the left shoulder. "Now in this one is a small mirror—"

"Oh, what, so I can see how beautiful I am in the middle of the ocean?" I broke in and was halfway through an eye roll when Matt finished.

"For signaling or starting a fire in a pinch. Though you are quite lovely, mirror-gazing seems a bit impractical during an emergency." He kept his tone very matter-of-fact. Matt is really good at calling me out when I say stupid things without making me feel like I'm a baby.

Mama chimed in, "Can you put a homing beacon in one of the pockets? That way, I can know where to direct my worries and when to fly in and pick her up?"

"No way. I don't—" I started to protest.

Matt's hand went up. "Of course not, Grey. Mama and I respect your judgment. Right, Kat?" I saw him look pointedly at Mama as Rini reached out for him. He took the little sweetheart in his arms and kissed her neck as she giggled. Then she leaned out of his arms toward me. I obliged by wrapping her up in my arms and twirling around, both of us laughing.

When I stopped the spin, she demanded, "Rini go Grey! Wanna yellow coat."

Mama responded fast. "Not a chance, Rini. A yellow coat, maybe, but you, I still get to put a homing beacon on. For at least a few more years." She looked at me with her warm smile, then reached out and ran a hand down my arm. "I do trust you, baby. It's more my issue. It's a long way, with people I don't know, on a very big ocean. Not really my comfort zone."

Though I absolutely hate that she still calls me "baby," I was still about to say something nice when she looked at Matt. "Cal wouldn't give you one of those little beacons either, huh?"

Matt shrugged. "Nope. I believe he said, 'If I didn't give one to the MC, why do you think I'd give one to you?'"

When I realized that they had actually tried to get some kind of tracking device from their friend in Bosch Intelligence, I stomped my foot and ground my teeth. How could they even consider that?

You see, my mama is the MC, or master commander, of Bosch, a mid-sized island of the Central Continent. It's my home. Well, mostly. My real papa comes from Edo, a group of islands way on the far side of the Great Sea, closer to China than the Central Continent. I was born on the northern island in a little cabin in the foothills of Mizueyama. My brothers and I used to visit there a lot. Since the Awful July in Haida, Mama still is nervous about us going to Edo without her. I think she doesn't really trust Papa, which sorta makes sense.

So, Papa and Hayami bought a little house in Bosch. They come and stay there with my other little sister, Sumiko. Before they moved to their house, my brothers and I were about the only people on Bosch who looked Edoan. Most people on Bosch are different shades of deep brown, like late fall leaves, with a few almost black-skinned folks and a few super-pale-skinned people, like Mama, but not many who look like me. The thing I like best about Bosch is that it is an island of pirates, which I guess makes me a pirate.

The thing I like least about Bosch is how everyone—and I mean, *everyone*—from my teachers to my cousins to people I meet at the grocery all say, "Oh, Grey, you are just like your mother. You'll be enlisting in the Force [that's the Bosch Pirate Force, or BPF] soon, and before you know it, you'll be MC." Ugh. No way.

When I was a little kid, there was nothing I wanted more than to be just like Mama. But I'm not little anymore, and there are lots of things I may want to do. Like racing a sailboat across the Great Sea to the Drowned Islands. Mama is the best air vessel pilot, but she didn't grow up in Bosch, so she doesn't really know how to sail. I do. Matt is a great sailor. I was struggling in sailing class at the end of primary, so he took me out on his boat and taught me all he could. The first time I took the *Rune* out on my own, I was hooked. By the next spring, I started racing in regattas. Lots of them and I got better and better. And that's how I qualified for the Great Sea Race. Which landed me here, floating on this little chunk of wood in the middle of the great, big, beautiful ocean wishing my mom's friend Cal had given her that damn homing beacon.

The ocean is my friend, always. Even after her temper tantrum last night, I still love her. Now she's calm, with small swells gently rocking me. The deep blueness of her shifts and brightens as she rolls, the sunlight decorating her with thousands of sparkles and the breeze stirring up patches of seafoam. Her song has shifted to a gentle hum, hypnotizing and comforting. Usually, it's my favorite way to spend a lazy day, watching and listening to her. But usually, I'm on a boat or on the sandy beach of Saltend Harbor.

I decide to pass the time playing with my mirror, catching

the light, and sending beams over the water and up into the sky. I guess I could signal someone, but who? There's only me and the ocean. She may be my friend, but she keeps her own counsel and is unconcerned with getting me to land. She'd be happy to keep me with her forever.

That thought ruffles me, so I refocus on the mirror. It has two sides, one regular and one that magnifies. I use the regular side and survey my face for a bit. It's gotten skinnier in the last couple of years but still is very oval and tan from the past weeks on the *Fascination*. My eyes are like Papa's, which are like his papa's, though mine are not as dark as theirs. My nose and mouth are more like Mama's, which is okay. I peer at my chin and the space between my dark eyebrows, where the skin is speckled with several pimples. There were more at the end of school; I think the sun and the sea have improved them. Leia said I should scrub my face more, but she has hardly any spots, so I don't think she knows. She also said I should cut a fringe of bangs, but I haven't ever cut my hair and don't plan to for a while. Thinking of Leia annoys me, so I flip to the magnifying side.

Matt said that's the one to use to start a fire. I try it on a chunk of wood that sticks out from *Chance*, which is what I have named my boat, or piece of boat, and I see a little smolder, so I stop fast. I don't want to burn up the only thing floating between me and my friend, the deep ocean. After all, she has lots of hungry things that live in her, and while I love her, I know she is pitiless.

I put the mirror back in the correct jacket pocket and pull out two desalination pouches from their place. I loop a piece of fishing line through the little handles on top, wrap the line around a sharp splinter of wood that sticks out from the edge of my raft, and then drop the pouches into the water. It will take a few hours for the water to filter through them. I wish I had some food in my pockets, but I don't. So, I decide instead to watch a few fish flit up and hide under *Chance* before dozing off under the cover of my jacket.

The cool evening breeze and my bladder wakes me. I pull down my leggings, peer into the water and around *Chance* for sharks, and then scoot to the side and let my legs float so I can pee. I think about paddling a bit, but since I have no idea where I am, there's really no point. I'll be more intentional—one of my mom's favorite words—with the mirror tomorrow. Since the sun is low, I take my jacket off entirely and sit on it. I have mastered moving slowly on *Chance* and keeping my balance. Riki, my Edoan friend, who also used to be my nanny, would be impressed. He taught me some great fighting moves he learned in his old job in Edo. Thinking of him makes me think of my brothers and sisters, which then makes me think of Mama, Matt, Papa, and Hayami. I feel a lump in my throat and a little sting to my eyes. *No crying, Grey, it'll make you lose water.* I know it's true, but I cry for a little while anyway.

After my cry, I shake my head, which feels a little fuzzy. I try to focus. My mouth is so dry. A cool drink… That will help. I pull up the desalination packs, now plump with drinkable water, and suck one down. I feel immediately better and decide to drink the second one. They have an odd taste—kinda salty and kinda sweet—not like plain, fresh water. I know they have some calories and stuff in them, which is good, but I start to fantasize about how at home there's all the freshwater anyone could want. I lick my lips. It's weird to wish for something that doesn't taste like anything. I put two more packs in the water. Eight packets left. I'll need to be careful with them.

Now the ocean is no longer fully blue, shifting to her

evening grays with an overskirt of gold and orange and a sash of light that leads to the setting sun. I let myself sink into an imagining. Usually, those are of dragons, elves, fairies, and swords, but right now, I see myself going for a swim at home in the Tamrood River, under the willow copse where the water spreads out and slows down to make a swimming hole. I roll onto my back, looking up at the darkening evening sky and the stars beginning to appear, envisioning that I am floating in the non-salty water, hearing my twin brothers laugh and splash and knowing that my grandma, Mama M, has her special picnic lunch packed with blueberry scones and the cheese she always buys from the Keya farm. The basket is just a few meters away on shore. I can eat all I want if I just swim.... I sigh and my mouth starts to water when something catches my eye.

I am immediately pulled back to the now. I roll carefully to my belly and squint—it's about 45 degrees off to my left, and its red sparks. Those bits of light jump around, and then they disappear, but I am sure I saw them. I pull out the waterproof torch Matt gave me and, slipping its wristband over my hand, scan the horizon, but the beam doesn't go far. I turn it off to conserve power. Matt said it takes a while to recharge and must be in bright sunlight. I weigh my options. Stay here alone or go toward where I saw the sparks.

I pull out my compass from its place in my right shoulder pocket and flick on the torch. Remembering the spot where the sun set, I orient myself. The sparks showed up at about 310° NNW. I turn the torch off again and shift my orientation on *Chance*. I hadn't wanted to just paddle randomly, but this is something real—a destination. A heading. The decision is easy. If I stay here, I may just die. Holding the compass firmly in my left hand and the torch in my right, I slip my legs into the water and start to kick, maneuvering *Chance* 310° NNW toward where I saw the light.

My legs are pumping furiously. I return to counting the same way I did while I was floating pre-*Chance*. Scissor-kick fifty times, frog kick fifty times, rest for the count of ten, turn on the torch for a quick look at my compass and the sea, reorient to stay at a bearing of 310° NNW, and repeat. I lift my chin to see if any other red sparks show, but there's nothing. I figure I'll just keep going in the direction I saw them and hope something good happens. I mean, I'm due, right?

There's no moon yet, and the sea is darkening. The sky holds a faint, greenish airglow, and the stars are plentiful though don't provide much light to see by. When I was little and would wake up, the dark felt scary, so I'd slide out of bed, rush away from the monsters I was sure were around me, crawl into the safety of my parents' bed, and then snuggle next to Mama. I realize I can't remember the last time I did that. I feel a pang of sadness. *Focus, Grey—kick. Forty-two, forty-three, forty-four…*

I've been kicking for just this side of forever. I've tried to pass the time retelling myself some of my favorite stories, pretending to be Nyra Jhone, Beverlee, or, for a while, just a nameless mermaid out on a lark, but I can't lose myself in imaginings if I'm going to survive. And I intend to do just that. I put on my torch and pass it over the water. There seems to be a darker splotch off to my left. I squint, but it just stays a splotch. Okay, that's my heading. I shift my angle and keep kicking. My legs are burning but are simultaneously so very cold. *Are there sharks here? Do they sleep at night? Will my torch wake them up?* That thought makes me kick a little faster, and I try hard not to look like a shark snack.

My rest periods are getting longer. I really want to stop moving altogether, but the dark splotch is now bigger and bobbing with the waves, so I push on. I imagine that I am on base, and my friend Flossie, who is a BPF sergeant, is yelling, "Keep going, Grey. You can do it!" like she did when I would practice the recruit challenge. I keep going.

I am on stroke thirty-six of my frog kicks when a small thump reverberates through my arms. *Chance* has hit something. The surprise and delight wash away all my fatigue, almost making me lose my grip on the torch but not quite. Instead, I snap it on. Immediately, I grin. It's a boat. A really little boat, but—and don't tell *Chance* I think this—it's better than what I have now. I call out, "Hey, anyone there? Can you give me a hand?"

PART II
Sailing in Bosch, Lesson Two

Cooperation and Trust

It is important to know and trust your crew. While the smallest boats can be sailed single-handedly, on medium and larger sailboats, you must develop the skills essential in working in a partnership or with multiple crewmembers. The ability to listen, to speak your mind clearly and without offense, to know what work needs to be accomplished on board and off, and to pull your weight and be able to work tolerantly with anyone, whether friendly with them or not, will create a smooth-running crew. A good working relationship can spell the difference between a pleasant day's sail in the bay or a miserable one, as well as the difference between successful survival or catastrophic collapse should an emergency develop.

The history of Bosch egalitarianism is one that stretches back to the philosophies of the Golden Age of Pirates in the sixteenth century and honors and amplifies their belief in equality: both in the equitable division of booty and in the equal voices of all the crew, including its officers. This tradition is upheld in Bosch business, the political arena of the Council, the pastoral farms and vineyards, and, of course, the Bosch Pirate Force. You will be expected to uphold the same beliefs and ethics on your group sails.

To that end, it is imperative you and your crewmates meet briefly on arrival at the dock at eight bells to determine roles and responsibilities. Also, after each day's lesson and sail are complete, at approximately sixteen bells, the crew will sit down with their assigned instructor for a debrief to discuss what went well and what could be improved. At this time, each crewmember should air any grievances or concerns in a reasonable manner. It is up to the acting captain, and your instructor as needed, to assist their crew in finding resolution. Without resolution, anger, resentment, and hurt feelings can develop and can result in your crew working antagonistically, creating a dangerous situation for all.

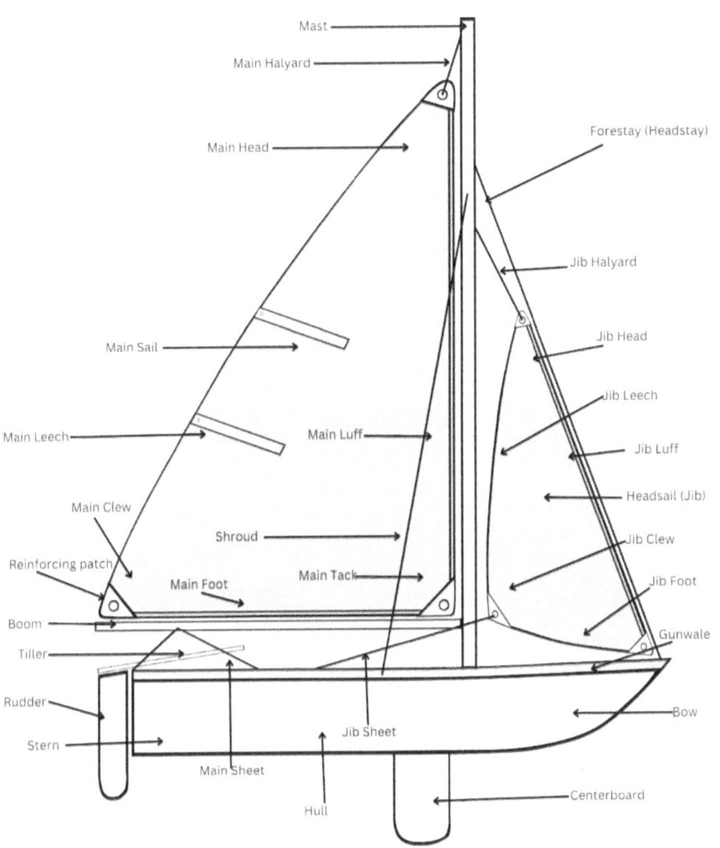

Parts of a Sailboat

SIX

Take My Hand

Stuffing my light in my pocket, I clamber over *Chance* and move toward the port side of the little boat near the bow.

"Here. Take my hand." A man's voice comes over the edge. Something about it stirs a memory in me, but I ignore my trepidation—that's a word Pheidon uses in *The Sword of Transformation* when there's something worrisome, but he isn't sure what. I chalk it up to thinking I might never have heard another voice again. A hand is thrust down in front of me. I reach up and take it. An involuntary gasp escapes my lips at the touch of another person as the realization of just how scared I actually have been surfaces. Tears threaten, and I beat them back. I'm not home yet.

I start to heave myself into a small boat, but then the hand gives an unexpectedly strong jerk, and I am pulled aboard headfirst, slipping over the side and smashing my face into the sole, which is covered with a sizable puddle of foul water. I jerk my head back from the nasty and excessive bilge water.

Looking around, I see someone's bare legs and feet in front of me. I swiftly right myself and pivot toward port, where *Chance* is bobbing near the bow. "Quick, I need to tie my...

raft…up." I may be in an actual boat, but I'm not ready to let *Chance* disappear. He's been too good to me.

I hear scrabbling. "Here," the same man-voice says, and a line is thrust into my hands. I lean over the edge, tie a bowline around the splintered edge, and then cleat it off. It won't hold in a storm, but there're no clouds tonight, so I am willing to bet that it will be enough until morning.

I turn around. "Hi. Thanks." It's still pretty dark, so I can't make out the man's face, only the dark smudge of him against the sky and sea. I hear snoring and squint toward the stern, where the sound is coming from. There's another dark, person-sized blob stretched out on the seat. Two people in this boat. That's lucky, I guess.

The tiniest bit of light from the rising crescent moon starts to give a little illumination, so I leave my torch in my pocket and squint to see who saved me. Because my brain is muddled, I say in Bosch, "My name is Grey. What's yours?" Then I realize my mistake and repeat the same in standard Federal Alliance dialect.

There is a long pause. I wonder for a moment if maybe the man doesn't speak either language, but he had used standard FA earlier. I say more slowly, "What…your…name? I…am…called…Grey."

The man at the other end of the boat finally speaks. "No freaking way."

Ashton stared at the girl at the far end of the dinghy. He couldn't see her face, but the voice was right, as was her name. It couldn't be. How could he be adrift on the damnable Great Sea and somehow end up with that nasty little shrew who had plagued him three years earlier? Her home was clear across the continent. There was no way. A zipping sound broke his thoughts, and then suddenly, torchlight was in his face. His eyelids shut tightly but not soon enough to protect them against this sudden intrusion of brightness.

She gasped. "Oh, no. No. Not you."

The beam clicked off, and he opened his eyes. All he could see was the ghost of the bulb that had just assaulted him. *Figures she'd do something to attack me. Even with light.* It really was her style. He rubbed his eyes with the heel of his hands, then dropped one hand to his right knee as he felt the not-that-old scar. While his eyes were trying to recover, and he was trying to collect his thoughts about this unlikely intrusion, another zipping sound started, and the boat rocked heavily. A loud splash followed, and water sloshed into the boat and onto him. *Did she seriously jump back into the ocean?*

He shifted to the side and called, "Hey, what are you going to do, swim to land? Or go back to whatever you were on before?" He squinted over the edge, blinking heavily as he tried to regain his night sight while looking at what was tied next to the dinghy. It was a slab of wood. Like, from a boat—likely from the one Brian had crushed. Holy shit. She must have been on that boat. Who takes a little girl out on an ocean race? He grabbed the rope she had tied it with. "Listen, I'm just as lost as you. Come on. Get back in the boat."

"I don't want to be anywhere near you. I hate you," her voice called from the water. Yep, that was her, all right. Unbelievable.

She was one of the last people on the planet he wanted around him, but he couldn't just leave her in the water. She was a little kid, for Earth's sake. He let out an exasperated sigh and said through his teeth, "Fine, I'll move to one end, and you can have the other. Just take my hand and get in the boat." He dropped his hand over the side of the dinghy.

There was a pause, and he heard swim strokes. Once again, he felt her hand in his, this time noticing how small it was. He pulled and she scrambled in, then she jerked her hand back and moved quickly to the very front end of the small boat.

"What the hell are you doing out here?" Ashton demanded of the girl as he squatted near the seat with the extension, trying to keep his feet out of the unpleasant water that sloshed in the center.

"Oh, for Earth. What do you think, just on a refreshing late-night paddle in the open ocean eight thousand kilometers from my home?" she growled. "What the hell are *you* doing here?" she shot back.

Ashton could feel the loathing radiating from her. He hesitated before answering and then motioned toward Brian, who still had not woken up. "We had a problem with our yacht and had to abandon it," Ashton loud-whispered.

A long, tense pause followed.

Please, please, Ashton pleaded silently to no one in particular, *don't let her figure it out. Why would she? She's just a child. A child, shit—what if her mother was on the boat too?* A stab of fear ran through Ashton, which he attempted to shake off. *Hell, she should just be happy we rescued her kid.*

"'Our yacht,' you say?" she began. His heart sank, and he could visualize the gears turning in her head. He was almost sure he heard the loud *click* as it all came together for her. "Sweet New Earth," she started, "it was you, wasn't it? It was your yacht that crushed the *Fascination*." There was a clear accusatory tone to her voice. Which, Ashton reasoned, was actually legitimate.

Maybe he had an out; there was someone else to blame. He pointed to the sleeping Brian. "It wasn't me. He did it."

Again, there was a *ziiip* from the front of the dinghy, and the light came on. But this time, it moved along in the direction he pointed, its beam scattering as it reflected off the dirty water at the bottom of the boat. A bit of the glow illuminated upward onto her. He could make out a yellow jacket and the wet ponytail slicked back from a thin face. He leaned slightly forward, studying her. It definitely was the same face from three years ago, though a bit longer, with more defined cheekbones. Definitely skinnier, and with a few spots that signaled she was probably a teen now, so, still a kid but maybe not a little kid. *How old had she been that July?*

"Oh, right, I'm sure nothing ever is your fault." Her scornful voice broke into his thoughts. He refocused as the beam passed over Brian, pausing on his red chest and blistered feet. "Who is he? And why is he burned to a crisp?" the girl asked.

Ashton looked at Brian, noticing his dry lips and the way his red skin seemed to sparkle under the torchlight. He did look like an overdone piece of meat.

"His name is Brian. He got seasick and then sunburned," Ashton stated.

The girl's voice dripped with sarcasm. "Oh, really? And did he blame me and my captain for that? Is that why he decided to destroy the *Fascination* and throw us both into the sea?"

Ashton sighed. Okay, so her mother wasn't on board. Well, that was good…and bad. She wouldn't come looking to kill him, but then, she also wouldn't come looking. "No. Of course not. He was being chased by some people who wanted to hurt him. He decided to use the yacht to get away, but it went sideways."

"How?" It was phrased as a question but sounded like a demand.

"Brian started up the yacht but didn't know how to steer, and the crew was in the village…," Ashton began.

"But it was his yacht?"

"No, it was mine."

"And you don't know how to captain your own boat?" There was that accusatory tone from her again.

"Well..." Ashton paused and felt his anger flare over his shame. He didn't owe this little snotty girl any explanation. "Look, I can drive a little boat, but the *Abundance* was always crewed, and...well, it's complicated."

She gave a snort. "Obviously."

"Now listen here, I don't need you to show up on my boat and tell me I'm a screw-up." He barked his response. "I get enough of that from my mother."

Now she was yelling too. "Fine! You definitely are not a screw-up. No. Obviously, everything you've ever done has been carefully thought out to get you here—sitting in the middle of the ocean on some half-swamped dinghy with a friend who is just this side of well done. Meanwhile, the two of you both put me and my captain in the drink—and he, likely, is still there..." She paused. "...and probably drowned." The light clicked off, and he heard her huff.

Brian stirred and said with a sleepy voice, "Hey, what's going on?"

Neither Ashton nor the girl took time away from their argument to acknowledge him.

"Yeah, and are you so different? You're here, too, just no friends with you. No surprise there. You probably broke their knees as well!" Ashton snarled back to her.

"Oh, poor baby. You got kicked by an eleven-year-old three years ago, and you are still crying about it? You were horrible and deserved it. You slapped my obaachan, and she was just an old lady. And you slapped me and made fun of me before..." Her voice started strong but ended in a small, sobbing gasp.

Ashton had been prepped with a scathing response, but the sob caught him. That had been an awful summer for him, the worst, and it clearly was for her as well. Up until that summer, Ashton had been willing to do anything—almost—for his father, and still, when it came to it, his father didn't choose him. He chose this girl and her pirate mother. And so, his father was gone, along with most of the markers that would have been his. The damn Bosch pirates were the reason Ashton had to go begging to his mother for every little extra. This girl, obnoxious as she was—and still is—had been just a kid then. Eleven. That would make her, what, fourteen now? Still pretty much a kid as far as he was concerned.

Brian had now sat up and was leaning forward, looking first at Ashton, then at the girl at the front of the boat. His voice was still dozy. "Ash, what's going on? Who is she? Are we rescued?"

Ashton and the girl, still staring at each other, chorused, "Go back to sleep!" with so much intensity that Brian said nothing more, simply scooting more to the back of the dinghy and under the tarp.

Ashton bit back the sharp retort he had considered and, instead, said in a voice taut with tension, "We can talk about all this tomorrow. I'm going to sleep. You ought to do the same." He shifted off the bench and felt the girl go tense and alert as he moved. He reached for the backpack to use as his pillow, then looked back at the girl tucked into a ball at the very point of the dinghy. Sighing, he unzipped the bag, retrieving a water bottle. "Here." He held the bottle out, but she made no move to come near, so he tossed it toward the front, where it landed with a damp clunk. "Are you going to be warm enough? I don't have another tarp."

There was scraping and then splashing as the girl retrieved the bottle from where it had landed near her feet. "I'll be fine.

Don't come up here. I'll kick you again, and I'm bigger now," she threatened. Then after a pause, she added in a softer voice, "Thanks for the water."

Ashton gave a quick nod of acknowledgment, laid on the bench pulling the edge of the tarp over him, and then shook his head as he tried to slip into sleep.

I am tucked as far forward as possible in the bow of this little boat, arms crossed, one hand clenching the bottle of water he tossed, hearing vague whispers from under the tarp, which makes my skin crawl. *How can I be stuck here with one of the worst people in the world?* An entire planet with huge oceans covering most of it, and I end up in a lifeboat—scratch that, a dinghy—with the one person alive I hate the most and some spare guy too. *The only person I hate more is your father.* How could he and that other man have been so careless? The *Fascination* was destroyed, and while I thought Darvin was ridiculous with lousy breath, he didn't deserve this. I really hope he didn't drown. I feel a lump form in my throat; tears sting the corners of my eyes and begin to flow down my cheeks. I guess I really didn't hate him after all.

Along with my worry for Darvin, the memory of the Awful July three years ago swirls in my head. I can't look toward where Appalling Asshole Abernathy is without remembering the horror of that time. So, I shut my eyes, pull up my hood, and take some breaths like Ruth taught me in therapy. Slooooow in. Hold it for the count of three, super slow out. The first one is pretty shaky, but the next few are better. Ruth also said I should sit with my thoughts, good and bad, not chase them away but not dwell on them either. Forget that. I can't bear them for even a moment right now. I shove them aside and focus on my current predicament. A-hole Abernathy isn't wrong—I can't swim to shore. There is no shore that I can see. And this tiny boat is better than a floating chunk of the destroyed *Fascination*. Sorry, *Chance*, but, as Unty Bailey says, that's the truth of it.

Peering out from under my hood, the thin moonlight gives a hint of light to the tarp that covers Abysmal Ashton and the toasted man who ran down my boat. I feel a little jealous grumble start in my head, and I begin to argue with it.

A tarp is pretty useful, Grey.

I don't care! I'm never going to share that with them.

Not even tomorrow? When the heat of the sun comes at you?

No! Shut up!

I blow out a breath. But my shoulders are tight, and my teeth are grinding. Another breath. A shiver comes over me, but I'm not particularly cold, just so very tired. I guess there are two things to be thankful for: one, it's the end of August and not the end of September, so the night air stays pretty warm; and two, though I hate to admit it, I'm glad my mom made me take the clothes from Bosch. Of course, that was yet another thing we had argued about. I remember trying to convince her that what I wanted to wear was better:

"Mom, haven't you seen the pictures of past races? The other women sailors wear those new artificial skin suits from China or just regular swimsuits, not stupid stuff like this." I had stomped and gestured at the two sets of leggings and long-sleeved shirts she had brought in.

Mama had taken a deep breath in, and I could tell she was controlling her temper. "Well, fine, take a swimsuit for swimming, but you are not buying those skin suits from China. That's not where any of our markers will ever go. And believe me, when it comes to working in the wet, nothing beats good Bosch wool. It'll keep you warm when you're cold and cool you off when you're hot." She paused. "And it's what you have, so make the best of it."

I let out my breath almost in a growl. "Fine, I'll take it. But I won't wear it." I grabbed the garments, shoved them in my backpack, and then glared at Mama, whose face contracted a bit as she left my room with a shrug.

I cringe a little, thinking of her hurt look. Of course, she was right. That's one of the things that bugs me the most about trying to talk to her. She thinks she is always right, and unfortunately, for me, she *is* right nine times out of ten. It turns out it was a damn good thing I had a set of those shirts and leggings on last night, because even though I am drenched from all my time soaking in seawater, I'm not really cold.

I break the seal on the water bottle and take a drink but am stopped short as bubbles fizz in my nose and throat. *What the...?* This is the kind of water that kids get to drink on fancy occasions on Bosch. Bubbly water while shipwrecked? I don't understand, but it is water, so I drink it down, slowly, carefully replacing the top and tucking the empty bottle in my largest jacket pocket.

I give a cursory scan of the boat before I settle in to rest. It must be only about three meters long and maybe a meter and a half or less across, but it looks sturdy enough. I glance toward the sole. All that bilge water has got to go. I remember the first day of Matt's Boating Basics lessons. He said, "Grey, I like a clean boat. One of the most important things to remember is that water belongs outside of the hull, not in it." He said it so seriously that I pulled out the notebook Mama had given me and started writing it down. Then I saw Matt's eyes twinkling, and we both laughed. But he wasn't completely kidding. He is definitely a stickler for a clean, almost-dry sole. And now, so am I.

Above the excess water are two thwart seats. The one near

me has an odd extension that juts toward the center of the dinghy, and the one farther aft of me extends straight across the width of the boat. I can see Arrogant Abernathy's hand and arm hanging off it and the feet of the other man—Brian, I think is his name. He must be leaning against the stern, but I can only see tarp-covered lumps.

I see several hatches along the inside of the dinghy. I'll check those out tomorrow. One of the men makes a noise, and I go on high alert, glancing over to be sure neither of them is coming toward me. The one near starboard rolls over in his sleep and pulls the tarp down from the stern. I can't believe what I see: A tiny moonbeam catches on what is clearly a motor. What on New Earth? Why aren't they using that?

I want to say something immediately, but since… I pause to find another insulting "A" word. Got it. Since *Aggravating* Abernathy has disappeared, I instead wring my dripping ponytail out into the bilge and tuck it back under my hood. I pull my arms out of my jacket and "good Bosch wool" shirt and cross them over my chest, wedging myself in the bow. I'll sleep first and ask about the motor when daylight comes.

SEVEN

Open Ocean

Dreams of deep water and heavy rain, smooth mountains appearing before me, guns that don't shoot, and steep cliffs that end in sharp rocks plague me through the restless night. I startle awake a dozen times terrified at being left alone until the sun breaks on the horizon and I give up on sleep. Aft, the two lumps under the blue tarp are snoring.

Body check time. Mama and the boys and I would do that every morning when we first woke up. Today, there is a kink in my neck—probably from how I slept plus the strain of keeping my chin out of the water as I kicked. My arms are really sore as well. The right one more than the left. My pelvis and lower belly are heavy and full. I really have to unload my body—both ways. Another glance at the tarp. Best move now before A… my urgency is too great to think of a word. Before either of *them* wakes up. The lumps under the tarp are off to port, so I get into a squat, pull my leggings down just over my behind, and then lift up to the starboard side of the bow and hang over just a bit. I haven't had to do this often as Matt's *Rune of Bosch* and the *Fascination* both had rudimentary heads on them. But I've been out on little boats and had to go, so I know the drill. Butt over the edge…and release. Ahhhh.

I glance down and give a little groan of annoyance. There is a smear of blood on my inner thigh—great. Not really the most convenient time. Since starting in March, I've only bled four times. Sure, it was good it hadn't come during the race, though Mama gave me some special bleeding underwear that I decided to wear all the time, and she also gave me a cup. I've never used the cup, though, which doesn't matter as it's somewhere at the bottom of the ocean with the rest of my things now. *At least you aren't there with it. Figure this out.*

I glance over my shoulder at the water behind me. Usually, I'd splash seawater on me to rinse, but I don't want to put my hand in the water if there's blood in it. Predators like blood. I envision a shark coming up to bite my rear and slip back to the boat like my bottom is on fire. A quick swipe on my under-wear crotch tells me there's not much blood yet. So, up go my drawers and pants. I sure hope this bleed is short like the first three. Those only lasted three days. The one I had in June, though, lasted for seven and was heavy, and I felt pretty crappy for most of it. Mama M, my Bosch grandmother, says it's normal for monthly bleeds to be unpredictable through the first year or so. She's a midwife, so I expect she knows. I know I'm supposed to be all thrilled about my body growing and being able to someday, maybe, have babies, if I want and all, and I kinda am when I'm home and have a bathroom, a change of clothes, and Mama to make me a cup of broth and give me a hot water bottle, but right now, I'd rather have my thirteen-year-old, non-bleeding body back.

In one of my pockets is the first aid kit Mama put together. I find it and click open the metal locks that keep the lid on securely. Inside there's a tube of antibiotic ointment, a small bottle of antiseptic, some bandages, a needle, two fishhooks, a pair of tweezers, four waterproof matches, and (bingo!) a reusable pad. I grab the pad, relock the little box, and then stick it back in my pocket. Then I stuff the pad into my underwear—double protection. *Thanks, Mama—again.*

My attention focuses on the quiet tarp. These men and I are the only crew for this dinghy until we reach land...whenever that happens. I don't have to like them, but I have to get along with them. *Keep your distance and keep your eyes on them.* My whittling knife is in my pocket, and I grip it. Okay, for now, they are asleep. I need to explore this boat and figure out a way to get back to land, but my arms and legs ache from last night's swim, and my head feels fuzzy. Plus, there's a deep crampiness in my pelvis. A little more rest—just an hour—then I'll feel better and can get to work. Decided, my feet move back to the bow, my arms shed my coat, my hands tuck it under me, and my eyes close. In less than a heartbeat, I slip into a deep sleep.

The morning sunlight heated the air under the tarp and created a blue glow through the makeshift tent. A few errant rays leaked under the tarp edges, one shining directly on Ashton's face, causing him to stir. He stretched a bit, turning his face away from the light, and took a deep morning breath in. The ripe smell of Brian's farts invaded his nose, and he gave a cough. He supposed his weren't any finer, but they certainly didn't offend him in the same way. Time to get up.

The night before, Ashton had, in a hushed whisper, filled Brian in on who the girl was and how she came to be in the dinghy. He edited the story heavily, leaving out the less-than-honorable actions he had taken three years earlier, but he did include the part where she had kicked him in the knee so hard it had cracked his kneecap, necessitating a rather painful surgery and several weeks of rehab, along with chronic mild pain that remained even now.

And what had Brian's response to the story been? "A girl? That could be fun. Too bad she doesn't have any Glitter with her."

Ashton had wrinkled his forehead and curled his lips in distaste while reminding the younger man that the girl was just that—a girl, a kid. He wondered to himself if there was really anything more to Brian than his pursuit of getting laid and finding his next cube of Glitter. Brian had gone quiet then, so Ashton didn't contemplate the issue for long before settling into sleep.

Now he nudged Brian. "We should get up." A groan escaped the sunburnt man. Ashton gave him another nudge. "C'mon, I'm not going out there alone."

Brian stretched, yawned, and peered at Ashton, narrowing his eyes. "Out where? Aren't we still on a boat?"

Ashton gave a small shake of his head. "Yeah…we are still on the boat." He knew he had to confess, "But that girl is mean, and I want someone else out there when she sees me in full daylight."

"Didn't you say she was a kid? Is the great Ashton Abernathy scared of some kid?" Brian laughed far too heartily to please Ashton.

The taunt hit home far more deeply than Ashton expected. His jaw clenched, and a wave of heat came over him. His vision tunneled as he glared at Brian sitting under the tarp, still chuckling at the jest. His arm tensed as he began to envision himself pulling back his fist and landing it somewhere in Brian's face. The gauge of his anger was close to entering the dangerous zone. With effort, he tossed the tarp back and wadded it into a ball, stuffing it under the nearest seat and giving a growl as Brian chortled, unaware of how close he had come to being pummeled.

~

The men had been awake for several hours, but the girl slept on, curled like a dormouse in her long, blue leggings and long-sleeved shirt, her yellow coat tucked underneath her like a nest.

Brian had peered at her early that morning. "Well, she doesn't look that dangerous," he had laughed. Ashton envisioned tossing the stupid, laughing man overboard.

Drifting on a boat was boring. They passed the time debating the outcome of the upcoming Toronto Oystercatchers vs. Truvale Firewhirls footy match and whether the Cipher Club would reopen after arsonists had torched it.

"Goes to show you need to keep up on your protection payments," Ashton said. "Too bad, too. I liked that place."

"Yeah, they made a great Mint Tornado there," Brian agreed with a sigh. "Damn. I'd like a cocktail."

The mention of a cocktail stirred something in Ashton's brain, and he grinned and reached over to drag the backpack close to him. "I don't have a cocktail for you, but..." He unzipped the bag. "How about these?" He extracted the two bottles of champagne and held them aloft.

Brian clapped his hands. "Wow, buddy! Now you're speaking my language. I had forgotten those. Hand one over here."

Obliging, Ashton passed one of the bottles to the sandy-haired man. They each unwrapped the foil tops, dropping the rubbish willy-nilly as they eased the corks out to prevent over-flow. Some bubbles still rose up and spilled over the neck of the bottles, prompting each man to quickly lick the sides, determined to get every drop. They both took a deep swig of the sweet effervescence and sighed in contentment.

Brian smacked his lips and held the bottle so he could read its label. "A good vintage. Course, it'd be better if it was cold," he observed.

"It'd be better if it was being served to me on board the *Abundance*," Ashton answered after another swallow of champagne.

Brian was almost halfway through his bottle already. "Yeah, man. In a flute and served with some cheese and nuts."

"Mm-hmm," Ashton murmured in approval. He took another long drink. "How about some lobster salad?"

"Stop it. I am really hungry now," Brian moaned. He took another long drink, wrinkling his face as the bubbles fizzed in his mouth, and waved any further food discussion off as he relaxed back on the seat. His elbow slipped and he barely caught himself from crashing onto the seat. "Whoa." His words were becoming slurred. "That was close. I saved the drink, though." He held up his green bottle as evidence.

Ashton laughed, draining a bit more of the bubbly goodness into his mouth. The bottle was close to empty, and he could feel his head definitely spinning. "It's getting hot out," he announced from his place on the shorter bench, his words slow as he slurred the *s* in "it's." "We should cover up and take a nap."

In a faraway tone, Brian asked, "Ash, are we ever going to get back to land? Shouldn't a rescue boat have found us by now?"

Ashton stared down at the sloppy bottom of the boat, then out at the unending blue of the ocean. He wondered the same thing; likely, there was not going to be any rescue boat. But just like in childhood as the oldest, he put on a good face. "Naw.

It'll take a couple days for them to get all the boats and planes out, and then we'll get rescued."

"Really?" Brian sounded very young.

"Yeah, really. It's gonna be fine. We got water and cakes. And we are healthy." Ashton tried to make his voice hearty and reassuring.

It seemed to work because Brian returned to the task of covering up. "Cool. Thanks. I'll get the tarp. Hey, my champagne is gone. That was fast…." Brian struggled up from his bench and dragged the tarp over to Ashton, who sat up to help spread it out. They both looked at the girl who had slept through the entire morning and still was breathing quietly in the bow.

Brian looked at Ashton, and his eyes narrowed and widened, clearly not focusing well. "We didn't save any booze for her. Shame on us."

Ashton considered this and then reached into the backpack and pulled out a bottle of sparkling water. Very slowly, as if afraid to wake a sleeping tiger, he inched closer to the girl and tucked the bottle next to her. Then he motioned to Brian, miming him handing one end of the tarp to him. It took a few moments for Brian to understand, but a bit later, the entire dinghy was covered, with the tarp shading all three people now aboard it.

Once back to his place on the bench, Brian sank into a boozy sleep. Ashton lay awake on his bench for a few moments and wondered if he'd ever see dry land again or if this was the way his frivolous life would end. Soon, the champagne drew a bubbly curtain over those dark thoughts, and he slept.

～

So, so hot… I can't get a breath of air. My eyes open, and the world around me glows blue as if the bluest summer sky has descended and wrapped itself around me. My arm extends to touch the sky. It feels somewhat rough. A bottle of water tumbles to the sole from where it was wedged by my left elbow. Its presence jostles loose first one memory and then another until they all come tumbling around me—shipwreck, sinking down into the ocean, gasping for air, red sparks, kicking and kicking and kicking, and…sweet New Earth… Abernathy. My head whips around, and I realize that while I am under a tarp—the tarp Abernathy had been using—I am still in my spot at the bow. Abernathy lies stretched out, blue-tinged and snoring on the near thwart, and the sunburned fellow, now looking lavender under the tarp, is in a similar position on the aft one.

It must be midday. I pull the tarp from my face, feeling the cool of the open air, and squint at the sky. The blue is deep and serene, and puffy clouds streak across it in tidy rows. Mama and Matt call them streets of clouds, probably because they fly among them so often. The sun sits midway past its zenith. So, not midday, more like fifteen bells. Dismayed, I blow out a breath. How did I sleep so long?

Body check: My mouth and throat are parched, so I duck back under the tarp and retrieve the bottle that fell and open it. Fortunately, I remember the bubbles from yesterday, so my mouth is not shocked. After drinking it down, though, I find I am still thirsty. I'm also sweating under this tarp. It could be better configured for air circulation, something I am desperate for.

Chance… The thought pops into my head. He will solve both issues at once. Little by little, I shift my body toward port and creep from under the tarp, leaving my coat to identify that space as my territory. Clamoring over the edge of the hull, I pivot and, with very deliberate movements, board my raft. The fishing line is still intact, and I retrieve the two desalination pouches I had placed there last night. After drinking one down, I immediately feel refreshed and focus on my matted hair. Untangling my ponytail holder is tricky and takes time, but once done, my scalp tingles as I rub it, alleviating the sensation of having my hair up for so long. I shake my head, sighing with delight at the free feeling my loose, wavy hair gives me.

My wools get stripped off, but I leave my underwear on because who knows when the men might wake. The pad gets a quick rinse and is set in the sun to dry. I tuck the leggings and shirt under me and, sitting with my knees up, lean back on my hands, delighting in the sea breeze that cools my skin. The dinghy actually casts a little shade onto *Chance*, so my concern for a burn is low. Time for a visual body check: my legs are sporting several bruises and scrapes, and the back of my right arm seems to be one big bruise—I'm sure I hit something as I was tossed from the *Fascination*.

I sip on my second water pouch, recalling some of the easy-weather sailing days on the *Fascination*, when we would catch a breeze and current together and cut through the water apace, generating a nice wake. Darvin and I would talk about home and family on these days. His teasing was pretty constant, but he wasn't mean to me at all. The thought, *I hope he isn't dead,* runs through my brain for the hundredth time, and a pang of remorse for my unkind thoughts about him bounces around my head.

Now I turn my attention to the dinghy, moving carefully on *Chance*. I run my left hand along its hull above the waterline. I need to get to know this boat if it's going to get me to land and, I hope, home.

I have developed a practice, whenever I sail, of pressing my palms on a new boat's hull to feel its spirit. Admittedly, I have been razzed about it by some sailors, mostly those close to my age, but other, more seasoned sailors have nodded knowingly and smiled. We seagoing folk tend to be a bit superstitious, and even though I know in my brain that a boat is just a boat, I like to believe each of them has its own vibration in the universe, and that, to me, is a spirit.

The vibration I get from this dinghy is one of uncertainty, which, given who it's been carrying up until now, is understandable. I'll fix that.

First, a name. All boats need names. Partly for identification, partly because you want to know who you are relying on, and partly because it's just more respectful. I wouldn't want someone just referring to me as *the girl* all the time. That's why I named *Chance*. He was the first boat (even if he is just a raft) I ever named. All the others I've sailed came named.

I press both hands on this little dinghy's hull again, close my eyes, and try to hear its name.

Pictures appear in my mind, and I let them flow through me as the raft and dinghy move in concert with the gentle swells of the sea and the soothing serenade of the breeze sings in my ears. Several heartbeats of time pass, and I smile. Her name is *Noĕlani*.

The name arrived with the image of my Aunt Gia, who isn't a real aunt but one of Mama's and Matt's friends. She's also my sorta-ex-best friend, Leia's mother. Her name is actually Gialani Ka'ne, and her people came from the Drowned Islands generations ago. The other image was of Noĕ, Beverlee's friend in *The Queen of the Marsh*, who carried her to the surface and onto shore after the witch had taken away her ability to breathe underwater. It took all of Noĕ's strength, and at the end, she slipped back into the water, having saved her friend, but we don't know if she's alive or dead. I guess we'll find out if the author ever gets around to writing a sequel. *Noёlani* will see me safely to land, and I will care for her.

She is not made of wood but of some kind of composite. Matt had said both the FA and Dihya, on the North Coast of Africa, were working on bioplastics that could float and not break down after extended contact with seawater. She is made of something else, though. Some combination of wood and bioplastic, but far stronger. I bet the material came from China. They have great technology—even some left over from Old Earth. A thrill knowing how much my being on a Chinese-made boat would piss off my mother goes through me. Not the kindest feeling, I know, but she always makes such a fuss about China. She didn't even like it when I learned a few Chinese dialects as my elective language last year, though my Edoan papa thought it was a great idea. Mama relented when I convinced her it might be useful for trade. Of course, that was a lie. I can't imagine ever needing to use it since China hasn't let outsiders in since the fall of Old Earth, and they seldom let anyone but diplomats leave their own borders.

My fingers detect a long seam just under the deck's edge. The edge is wide enough to sit on, maybe fifteen centimeters. There may be a storage place here. My curiosity is piqued, but I'll have to get on board *Noёlani* to investigate it more.

The hull seems in good shape as far as I can see. If I were somewhere else, I'd take a light and go underneath her and inspect, but the middle of the ocean during my bleeding time is not the time for dives. Instead, I take my wools and rinse them in cool ocean water and wiggle back into them. The dampness will help keep my skin cool in the afternoon heat.

I climb into *Noёlani*, then fish in my coat pockets for more line and my first aid kit. Pushing the tarp back almost to the first thwart where Abernathy sleeps, my toe bumps into something hard in the filthy bilge water. *A champagne bottle?* I stare, not ready to believe my eyes. But it is. I've seen these at home when Mama and Matt would break them out on birthdays or after BPF graduations. I've even tasted some a couple of times. It was cold and put bubbles up my nose like bubbly water, but it was also sweet, leaving a warm feeling in the back of my throat. Mama had said that was the alcohol in it and I could only have a small taste. That's pretty much my entire experience with alcohol, though I have tried sips of beer before but didn't enjoy them. One thing I do know is that alcohol makes you thirstier. So, why is it onboard after a shipwreck, and why would they drink it?

I duck under the tarp and peer at Appalling Abernathy. Sound asleep. Lifting the tarp a little more, I see the other one. And there's another empty bottle in the water near him as well. They are idiots. That can be the only explanation. I pick up one of the champagne corks that bobs in the dirty water and tilt my head. This could be useful. A bit more contemplation and I pick up one of the bottles as well.

I move on in my inspection. The bilge water is almost to my ankles. First step: Get this water gone. Then I'll go fishing. I begin my plunder of the storage areas onboard.

EIGHT

Noëlani's Gifts

The cook was kneading dough for breakfast pastries and had left the faucet running for some reason. Ashton was looking forward to a tray with croissants and coffee. He came fully awake to the sound of running water and a recurring slapping sound. Looking up, the tarp was suspended about half a meter above him. He looked to his left at the front of the boat and saw one of the oars he had discovered holding the edge of the tarp up. He could see out to the ocean and felt a cool breeze on his face. He looked to his right and saw a second oar fastened with ropes on either side, holding the tarp in the center of the boat. Brian was still napping on his bench, and the tarp came down behind him. He sighed. There would be no coffee and no pastry. He reached out and shoved at Brian. "Hey."

Brian roused with a "Whaa...?" Then his eyes opened and flicked around at the tented tarp. He turned his head from side to side. "What's that sound?" he whispered.

Ashton shrugged. It was coming from the back of the boat. The two men pulled the edge of the tarp back and peered out.

The girl was crouched near the defunct motor. Her yellow coat was draped over her like a shawl. Her shoulders were curled forward, her right elbow moving back and forth like a piston, and she was breathing in sync with the motion of her elbow. Some kind of tube hung over the back of the dinghy; this is where the sound of water flowing sporadically was coming from.

The men exchanged a confused look. Ashton spoke. "What's going on? What are you doing?"

The girl, Grey, looked over her left shoulder and gave a vague scowl. "Oh, you're awake, finally. I'm pumping the bilge. It's a mess." She turned her head back and continued her repetitive motion.

The men looked at each other again. Brian whispered, "What's a bilge, and what's she pumping with?"

The girl answered, "You needn't whisper. *Noĕlani* is not so big that I can't hear everything on her. And bilge water is all this dirty water on the sole. And this…" She turned a bit to display a red tube about a half-meter long with a black handle and a tube running from near the handle to the edge of the boat. "…is a bilge pump."

Ashton watched, with astonishment, the miracle of water leaving their boat without him having to bail it. "Shit," he murmured as he rubbed his knuckles, which were still raw from the first night's bailing session. "Where was that before?"

There was a slurping sound as the last of the water was sucked into the pump. Grey leaned over and pulled the tube from the edge. A tiny bit of water drained from the pump back to the bottom of the boat. She tilted her head. "Well, I'd have to guess the pump was right where I found it—in the forward port hatch. Unless maybe it's a magic bilge pump…" She waggled the pump. "…and it can disappear and reappear in different spots."

Brian gave a guffaw and said, "Magic pump."

Ashton studied the girl in daylight. *She's not big*, he

thought. Her arms and legs had that early-teen, gangly look, but her face was pleasant enough, with oval, almost heart-shaped contours. She had deep brown eyes, almost black, and when they glanced around, they were sharp and intelligent. Her dark hair was still pulled back in a ponytail, but it looked neater than when she had been asleep up front. She leaned back on her heels and looked at both men, puffed her cheeks out, and blew out a breath, shaking her head, clearly disappointed in what she saw.

Brian asked, "Why do you call *that*..." He pointed at the now almost completely dry bottom of the boat. "...a sole?"

"Because it is *the* sole. And it's one precise word, which is more efficient and clearer than your five words: *the...bottom... of...the...boat.*" She ticked off the number of words on her fingers as she accentuated each of her last five words.

Brian grinned. "Cool." He nodded. "Did you stick the oars under the tarp too?"

"I did. It lets the air circulate but still protects from the sun," the girl said, and Ashton heard no animosity in her voice.

Again, Brain nodded. "Double cool. So, I have to pee."

Ashton shook his head to himself at this abrupt announcement, but then realized he did as well. He looked at Grey. "Turn around."

"Oh, definitely," she hastily agreed as she pivoted her body around. The two men assumed positions on opposite sides of the boat. "I grew up with brothers and a bunch of pirates, so I don't shock easily."

"Still, stay where you are," Ashton instructed as he finished his business and tucked himself back into his shorts.

Brian finished as well, and Ashton saw a sly smile on his boatmate's face.

I squat with my back toward the stern as Abhorrent (at least I am stretching my vocabulary—my reading teacher back in Bosch, Mr. Pagareli, would be thrilled) Abernathy and Bashful Brian pee off the sides. They hadn't been so careful about placement before I came aboard, given the smell of the bilge. As I wait, I eye the fishing line I had dropped astern. I tied one of the hooks from my kit to it and carved a slit in the champagne cork to act as a bobber, using the bottle as a weight in the boat. No bite yet. *Patience, Grey-chan*, I hear Riki say in my head. The motor stares at me, and I stare right back. I need to ask…

"Okay, turn back around," Abernathy's voice comes from behind.

I turn and sit on my bottom, extending my legs out in front of me on the clean sole. I lean over, stretching my sore hamstrings. Now to address the motor situation. But the man with the sunburn says, "So, I'm Brian, and you're Grey, right? Do you want a cake?"

Did I hear him right? "Cake? You have…cake?" *Who brings cake to their shipwreck? Obviously, the same people who bring champagne.* I guess it all fits together. Arch-Enemy Abernathy is in some kind of silky, rich-guy pajamas, with little embroidered stars on his robe, and Burnt-Up Brian looks like he should be poolside at some snooty club. Clearly, these guys did not attend sailing school in Bosch.

"Yeah. The cook made them as a treat. We don't have much, though. But I'll share." The burnt man pulls the tarp down from the oars, stuffs it under the aft thwart, and reaches into a maroon-colored backpack. His hand emerges, holding out what appears to be a beat-up green cube of about four or five centimeters. He grins at me in a friendly way, his white teeth a contrast to his red face.

Food. Cake! I forget about the motor for a moment as I reach out, take it, and nibble the side. My eyes get big, and I can't help but let a small smile out. It's kind of stale, but it is sweet and rich and tastes amazing. I eat it in three bites, which I realize belatedly was far too fast because I am wishing I had another bite.

Brian laughs at my expression. "It is pretty good. But I wish we had more."

Awful (I think I may have already used that one) Abernathy sits quietly nibbling on his cake cube, eyes shifting between Brian and me. Whatever. Just because Brian is with Aggravating Abernathy doesn't mean he is like him. He seems nice.

I say to him, "Don't leave saltwater on your burned skin. It'll make it hurt more in the long run and can make it burn even more in the sun. Rinse it, then dry it and cover up, and the burn will heal faster."

"Really?" Brian replies in a surprised tone. "I didn't know that." He smiles at me. "Thanks."

I nod back, though I am not willing to smile yet. "Also…" Now, I address both men. "…don't drink alcohol until we get to land and have plenty of water. It'll dehydrate you."

"Well, it doesn't matter 'cause we don't have any more anyway," Brian says, sounding a bit melancholy.

"Good. Just drink water," I reply, pleased that there is no more aboard.

Adversarial Abernathy nods. "Agreed." He pauses. "Hey, earlier, you called this dinghy something. What was it?"

"*Noëlani*. It's what I've named her," I say with pride and a hint of contention.

"Why?" he replies, a definite undercurrent of disapproval in his voice.

"Because everything deserves a name, especially things our lives depend on." I gesture at the open ocean. My answer is met with an impassive shrug from Atrocious Abernathy.

Brian looks a little impressed. "That's really smart, Grey."

Having now shared a breakfast of cake with my new boat-mates, I point to the stern, indicating the super-compact engine near me. "So, I see there's a motor on this boat." I say this slowly, enunciating each word carefully to be sure I am understood.

Brian glances aft at the motor. "Yeah, but it doesn't start. We tried."

I frown. "I know. I looked at it."

Brian laughs. "What do you know about engines?"

This annoys me, so I lean toward him, narrow my eyes, and say, "Enough to have kept the motor functional on the *Fascination*—before it was crushed."

This quiets Brian, who looks to—ummm, hell, I think I have used all my "A" words—Abernathy who then stares at me, face expressionless, for almost a minute. "So, what's the problem then, if you are so expert?"

I actually don't know that much about motors, but I sure as hell know more than these two. So, I allow myself a glare. "The battery is dead. Where's the charging cover?"

"The charging cover?" Asinine (back with an "A" word! Yes!) Abernathy responds, clearly confused.

I swear, we don't speak the same language. "Yes, the charging cover."

He blinks, and I hear his voice waver as he asks, "It has a charging cover?"

I narrow my eyes. "Yes. The cover: The thing that attaches magnetically to the engine when you aren't using it—that has built-in solar panels." I'm beginning to get an inkling of the issue. So, I then add, making sure to provide plenty of emphasis, "It is what keeps the engine charged."

The two men look at each other; I can almost see the blame flowing from one to the other. Finally, Brian makes a tossing gesture. "We tossed it off when we went to start the engine, and it blew off in the storm."

I gaze at these adults, unsure if I heard the one correctly. There's no way. Even my brothers know better than that, and they are still kids. My voice starts in a reasonable tone, but I hear it getting louder and higher as I rant, "Into the water? You just tossed it? The one thing that keeps the motor working. Tossed?" I am stunned by this stupidity and devastated that we could have simply driven to land if not for these clowns.

Mama says I can be overdramatic, but I'm pretty sure this calls for a bit of drama. What these men deserve is a screaming tirade and to be thrown overboard to fend for themselves. But as I take a breath to start my rebuke, I realize it will do nothing. I need to use my brain. I rotate my neck in anger but stop suddenly, recalling that move is my mom's. I will get a hold of my temper.

After several breaths in and out through my nose, because my chin is now too tight and my lips too pressed together for any air to move through them, I speak up. "Okay. Okay. We can't do anything about it now." I am racking my brain for a solution, but the only one I can think of is unlikely at best. "I guess I could try to hook up the panel from my torch, but I don't know…" I trail off as I look first beyond the stern and then toward the bow. There's nothing at either location, just empty water as far as I can see. Oh, no. This is a more immediate issue—one I am shocked I didn't see earlier. I was so fixated on pumping the bilge, I missed it. "Don't you have a sea anchor or a drogue?"

Brian responds, "Well, no. Isn't the water too deep?"

I use all my strength not to grab my forehead and yell, *Idiot!* I shut my eyes and take a breath, trying to relax my chin. Survival. That's what I am seeking. I say in what, to me, is a pretty reasonable voice, "No, Brian. A sea anchor doesn't go to the bottom. It keeps the boat oriented in rough weather, so a wave won't roll it over. And a drogue can slow our rate of drift, making it easier for a rescue to find us." There is a significant pause. Then I say because I cannot help myself, "How did you two stay afloat during the storm? Was it just dumb luck?"

A combination of astonishment, dismay, and terror grows on the faces of these two sort-of adults as they look at each other and then back to me, both shrugging like in some sort of choreographed idiocy play. I think of my books. *Trolls. I am on a boat with stupid trolls.* They have no idea about anything when it comes to boating. Well, I, for one, want to get home. Okay then, it's up to me to keep *Noĕlani* afloat and get us rescued. I focus on the task. "All right, do you have a line we could use?" The faces look back at me, empty and confused. "Er...a rope?"

"Oh, yeah. I found some rope last night." This comes from Apelike Abernathy.

Brian looks at him. "When? Before you screwed up those flares?"

"Yeah. While you were doing nothing—but sleeping." There's disdain in his tone.

There is no time for their little spat. So, just like at home with my brothers, I cut to the essentials. "Look, this is a really big ocean and I just want to make it as easy for us to be found as possible. I assume that's what you both want as well. Honestly, we can't be out here too much longer. Water will eventually run out. There's no sign of storms, which is good because a storm could sink us. But it's also bad because we could use the rain for drinking water. Either way, I need to slow our drift." I point to a red item in the center of the boat. "Is that a bucket?" A few minutes later, I have cleated off a makeshift drogue from the stern. It'll help slow us, but I will search for a real sea anchor regardless. There ought to be one on board. An image of the men throwing it overboard comes to me. I won't ask. I don't want to know. I just hope we don't run into any heavy weather.

My mind starts to devise a list of the tasks required to survive and get home. The champagne bottle rattles as my line jerks. "Fish!" I yell, jumping to grab the bottle. I start rolling in my line, letting it move back and forth as whatever is on the other end darts about. The pull gets heavier and heavier. *What if I can't bring it in?* I worry. Then, Accommodating Abernathy is next to me, dropping his robe on the deck.

"Here, I'll reel. You and Brian can use my robe to scoop it when it gets to the surface."

I see the wisdom in this right away and hand the bottle to him. In minutes, we have a skipjack almost as long as my arm on board. I hit it hard on the head with the base of the champagne bottle and pull out my carving knife. "Hold it over the edge," I instruct the men.

There's a pause, and when I look up, both men are staring at the knife in my hand. I shrug and look at it as well. "I like to whittle." There is a small beat before the men come back to the task at hand and hold the fish near *Noēlani*'s side.

I quickly slit its throat, whispering to the fish, "Thank you for the sacrifice so we can eat," as Riki taught me and my brothers to do on those summer mornings we spent fishing with him in the rivers back home. The blood flows into water. After the last drops ooze out, I direct them to put the fish on the stern thwart.

Knife in hand, I gut and clean the fish. Picking through the innards, I pull out the heart and liver, cutting each into three pieces. I consider the rest and think, *Maybe I can use it as bait.* Then I realize it won't keep and toss it overboard.

"Here," I say, holding out the organ pieces to the men who helped land the catch after quickly eating my share. No one moves.

"Did you just eat fish guts?" Brian asks, horrified.

Right. These are the men from a yacht with a cook who provided them with what they view as staples: champagne and cake. I sigh. "Just the heart and liver." Their expressions are still repulsed. Time for an alternate strategy, the one I use to get Rini to eat new things. "You know, they are considered delicacies in Edo." A smile with questionable legitimacy crosses my face.

They look at each other, then reach out. I drop the fish gifts into their hands and return to prepping and scaling the tuna.

Aloof-but-Assisting Abernathy chews and remarks, "It's actually good. Buttery."

Brian grunts his agreement.

I begin the task of scaling when suddenly there is a clear *thump,* and *Noëlani* rocks heavily in the water. *What…?* My brows furrow, and I stab my knife through the fish into the thwart to hold it there. Both men move to starboard, causing the boat to lean heavily in that direction.

Assuming Abernathy has excited hope in his voice. "Maybe it's a sandbar. Maybe we are close to land."

I pivot my head; we are not close to land. A bad feeling comes over me…. There is another bump, and the men scrutinize the water. For a millisecond, all is silent, none of us even breathing. Then, a sizable splash and Brian lets loose a high-pitched screech. "Shark!" He and Alarmed Abernathy tumble toward port, causing *Noëlani* to lurch in that direction.

I curse myself inwardly for tossing the guts over with such

nonchalance. *I should have thought that through.* A third thump occurs, this one from the port side, sending the men again to starboard and causing *Noĕlani* to pitch even more. There's more than one under her. Swear words are flowing from the men, and their voices are loud and panicked. *Oh, shit, Grey. You have to do this.*

I have no intention of tipping into shark-filled waters. I yell, "Stop moving!" Without waiting to see if they follow my command, I grab the near oar and shift to the side, holding it like a bat above my right shoulder. My eyes dart across the water, waiting to see something, and my heart is beating so fast, it just may burst.

There—a shadowy form undulates in the water toward *Noĕlani.* I wait—one breath, two breaths, as it approaches the surface, and then—*slam*—I bring the oar down on the creature's head. Another form comes under the boat. I re-cock the oar, and—*slam.* The adrenaline running through me made me swing early, and the second hit splashes more because the shark is deeper, but it still meets its mark. I lean heavily over to watch and suddenly feel unbalanced.

"Ahhh!" My body tips forward as I yell. Hands on my waist and they jerk me back to sit on the sole hard, knocking the air from me as I collide with whoever grabbed me. It takes a moment for my breath to return. "Thanks."

Advantageous (a negative name seems wrong right now) Abernathy is behind me, looking first off the port side and then starboard. Brainless Brian sits and shakes in the bow; even with his sunburn, he looks as pale as sand, and his mouth is open in a silent scream.

"Well done, kid! They are swimming away," Abernathy cheers. He looks at Brian and laughs. "We sure are a couple of big, strong men, aren't we, Brian? Had to have a kid save our screaming butts from the sharks." He turns toward me. "I guess having a pirate aboard is an advantage." He grins in a very sincere way.

I grin back, but don't know what to say. Pirate? Well, sure, I'm a pirate's kid. But it's not like we are all out wrestling sea life on the regular. I mean, my mama grew up a farmer and now is a pilot who only goes on sails for fun with Matt. Everything I know about how to defend against sharks came from Beverlee in *The Marsh Queen*, the book I read last month. Beverlee had a run-in with sharks and hit them on the head with a rock in chapter sixteen. Honestly, that's the closest I've ever seen a shark in real life. I keep that to myself though, because both men are smiling and looking at me with admiration.

Lips pressed tightly in a smile to keep my own screams within, I swallow heavily and move back to the thwart. My knife comes free with a quick jerk, and I return to fileting the tuna, breathing deeply as my heart slows itself to a normal rate and rhythm. Once I feel I can speak without my voice shaking, I channel Beverlee again, this time from chapter twenty-five, and say, flourishing my knife a bit, "For dinner tonight, we have sushi."

NINE

True Colors

The sun is dipping low, bringing magnificent oranges, purples, and pinks to the sky as the sun angles its brightness through the clouds, bouncing its beams and about to put on its final show of the day before it jealously takes its light and rolls to the other side of New Earth. We are all in high spirits, having avoided becoming shark food. My stomach is pleasantly full after our feast of raw tuna. I sliced the remainder into pieces to dry in the sun, though we had to take turns defending it from an opportunistic seagull.

I am comfortable beneath the stars with my jacket, but the men prefer to have a shelter overhead even at night. So, before the sun set, we used both oars to fashion the tarp into a sort of fort to cover both the fish strips and the men. The bow oar can be removed, effectively creating a closed tent. At the edge of the tarp, close to the center of the boat, the solar lantern I found provides a tiny pool of light as the darkness falls. The light isn't wide-reaching, but it illuminates two depressions in the sole under the thwart seat extension; one is circular and about ten centimeters in diameter, and the other, rectangular, directly below the caps on the seat. I hadn't noticed them before the water was pumped out and because I had stayed aft until now. *You don't suppose…?* I scan the bulkheads for hatches I may have missed and recall the long one by *Chance*. I got distracted and didn't investigate it. That will happen first thing tomorrow.

Sleep sounds marvelous, but Absurd Abernathy and Batty Brian are still awake, stretched out in their tent on the cleared sole, feet up on the aft thwart, talking with each other. Maybe I should stay awake and keep my eyes on them. My body seems to be making the choice for me as my chin keeps dropping to my chest. My brain goes blank for a moment until I jerk my head back up, eyes popping open to be sure my foe stays aft as he promised.

The third time this happens, Ashton Abernathy is breathing steadily with his eyes shut. I flick my glance at Brian. He is near the lantern and looking in my direction, his red face pleasant. He grins at me, hoisting a thumb toward Abernathy and rolling his eyes. I can't help but smile a bit back, partly because it's nice to have someone act in a friendly way, and partly because I'd like to have an ally against that awful man. Satisfied I am safe from Abernathy for the night, I close my eyes and let myself drift off, but then I sense something that warns me, *Wake up!* and I do. Brian startles me. He is very near now and looking at me, hardly blinking. He leans in and says in a low voice, "Grey, you are so cool. All those things you did today. The boat's all clean, and we have a tent, and you put the thing—that drog thing—out. You are real smart."

I lean away a bit and say, oddly finding it hard to keep my voice steady, "Thanks. I-I've been on lots of boats the last few years."

He grins and leans in, and I can smell his breath. It doesn't smell revolting like Darvin's. It actually smells okay. But it still makes me uncomfortable. "It shows," he says. "You know a lot of stuff, like how to fish. And you are real brave. You really handled those sharks." He grins a shy grin and acts like he's blushing, but with all that burn, who can tell? Without waiting for me to say anything, he continues, "I was scared, I'll admit it, but you inspire me. I watched you—carefully. Don't worry, I'll take care of them the next time." I want to say that I'm not particularly concerned about a repeat attack, but his hand comes up and gently brushes against my forehead as he moves a lock of wet hair from there. Then he leans in a few millimeters closer, and his voice is huskier as he adds, "Grey, you are real pretty, too, you know. Especially when you smile." He gives a small laugh. "That fish isn't the only Edoan delicacy on board."

His words are sort of kind, but his eyes look greedy, and something in his voice makes me scoot to port a bit. "Thanks. I'm going to sleep now."

As I scoot, he moves with me, narrowing the very small distance between us. One arm of his reaches to hold the port railing, blocking my escape scoot. He starts to lean closer, and his hand reaches for me as he urges, "Aww, c'mon, Grey. You want to be friends, don't you?"

Abernathy's voice from the stern makes us both look aft. "Hell's fire, Brian. Leave her alone. She's a kid." It is said casually but clearly.

Brian doesn't move; his eyes stay on me, and his grin grows. "Aw, Ash, she's big enough to be out here and big enough to teach us some things. I'm just offering to even the score. You know, teach her a few things in return. Then she could leave being a kid behind."

Suddenly, I flash on a description of Pheidon when he meets a young fairy princess, and now, I know exactly what the word *leering* means. His hand starts to snake its way into my hood and curve around my neck.

Everything Mama, Matt, Riki, and Flossie have taught me about self-defense and fighting seems to evaporate from my mind. Instead, I shake my head and try to shout, "Stop it!" But I am stunned when all that I can muster is a strangled whisper. I glance to port, where his arm blocks me, and then to starboard. *Noĕlani, help me,* I think. But she is so small. There's nowhere to go except the ocean. The sharks are no longer in the water near the boat. But one appears to have materialized right in front of me. I coil my legs, tensing the muscles to be ready to leap, when Brian's hand is jerked away from my neck. He falls back over the forward thwart onto his butt, upsetting the solar lantern, his arms shooting behind him to keep from landing full on his back.

He whips his head around behind him. "What the hell was that for?" His voice is no longer smooth and sultry but angry and a little dangerous.

Behind him, Astonishing Abernathy's hand slips into the pocket of the ridiculous robe he has wrapped around himself, and he sits back, his face impassive. "I said enough, and that's what I meant." His tone is one that will brook no argument.

Still, Brian glares at him and begins to form a retort, but Avenger Abernathy's hand comes back up, and he points a single warning forefinger at Brian, who quiets, pulls his legs under him, and then slinks back astern, mumbling. There is a long look between them, and it is Brian who looks away first. Ashton glances at me. "Go to sleep, kid. The two of us will stay right back here, guaranteed." He gives who I now have newly christened Creepy Brian a glaring look as he says this last word. I nod but say nothing. He pulls the forward oar out, dropping the tarp awning, and they both disappear from my sight.

I never thought I'd be thinking appreciative thoughts about Asshole Abernathy, but at least he isn't Creepy Brian. And while I don't like being called a kid as a rule, right now, the way he said it, there's something really comforting in the term.

Brian snarled at Ashton as the tarp tent closed. "What I do with her isn't any of your goddamn business."

"You realize what you were attempting is actually illegal in most of the FA, right?" Ashton worked to maintain a calm exterior, though inside, he was ready to throw a punch.

Brian just shrugged and pointed out. "We aren't in the FA, now, are we? And when did you start to give a shit about Grey?"

"That is not the issue at hand," Ashton said levelly. "The issue is that you *will* leave her alone." The two men locked eyes, then Brian turned away, settled himself against the hull with a huff, and closed his eyes. Ashton decided he would not even attempt to return to rest until he knew Brian was fully asleep.

As he lay stretched out blocking the front entrance of the tent, one thought was clear in Ashton's mind: *Brian is an asshole.* He was beyond glad he had opened his eyes when he did. It was unbelievable that sunburnt bastard was actually pursuing the child Ashton had pulled from the sea. Now, to be clear, he still didn't like her. As far as he was concerned, she was still a mouthy little brat who had broken his knee, but after all, they had crashed into her boat and had likely killed her captain, so there was some obligation to protect her. Kids needed that. After all, he used to be the one who protected his sister on the playground when they had attended school. He had kept Farris safe for many years…just not safe enough.

He rubbed his knee and considered the girl in the boat. So, she had gotten a lucky shot at him years ago. Today, she had pumped all the water out of the boat, made sense of the engine, rigged their tent for better daytime air, and actually caught a fish and fed them. *I'm pretty sure that balances every-thing out. And I was kind of an asshole, too, three years ago.*

TEN

To Set Sail

An odd rattling sound woke Ashton. He looked left to be sure Brian had remained in the tent. He had already roused and checked this a few times through the night. And, indeed, Brian was still reclined on the bottom of the boat—he grinned to himself. *Excuse me, the sole*—snoring, hands behind his head. Ashton shifted the tarp aside just a hair, saw the soft, blue light of morning that came just before the sun made its appearance, then looked to the point of the dinghy. Grey was kneeling on her raft, both her hands on the dinghy pulling open a hatch and withdrawing something large.

He peered over the side. "Grey? Kid? What are you doing?" She withdrew something from inside the dinghy.

To her credit, she didn't startle. She looked up and was actually smiling. It was the first time he had ever seen the expression on her face so unguarded.

"Check it out," she said, withdrawing a fabric-wrapped length of pipe. "It's an emergency mast and sail."

Ashton stared at the contraption in wonder and then grinned back. He knew for certain he wasn't a sailor, but the importance of her find was not lost on him. They could stop just drifting. They could get to land. They were saved.

It is almost noon before I rotate the bottom section of the mast, then hear a reassuring *click* as it locks into place in the depression I had seen earlier. With no written instructions, only a bag of parts, I had spent several hours looking at each piece and assessing where it would go. I certainly didn't want to screw up and have a vital section go overboard, leaving us stranded. It would be worse than it is now because we would know we had lost our opportunity. And as Mama always says, "Opportunity, Grey, is key. Wait for it, use it, don't lose it."

Abernathy and I have put the parts together and taken them apart a couple of times, discussing what should go where and in what order. I have decided not to use any qualifiers before his name, at least for today, since he stepped in last night and has been helpful this morning. Creepy Brian woke and had little to say to either of us until he finally could no longer contain his interest in what we were doing. Then he became excited and began to chatter.

"As soon as I get back, I am going to buy a huge bottle of rum and a chunk of Glitter the size of that fish you caught and gather up several lovely women—don't worry, you two, they'll be *of age*." Here, he cast a scathing glance to Abernathy, who simply shrugged.

He went on for several minutes about the indulgences he would provide himself once we made landfall until I asked, "Aren't you going to want to go home?"

Then his face darkened. "Why? No one there cares where I am."

It made me feel a little bad for Creepy Brian. But I'm not changing his name in my head just yet.

Now, with Ashton's help, I extend the three telescopic tubes upward and lock each with a twist. Then we connect the rigging I had prepped earlier, attaching the shroud and the forestay to help support the mast. I place the centerboard, but I leave the boom in its place, folded against the mast for now. It will take up quite a bit of space once the sail is hoisted and the rigging is complete. And space is already at a premium onboard *Noĕlani*.

I sit back to look at our handiwork with a grin. Ashton and Creepy Brian are clapping.

Ashton is the first to speak. "Well, Grey Shima, that's a job well done."

My grin expands. "Thank you. It was a team effort."

All this success means I am feeling forgiving and celebratory, willing to put my dislike of and distrust in both men on hold for the moment. "Here, let's toast our success with my water," I say, pulling up my precious desalinated bags of water, sugar, and salt from the port side near *Chance* and offering them up.

This causes both men to give a small cheer, and Abernathy suggests, "We should finish the cakes!"

He turns and grabs his backpack, then pulls out two cakes, handing the first to me and the second to Creepy Brian. I am thrilled to have another cube of sweetness—this time, mine is blue, and Creepy Brian's is red. Abernathy announces, "I'll have the crumbs." He then reaches into the backpack he has and mashes his hand around, pulling out a ball of squashed-together cake crumbs. We all laugh and toast with the cake ball, cake cubes, and bags of pinkish water.

"So, when do we set sail?" Creepy Brian asks as he chews.

"Well," I begin, "we need to figure out where we are, so we know which way to go."

"How are we going to do that?" Abernathy tilts his head, looking at me with honest interest.

I grin, put a finger up to signal them to wait, and then clamor over the side of the dinghy onto *Chance*. The men watch me pull out my knife and hack a piece of splinter off the raft—one of the several that has been sticking up out of the water and is pretty dry. I take one of the matches from my first aid kit and light it, using it to set the splinter's end on fire. I turn the wood, carefully shielding it from the breeze and keeping it well away from the dinghy. Then, before it can fully flame, I blow it out, leaving a charred end. This takes several minutes, giving me time to think. Three years is a long time and Ashton has helped me both with Creepy Brian and with the mast. And Brian, well, I resolve to myself that I won't be intimidated by him and his creepy nature. I'll just tell him to back off. I decide to now use both men's first names, no descriptors. They are my crewmates, after all. Grievances have been aired. It's time to work together to get back to land.

I climb back in with my improvised marker and, using the side of the hull, proceed to draw two circles next to each other, one bigger than the other, and then several small dots extending off to the left. "Okay, Brian, Ashton..." Abernathy's first name feels strange in my mouth, and I glance to see if they notice my use of their first names. Brian seems oblivious, but Ashton half-smiles, so maybe he did. I refocus on my map. "So, this is Moku-o-keawe, and this..." I point to the smaller circle. "...is Maui. The rest of the dots are the tips of the Drowned Islands. The wreck happened about here..." I point to an area just off the harbor of Moku-o-keawe.

"Now, the storm winds that first night were coming mostly easterly, so it's unlikely we were pushed south into the North Equatorial Current, which runs here." I make an arrow that comes at Moku-o-keawe from the right, or the east, and drops around the far southern end of the island, flowing away west. "If we were in that current, we would have been pushed fifty kilometers or more south. It's far more likely that we were pushed toward or into the Hawai'ian Lee Current." I draw another line skirting the line of dots and make an arrow that veers along it to the west. "So, if we can sail northeast toward one of the minor Drowned Islands, then we can turn east, make our way to Maui, and then to Moku-o-keawe."

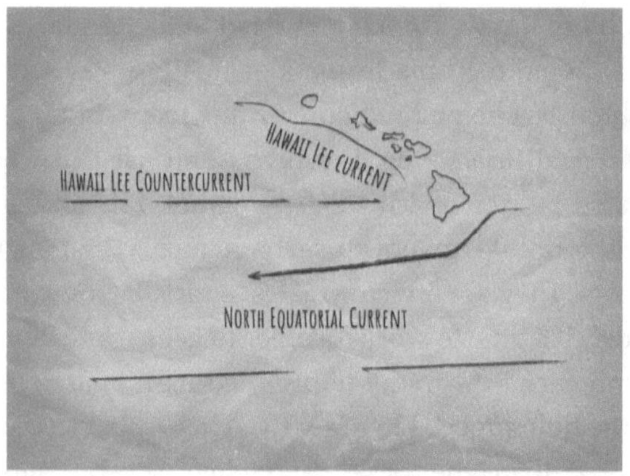

Ashton speaks first. "I understood maybe every third word you said, but the drawing—I get it."

"Well, I don't," Brian chimes in. "But I don't care. As long as we get back to Moku-o-keawe and then back to Karuk."

I cringe and look at Ashton. "You are living in that horrible place? How can you?"

He looks at me, wrinkles his face, and tips his head to one side, almost apologetically. "I didn't have much choice. All the other properties were taken by FA authorities. Karuk happened to be in my mother's name. And she decided I should be there."

That's the second time he has mentioned his mother. It's funny… I only ever thought of him as having a father before. "Oh, I guess that makes sense," I respond with a tight-lipped smile.

He changes the subject. "So, how do you know we aren't here—in this current?" He points to the North Equatorial Arrow.

"Well, I don't completely. Plus, there's the smallest possibility that we got pushed through the channel and are on the windward side of the islands." I point to the area above my circles and dots. "So that's why I don't want to start really sailing until we can look at the stars."

Brian looks at me. "What do the stars have to do with sailing?"

I start to say something snarky, but pause, remembering my need to get along with my crewmates. Before I can start to explain, Ashton gives a laugh. "Of course. Polaris. That makes sense."

I look at him with curiosity. "You know what I'm talking about?"

He nods. "I had a tutor, Professor Fry, that showed me how to figure latitude with my hands when I was about your age." He gives a small laugh that sounds a bit sheepish. "At the time, I thought it was a stupid waste of time, and maybe it was for a rich kid in New Detroit and Truvale. But since I've gotten older, whenever I travel, I've found myself looking up at the stars and holding my fist and fingers up." He reaches his arms out and demonstrates, but his eyes are somewhere far away. "I never really understood the real use like you do, but it made me feel like…" He squints and pauses, a smile playing at his mouth. "…like, maybe I could at least know where I stood."

I stare at him and feel my breath catch. Three summers ago, this man was cruel and pitiless, a lackey to his even crueler father, rough with my little brothers, my obaachan, and me. I still despise him for that. But this recollection of something so simple, so ordinary, has me flustered and confused. I am at a loss for words. Fortunately, Brian steps in with a ridiculous comment to cover my discomfort.

"Like, do you punch at the stars?" he asks, his face perfectly serious.

Ashton and I both look at him and start to laugh, and I clap a hand over my mouth to avoid being too unkind.

Ashton morphs his laugh into a cough and then says, still chuckling, "No, Brian. You use your hands to measure the angle from the horizon."

Recovered now, I explain, "Exactly. A sextant…" I ignore Brian's snicker at the word. "…would be better, but it'll give us a rough estimate. Honestly, as long as we are below twenty-two degrees, we'd sail north, because if we were in the North Equatorial, we would catch the Hawai'ian Counter Current back." I draw another arrow pointing back to the Moku-o-keawe.

Brian pauses as if considering all this new information, then he looks at me and frowns. "How does someone like you know all this?"

Offense overtakes me, and my temper flares. I know he is commenting that I am too young and little to be trusted. "Well, it just so happens, actual sailors learn how to sail and guide their ships instead of just steaming off into the night flattening other boats." My eyes flash the rest of the anger my words can't convey.

Ashton starts to laugh again, and at first, I think he's laughing at me, and I am ready to lash out until he says, "Good Earth, Brian—she's really got your number."

It's weird to have an Abernathy side with me. My mother hated his father, and his father was horrible to my mother, brothers, and me, but here his son is backing me up. Again.

"Okay, whatever," Brian interrupts my thoughts as he scowls at me and then at Ashton. Then he looks off into the ocean and sighs. "Grey, you just tell me what I need to do to help get us to land."

And just like that, I'm a captain with two crewmates.

PART III

Sailing in Bosch, Lesson Three

Reading the Wind

As a sailor, you must come to understand your most important medium, the wind. While nowadays we have many instruments that provide a boater with the wind direction and speed, a true sailor must be able to read the wind without the gadgets of today.

Winds are named for the quarter they blow from. A north wind comes from the north and blows to the south, and so on. But winds seldom stay the same as you sail, so here are ways to determine wind direction as you sail.

The sailor themself can use their body to assess wind in multiple ways. A simple wet finger extended to the sky can give you a good idea of direction. Putting your face to the wind and turning your head slightly from side to side to feel the specific direction on your cheek as well as the variation of sound in your ears is another method.

Your boat can also tell you with the yarns or tell-tales on

your sails that catch the wind, and your sails themselves will fill and luff depending on the wind's direction.

Finally, the waves in the body of water can clue you in as small ripples will run perpendicular to the wind.

Wind speed can also be determined by observing the color of the water. The darker the water and the closer together the ripples, the faster the wind is blowing.

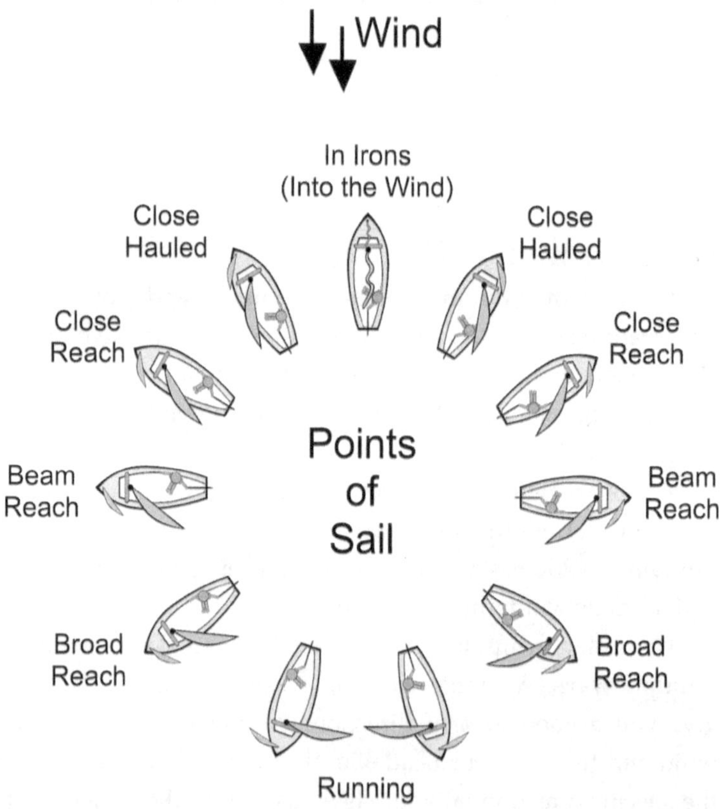

ELEVEN

Last Chance

"Okay, we have a nice breeze—let's see what you remember." I have hoisted the mainsail and *Noělani* is on the move. "What's our point of sail?" I call to my crew. There's murmuring between the men. As I wait for some answer from the novices, I feel *Noělani* lurch a bit on her port side. My stomach drops as I realize *Chance* is dragging her.

Ashton finally replies, "Broad reach?"

"Yes, good. Broad reach." I'm distracted by the weight of what I have to do as I pull in the sail and heave-to.

"Why are we stopping?" Brian asks. "That was fun!"

I swallow hard. "We need to cut *Chance* loose. He creates too much drag."

The men shrug. "Okay," Ashton says. "Seems reasonable to me." And it is reasonable. Our task is to get to land and then get home. *Chance* will make our travels unwieldy.

Brian jumps to untie the line that holds *Chance* close. I speak up. "No, wait. Let me." He pauses and frowns a little. "Okay…" I realize I am contradicting myself, but I need a moment.

I climb over *Noĕlani*'s side and onto the slab of the boat Darvin and I sailed over three thousand kilometers together. I press my hands onto the blue surface and whisper, "Thank you. You saved me." I feel tears sting my eyes, so I try to blink them away. I am sure the men think I am a toddler weeping about a chunk of wood. Still, I lay down and press my cheek to *Chance*. Then as quickly as I can while still maintaining balance, I scramble back onto *Noĕlani*. "Okay," I say with a shaky voice. "Go ahead."

But they don't. After the tiniest of pauses, Ashton picks up one of the empty champagne bottles and fills it with seawater. Then he leans over, partially loosens the line from the splinter of wood holding the raft, and pours the seawater over *Chance*. "To *Chance*," he says with dignity, "who started life as the *Fascination* and became a hero in a storm. We send you out to the ocean to find your ship, and we thank you for bringing Grey to us."

His speech causes my breath to catch, and I feel the lump in my throat thicken and grow. Tears are now flooding my eyes and flowing down my cheeks. He hands me the end of the line to pull. I stare down at this strange man's sun-browned hand holding a line out to me. A glance at his face reveals a sad smile and eyes that seem to understand. He gives a little nod. I snuffle heavily, wipe my nose with the back of my hand, and smear my tears away with the heels of both hands before I take the line from his hand. I feel the weight of it and run my fingers over its roughness, then I take a deep breath in and pull it sharply. *Chance* bobs, now free, staying near *Noĕlani* but shifting away little by little as the ocean swells take him home.

~

A bell later, *Chance* is barely visible, a small smear of blue surrounded by the immense blueness of the ocean. "Okay." I turn away, intent on shaking off my melancholy. "It's time to put the lesson I taught you both to use."

Ashton goes first and does reasonably well, though his shoulders are tense and tight, and he is reluctant to trim the sheet in when *Noëlani* picks up speed. "What if I flip her?"

I laugh, recalling the same worry as a beginner. "The word is 'capsize,' and if you did, you'd just have to learn to right her then. But let's skip that lesson right now. I need to stow things first."

"I'm happy to skip it." Ashton shakes his head as he gives a nervous laugh.

We work on tacking, which is basically sailing in a zigzag fashion into the wind. Ashton ends up in irons—or headed straight into the wind, which makes it impossible to make any progress—a couple of times, so I show him how to both sail backward to get back in motion and push the boom out so the sail catches wind as he adjusts the tiller.

"A good first sail." I nod my approval.

"Thanks, Capt'n. Though, I'm glad I don't have to do that alone," Ashton admits as I take over. I grin at the title.

Brian's focus is speed, and he moves *Noëlani* into a beam reach and scuds along. Trouble is he forgets to pay attention while the winds blow past him. Twice, he tacked and didn't watch for the boom, ending up in the drink once.

"It moves too fast," he complained as he shook himself dry, reminding me of the farm dog Mae and Stephen have out in District Seven.

I shrug. "You are in control of the boat when you have the tiller and the mainsheet. It's up to you to let the sail out and slow it a bit if you can't duck faster."

After the two lessons, I heave to again, this time lashing the rudder. We configure the tarp like a canopy over us to block the sun, so we don't all end up like Brian, whose sunburn, while improving, still looks painful.

Brian scratches at his beard. "I really wish we had brought some Glitter. This is the longest I have gone without Glitter in a year or more. I think that's part of why I still feel sick."

"You sound like a Glitterhead," Ashton remarks with a frown.

Brian nods and narrows his eyes thoughtfully "There's a good chance you are correct, Ash."

For some reason, this bothers me. Glitter is the main thing we export from Bosch. Mama and Matt say it makes people laugh and feel relaxed, so I always figured it was like wine or something. But the way Brian and Ashton talk makes it sound different—and not in a good way.

I decide I will need to think about this, but it will have to be later, when my feet are on land. I shift a little, lean back on the hull, and announce, "Well, I'm going to take a nap. Wake me when the stars come out."

Brian leans slightly toward me and says in a voice just a little lower than normal, "You could put your head on my lap and rest."

"Hey, Walsh. Remember what I said." Ashton's voice is sharp.

Brian rolls his eyes and grins in a conspiratorial way. "He's no fun," he whispers to me.

This time I have my voice and assert, "I'm not interested, Brian."

"What, you don't like boys?" he asks.

My brows come down. He isn't the first person to ask this of me, and I have my answer at the ready. "I like boys just fine, and I like girls just fine, and I like middles just fine. I just don't like anybody like *that*." I give the word *that* a bit of a warble.

I'm not naive. I know about baby-making and fun sex and all the stuff we learn about in our Healthy Bodies classes, as well as the stuff Mama and Mama M have talked about. Leia and my other friends are starting to try out kissing and sometimes more, which…well, it's fine for them. I just… I don't know… I just don't want to do any of that with anyone. Not right now at least.

Now Brian snorts. "Oh, you will. And you never know, maybe it's like Glitter—you need to try it to know what you are missing."

"I don't think so." Again, it's not the first time someone has made a comment like this to me.

During the second to the last week of school, Ronan sat beside me during math and kept trying to hold my hand and touch my hair. I finally got mad, told him in a pretty loud voice to stop it, and moved away, and then the whole class laughed. He got up and moved next to Anya, saying, "You're ugly anyway. I was trying to be nice." After that, he didn't even look at me for the rest of the year.

Leia told me when we were talking about it after school that day that I was probably a late bloomer. But Anya, who started holding hands with Ronan later that week, had said that maybe it was because I was half-Edoan, and since it was such a little island, they couldn't have many kids on it. I told her she was stupid and didn't know anything because Edo is bigger than Bosch *and* because my brothers, I, and Hayami's baby were born there. We got into a fight. Leia sided with Anya, so I ended the year with hardly any friends.

Now, I simply extract myself from the conversation and head to the bow. Instead of sleeping, I turn my back on the men, take out my knife and the remainder of the chunk of wood I had cut from *Chance*, and start to whittle out a shape. I'm thinking dragon, but we'll see what the wood tells me. The boat isn't big, so when Brian and Ashton start to quietly argue, I begin to hum a tune to cover the words.

TWELVE

Sea and Stars

Ashton sat between the seats, Grey in the front—rather, in the bow—of the dinghy she had named *Noĕlani*, and Brian snoozing in the… What was the word? Stern. The two men had exchanged a few heated words after Grey moved forward. Ashton was surprised that he felt the need to act as a shield against Brian's dog-like enthusiasm with Grey, but he did. Surely, the pirates must teach their children to take care of themselves, but still, he felt responsible for the first time in a long time.

The four-day-old beard that had sprouted on his face was annoyingly itchy, and he scratched at it with both hands. As he did, he tipped his head, regarding the girl sitting on the bow, her back to him, her long, black ponytail hanging down to the middle of her back, its ends fluttering in the sea breeze, distinct against her yellow jacket. The sun was sinking into the western horizon to her left. The long shadow of her extended to the right of the boat and onto the surface of the water, where it rippled with the swells as the orange and purples of the sunset created a glow around her. *That light is perfect*, he thought.

The itch of his beard forgotten, Ashton reached into his pocket for the chunk of charcoal Grey had used to draw the map of the currents and the points-of-sail diagram. Not wanting to lose a moment of the light, he withdrew one of the champagne labels he had salvaged and dried from the sole after it was pumped and began to sketch.

Though he was pleased with the rough outline, the charcoal chunk was awkward, and it took several errors and smudges for him to grow used to its behavior. He found himself wishing for his drawing pencils or even the pastels he had at home. Brian might have been having Glitter withdrawals, but as for Ashton, he needed to draw. Now he fussed and refined the piece until the light faded and it became impossible to continue. *I'll add to it later*, he thought as he slid the slip of paper into the backpack pocket.

He could just make out Grey sliding whatever she had been working on in the bow into her own pocket as she moved back toward the center of the dinghy. "So, that's north." She pointed forward. "As soon as we see Polaris, we can measure."

"I think it needs to be darker," Ashton commented. He squinted into the vastness as first dozens, then hundreds of stars began to appear in the darkening sky.

Grey nodded from her seat on the sole. "Shouldn't take long. Night falls fast out here."

Ashton silently scanned the horizon from his place on the aft bench.

"So, what are we looking for?" Brian asked. He was staring upward while sitting next to Ashton. "There're so many stars. Even more than at home."

Ashton paused to wonder where *home* actually was for Brian. He had never asked before. But that wasn't the conversation for tonight. Tonight, they had to get a fix on their position.

"We are looking for Polaris, the North Star." He had already found it but decided to share his knowledge of the stars with his younger friend. "Look—see that group of stars that look like a little house on its side?" Ashton pointed.

"Yeah, it looks like it has legs," Brian responded with a little laugh.

Ashton laughed as well. "It does. I know it by the name Cepheus. But I imagine it goes by different names for different people." He pointed again. "Now near it, there is a group of stars like a *w*. See them? That's Cassiopeia. It's my sister's favorite constellation."

"I see it, yeah." Brian nodded, then asked, "Isn't your sister dead?"

Ashton held his breath to keep from yelling. He glanced up and saw that Grey had turned and was listening. He answered in as controlled a voice as possible, "She's missing. Not dead."

"But I thought you said your dad killed her," Brian pointed out.

Now the fuzzy memory of a drunken night and him telling angry stories around the pool came back to Ashton. "No, I said he *might* have killed her. But I hope he didn't."

"Sorry to say this, Ash, but your dad sounds like a real nasty guy."

"You have a gift for stating the obvious, Brian." Ashton's pleasant mood was turning rapidly.

Grey had shifted back from the bow and was sitting near the centerboard. She said, "My friend, Flossie, says Cassiopeia is her favorite as well. But I like Draco, because, well…dragons." She laughed a little. "See, Brian, Draco weaves near Cepheus…"

"Yeah, and there's the Big Dipper. I know that one." Brian's voice was excited.

Ashton smiled at Grey, appreciating her re-steer of the

conversation. "Now, follow the two stars of the dipper, and that star right there is Polaris."

Brian squinted and his pointer finger made a sweep across the sky. "Wow. This is so cool."

Both Ashton and Grey were now stretching their arms out in front of them. Brian watched as they each first made fists with both hands and stacked them as they held them to the horizon.

"I get more than twenty," Ashton said.

Grey nodded. "Me too, but not much more. Let's try again."

This time, they both just extended one arm, stretching their five fingers wide and peering down their arms toward the horizon and Polaris.

In a chorus, both announced, "Twenty."

Grey's hand was still outstretched, and she put first the small finger of her opposite hand on top of it and then her thumb. Ashton did the same. Grey finally dropped her arms. "I get just under twenty-one degrees."

"Same," Ashton confirmed, dropping his arms.

"Well, that's good news. The trades haven't been that strong, so we can't be too far from land. So, let's split the last two hydration packs, get some sleep, and we will sail at dawn."

"Those are your packs, Grey. You use them. Brian and I will have plain water," Ashton objected.

Grey shrugged and said with a smile, "I'm doing okay. You shared your cakes. And there's not much to me that needs to be fed. I can always fish again if necessary. But after all, we'll be cooking fish and eating coconuts this time tomorrow on one of the Drowned Islands!"

Brian laughed with delight and then paused. "Huh. I heard a weird story about the far islands from Mahina, the girl at The

Volcano House in Moku-o-keawe. She serves drinks there. We were getting cozy before those jerks showed up the night of the wreck and ruined everything."

"What sort of story?" Grey sounded eager reminding Ashton that even though she knew how to manage a boat and do all sorts of things he couldn't, she was still a kid who loved tales.

Brian began, "I can't tell it fancy, but she said that the Drowned Islands used to be a popular place to go to back during Old Earth days. There were huge buildings that thousands of people from all over the world would stay in for holidays, and the beaches used to be covered with people, shoulder-to-shoulder, playing in the surf. But according to Mahina, it wasn't the diseases, fires, earthquakes, or even the sea rise that destroyed the islands—it was a curse."

Ashton saw Grey's eyes get big at the word "curse." "Wow! What sort of curse?" she asked.

Brian leaned toward Grey. "Well, Mahina said that the people of Moku-o-keawe, which was called Hawaii then, and the people of Maui blocked their islands from any outsiders because some priest had a dream that said some of the visitors carried evil spirits and the islanders must keep visitors away for, like, two hundred years."

"Really?" Grey was breathless. Ashton, on the other hand, was skeptical but said nothing.

"Yeah, really." Brian began to use his hands as he spoke, clearly enjoying being center stage. "But the locals on the other islands didn't listen, and so they were cursed with evil spirits who called the sea over the land, and that's why those islands drowned and Maui and Moku-o-keawe didn't. Mahina even said the curse is why no one ever goes to any of the other islands—because the spirits are still there, haunting the islands, drowning anyone who sets foot on them. And that's why anyone who has ever tried to visit has never come back." Brian slapped his hands onto the seat he was near for emphasis.

Grey jumped a little. "Not since Old Earth times?" Her voice was breathless.

"Nope. Never," Brian declared.

"That gives me the shivers," Grey remarked with a little sigh.

Brian leaned toward the girl. "You know…"

Ashton cut him off, "Okay. We all better get some sleep before we sail. I'm pretty sure that'll counter any curse the islands have."

Grey laughed and moved away to her spot on the bow as Brian gave Ashton a scowl before moving off himself. Ashton grinned to himself and shook his head. A curse. Ridiculous.

I wake after a bit of sleep, feeling crampy and needing to pee. While my pants are down, I find my pad and underwear are soaked through with blood. *Of course*, I grumble to myself.

I cast a glance aft at the tarp. I don't want to pull the saturated stuff back on, so I decide to take the late-night opportunity of the men being asleep. I scoop some seawater into one of the used water bottles and do a solid triple rinse of both items in the bailer, dumping it into the ocean on one side and scooping on the other. It's all part of my confuse-the-sharks plan. Though I haven't seen any since the wreck, I still know they are around.

There's a solid headwind, so I squeeze my garments as dry as I can and then stand and hold them up, hoping the wind will dry them further. Note to self: Put clothespins in my pockets next time I get shipwrecked. I really want that chocolate iced cream I thought of earlier. I wave the underwear around, trying to speed up the process. I am literally half-naked here since I don't want to bleed on my GBW, my new name for the "good Bosch wool" I am thankful for again and again.

I don't know if I ever want a kid, but if I decide I do and have one, I'm going to make all their clothes out of this stuff. That'd make Grandma Kat happy. Thinking of Mama as "Grandma" makes me laugh inside enough for it to come out as a silent giggle. I try to picture Papa as an ojiisan. He'd be like his papa, my ojiisan, was—very dignified. Papa has become very proper with me in the last few years; it's like either he's forgotten how to play or doesn't think *I* should be playing. Growing up stinks sometimes.

One of my crew moves under the tarp, so I quickly pull my underwear back on. The pad is still too wet to be of use to me, so on go the GBW leggings. I stuff the pad in my trusty yellow jacket pocket and then slip my arms into it and zip it up. There are no further moves from the tarp. I look to the east and see the sliver of a crescent moon rising. I get low in *Noĕlani* and peer at it as the waves chop about. The moon always looks so big as it rises, and if I get it just right... There. A swell comes up and seems to bisect the crescent, and for a moment, it looks like the ocean has a set of glowing horns. It creates a glimmer that spreads near the horizon, and I watch the waves play. I even see a little bioluminescence in the sea off to the west. I sigh. I love the night watch, and I love night sailing. I wonder...

I peek at the tiller where it is lashed to the side when we hove to. It lies on the tarp, creating what Ashton said was a two-bedroom suite. Hardly, but both men were good-humored about it. I know we are all looking forward to being some-where we would have more space. I could do it.

I release the lashing, then, turning to the mast, I shake out the reefed mainsail. Immediately, *Noĕlani* starts responding. Keeping the mainsheet line in my hand, I take a seat between the two sets of large, bare feet that extend from the tarp and grip the tiller. I look at Polaris and glance at the thin crescent moon off to port, trim up my sail, and we are off and picking up speed.

The moon is now so high and thin that it gives barely any light, but I can keep my bearing with my compass. The creak of *Noĕlani* and the sound of the wake she is cutting is rhythmic and hypnotic, and I start to hum a bit, then sing. I sing the old shanties and folksongs that Uncle Aaron and Matt taught me: "Ring Down Below," "Mairi's Wedding," "Roll the Old Chariot," and "Blow Ye Winds." Then I take a breath and roll some spit around in my mouth before I continue to sing into the dark as my boat moves through the Great Sea.

THIRTEEN

The Cursed Islands

Ashton came half-awake, roused by a clear, pure alto voice. At first it was just sound, but as his brain came more fully awake, he heard an unfamiliar melody. But where was it coming from? He concentrated and realized it was Grey singing.

He lay, quietly listening for a song or two before he sat up and opened the flap of the tarp a bit. It was still dark, and he could just make out her back immediately in front of him, her body turned slightly and her right hand on the tiller. To Ashton's surprise, they were under sail.

He rubbed his face to wake himself fully, yawned, shook his head, and quietly shifted next to her on the seat.

She glanced over, and the singing stopped. "Oh, dear, I didn't mean to wake you." He could barely make out her face in the dim moonlight.

"Don't stop," Ashton requested, keeping his volume as low as possible. "You have a nice voice. It was pleasant to wake up to."

She gave a quiet laugh. "Thanks. I have always liked singing." So, she continued:

"Well, me father often told me when I was just a lad
A sailor's life is very hard, the food is always bad
But now I've joined the navy, I'm aboard a
*   man-o-war*
And now I've found a sailor ain't a sailor any more
Don't haul on the rope, don't climb up the mast
If you see a sailing ship, it might be your last
Just get your civvies ready for another run-ashore
A sailor ain't a sailor, ain't a sailor any more..."

Ashton listened closely. By the time she had gotten to the chorus the second time, he was able to pick up the lyrics, and his baritone and her alto blended together.

"Who taught you that one?" he asked when the song finally concluded.

She paused with a long "Ummmmmm," then answered, "Probably Uncle Aaron. He knows lots of them."

"You sure seem to have an awful lot of aunts and uncles," Ashton commented as he watched the sail catch the moonlight.

Grey laughed. "Most of them are just Mama's friends and parts of her old unit. But we kids still call them aunt, uncle, or unty."

Ashton reflected on the adults he'd had in his life, other than his parents, while he was growing up. They all were either thralls or hired in. He saw his mother's conservative parents twice a year: once on Hardship Day and once during the winter holidays. His grandparents still celebrated Christmas with all the Old Earth traditions of a tree, lights, and presents. While they were not particularly warm to either his sister or him, those visits were still some of Ashton's best memories.

"So, why did you start sailing in the middle of the night?"

he inquired, not wanting to dwell too much on his rather miserable childhood.

A warm laugh came from Grey. "Well, I was up and didn't feel like sleeping anymore, and I knew we needed to get to… somewhere other than the middle of the sea. I heard my mama say, 'Sooner started, sooner done, Grey.' So, I started."

Ashton could easily see her shrug and make a wry smile as the eastern sky was shifting rapidly from black to deep blue. "You talk about your mom a lot. You two must be close."

Grey wrinkled her face and narrowed her eyes. "Well…we used to be. But lately, all we do is fight. It's like she has no idea who I am, and she's always trying to tell me what I *should* do— which is never what I *want* to do."

Now Ashton gave a muted laugh. "Well, that tracks. I mean, you are fourteen."

"Why does every adult say that as if it is somehow the answer?!" Grey turned and snapped back.

Ashton took in her flashing eyes and her chin that was set. She was definitely ready for battle. "Because we've all been fourteen and, if we are smart, we remember how it felt. You're not a kid, but you're not an adult. And you want to be recognized—seen—for who you are becoming…not who he expected you to be." The first three fingers of Ashton's right hand came to his lips and tapped as he looked off at the horizon and trailed off.

After a little pause, Grey's voice, small and soft, asked, "Who did he expect you to be?"

It was clear both knew who *he* referred to: Ashton's father, the infamous Rob Abernathy. Ashton's answer was monotone. "He expected me to be him. Or, at least, a servile version of him. The times I tried arguing my views around fourteen, I got slapped around—or worse. So, I decided the smart path was to comply. I'd become a copy of dear, old dad." He shook his head. "Smart…" Ashton scoffed as he remembered. "Stupid of me, really."

There was an extended pause from Grey. The sail flapped a bit, and she shifted the tiller, pulled on the mainsheet, and said, "Tack." In concert, both man and girl ducked down and shifted to the opposite side as the boom swung over their heads. She seemed intent as she looked out at the sea. Finally, she spoke. "Well, I met your father. You aren't like him."

For some reason, this simple statement filled Ashton with more hope and joy than he had felt in years. Sure, they had smashed a boat, lost a yacht, and ended up shipwrecked and lost on the ocean, but, hey, someone on the planet, and who had cause to know, didn't think he was like his father. Now, he chuckled. "Well, I only met your mother once, under…less than ideal circumstances. You aren't her either, but there are parts of you—good parts, like strength and determination— that I'm guessing come from her." Ashton looked toward the girl to see what effect his words had.

A fleeting smile crossed her face, but in a flash, it was replaced with a face lined with worry. "Mama probably has the whole Force out looking for me by now," she muttered. "But what if she thinks I drowned?" Her voice took on an edge of panic. "Maybe she'll think there isn't any reason for a search. Ashton, what if we don't find an island? What if a storm comes? What if…?" She gasped a bit and started to cry, still keeping a firm hand on the tiller and the mainsheet.

There was nothing Ashton could say to this. He had wondered the same thing. They might all die out here if they didn't find land. Hell, they might all die even if they did, though he suspected Grey had not only the will to survive but the learning and talent as well. He decided distraction was the best approach. "Tell me about Bosch. Describe it."

There was a snuffle and a small cough and then a quiet

spell that went on so long, Ashton thought perhaps she had decided not to answer. Then: "I love walking home after school. My brothers and I would always cut through the field behind the school building because there's a path that wends through a meadow. In the spring, we picked wood sorrel and nibbled the leaves, and every time, we'd wrinkle our faces and comment on their tartness." She laughed lightly.

Her voice now lifted as if she was part of the rising sun. "A little farther along, we go off the path to the left because there's a whole stretch of wild strawberries mixed in with the grasses. They are tiny things, most only as big as my thumbnail, but they taste so good. After that, the path moves through a little wooded space that is cool and smells green. There's a stump that I would race my brothers to, and whoever got there first was crowned Stump Ruler."

"Stump Ruler?" Ashton asked with a grin.

Grey nodded. Her face was now relaxed, and she sounded happy as she remembered. "Absolutely. The Stump Ruler got to order the others about for the rest of the walk home, which usually entailed having someone carry your books or send a lackey back to fetch more berries.

"Oh, and just after the woods, there is a section of blackberry brambles. They are ripe now, in August. We would make a special trip, even when school was out, to pick some. I would always pick some from as high as I could reach, where the animals hadn't peed, and pop them in my mouth, all warm and sweet. Sometimes, if there were lots, we'd gather a bunch, and Mama would make them into a pie. I'm not sure if her pies are the best or Mama M's."

"Who's Mama M?" Ashton was now leaning back on the seat, eyes half-closed, listening and enjoying the peaceful scene Grey was describing.

"She's my grandmother. She and Papa T adopted Mama after she arrived on Bosch," the girl explained.

"Okay. Makes sense. What comes next?" Ashton was not ready to leave this pastoral walk.

"Well, before you know it, we come up the path that is a bit overgrown with grasses that tickle your legs and feet if any skin is showing. The path comes out next to the little yellow house that backs up to the woods, where Old Mr. Rahman lives. Sometimes, he is out on his porch, and if he is, we share some blackberries with him, and he gives us each a cookie that his granddaughter made—usually oatmeal with dried fruit, but sometimes chocolate chip."

"I bet I know which you like best," Ashton laughs.

"I gave that away with my iced cream wish," Grey said with a giggle. "So, Mr. R's place tells us we are close to our neighborhood. We veer left onto the grassy side of the road and begin to see all the familiar houses on either side: the Azizi house, the Palmer place, Mrs. Okiro's neat little cottage. A few more minutes, and there's the little white house with its picket fence and the blue door Mama painted. In front are two big trees that my brothers and I used to climb daily up until a couple years ago." She paused and gave the barest sigh. "If I get home, I think I'm going to climb one again."

Ashton heard the *if* but left it alone.

If I get home? The words bounce from my mouth to my ears and back and forth in my brain like some mis-hit ball in a racquet sport. I have tried not to let myself think about any other option. Now, I do again, and I feel tears start—again. In the books I read, I never worry about whether Pheidon or Nyra will make it through their adventures alive. Because they always do. They have to. But this isn't a story. This is real, and I'm here. On a tiny boat in the middle of a big ocean. There's only one more bottle of water, and there are three of us.

I don't want to cry again in front of Ashton. It was nice talking to him this morning, but I'm sure he thinks I'm just a baby, weeping about our situation. I remind myself, *Mama cries, too, and she's definitely grown up.* Singing makes me feel better, so I start up one of my favorite Old Days sailing songs.

Farewell an' adieu to you fair Spanish ladies,
Farewell an' adieu to you ladies of Spain,
For we have received orders for to sail for old England,
We hope in a short time to see you again.

We'll rant an' we'll roar, like true British sailors,
We'll rant an' we'll roar all on the salt seas,
Until we strike soundings in the Channel of Old
    England,
From Ushant to Scilly 'tis thirty-five leagues.

We hove our ship to, with the wind at sou'west, boys,
We hove our ship to deep soundings to take.
Twas forty-five fathoms with a white sandy bottom,
So, we squared our main yard and up Channel did
    make…

Now I hear rustling behind me, and Brian pops his head out. "Hey, keep singing. It's pretty." He gives my ponytail a little tug and nudges me as he climbs out of his tent and clambers over to the bow to pee. The turn-your-back-for-peeing issue disappeared quickly, and now, I simply avert my eyes, though I say, "You may need to turn a bit, or your pee will blow back at you."

He laughs. "Trying to get a peek, huh?"

"Oh, for Earth's sake, Brian," Ashton gripes. "Don't be so crude." Brian just laughs.

I roll my eyes and softly sing another "Spanish Ladies" verse or two—there are many.

The glow on the eastern horizon brightens as from the other side of the world the sun comes rolling up through the clouds that are heaped on the eastern horizon. It makes its day's debut in a grand fashion, beams bending and bouncing through the tiny water droplets, creating a sweeping, deep red glow with a bright orange center and purple edges. It's beautiful, but it likely means we may see some heavier weather. That worries me. Maybe it'll just be clouds rolling by.... *Keep an eye on them, Grey.* I hear Matt's voice from my lessons reminding me, *Never assume good weather. Prepare for bad. Squalls can come up fast.*

I'll be ready. But for now, I watch as the sunlight brightens the ocean waters from their deep, nighttime blue-black to more pleasant and varied shades of blue. I entertain myself by naming them—cobalt, cornflower, sky.

A yell from Brian interrupts my color study. "Look!"

Given our most recent conversation, I quickly respond, "Oh, please, Brian. I'm not interested."

"No, not that. Look!" His tone is eager, and I glance up. He is pointing at the sky.

Now, he has my attention and Ashton's. He is pointing to the sky in the northeast. I follow his finger with my eyes. There's a series of moving dots, and they are getting larger. Then a faint bird call reaches our ears and then another, and the dots sprout wings. While we've seen an occasional solo bird, there are at least a dozen seabirds now, looping and calling to one another. I start to laugh. "Terns! They are coming out to fish. They must be coming from an island nearby!"

I am adjusting *Noëlani* to take a slight eastward bearing when Ashton points.

"What's that?" His voice is as excited as I have ever heard it. "It looks like… It is! Land!

Brian moves next to him and whoops. "I see it too!"

As *Noëlani*'s bow shifts to point to the east, I fasten the tiller and the mainsheet, so I can stand. Squinting, I try to make out what they are seeing, but I only see the pile of clouds lying on the northeastern horizon even from the thwart. "Where?" I shout to be heard over the men's hollering, yelling, and back-slapping.

Ashton is laughing as he moves over to me and points. "Do you see it?"

"No. I only see clouds. Are you sure?"

"I'm sure! Here, shorty." And before I know what is happening, he has taken me by the waist and lifted me up, so my head is higher than his. I want to complain about him doing so without asking, but then I see it as well: The clouds on the northeastern horizon now part slightly to reveal a low mound, like a dull shadow, beneath it.

I gasp and then shout, "An island. I see it." I start laughing, and Ashton lowers me to my feet. The three of us grab hands and look at one another, our faces alight with hope and excitement. I let go and drop to run my finger along the current map I drew on the hull. "I wonder which one it is?"

"I don't really care what island it is." Brian shrugs and then grins at Ashton and me. "Unless it's cursed. That would be bad." He throws back his head and laughs.

Ashton and I laugh as well. My laugh ends with me biting my lip and making a small *mmhm* sound. Stories of cursed places are found often in the books I love, and nothing good ever comes from traveling in haunted lands.

FOURTEEN

The Squall

Our moods are buoyed as we now have a real destination. One we can see. The sun is past its zenith, and *Noēlani* continues on her course, north-northeast. The dull-gray, low mound has now transformed as we draw nearer into what is clearly a mountain or mountains rising from the sea. It is still distant, but we can see a green mist on it, and it has buoyed all our moods.

I have had a couple of breaks to stretch and pee, but my shoulders are getting tired. "You take over the helm," I say to Ashton, who kneels near me, holding my compass in his hand as he watches our progress. "The wind is just right for me to coach you through a couple tacks."

Ashton looks at me, and his face is filled with doubt. "I don't know…"

"Oh, c'mon. If a fourteen-year-old kid can…," I tease.

"Yeah, that might have worked a couple days ago, but I've seen the stuff you can do." He laughs. "Are all pirate kids like this?"

I consider the question for a decent amount of time. "Yes. If by *this* you mean *able to sail*."

"Well, then, how come more aren't out sailing in the GSR?" he asks.

I ponder this question. "So, all Bosch kids learn to sail in their last year of primary. It's all wrapped up in 'historical memory' and 'honoring our ancestors.' For most, that's it. Unless they are actually from District Four, where the harbor is, or have family with a boat, they don't do much sailing. I came back from That Summer…" Ashton's face darkens a bit as I reference that time, but he says nothing. "…feeling pretty scared. Ruth the therapist said I had exposed my vulnerability, or something like that. When the sailing unit started, the sea scared me…. It kept reminding me of the bluff in Karuk, and so, I froze and couldn't bring myself to sit alone in a boat, much less try to sail one. But then Matt took me out on his sloop and away from all my friends. He made it fun and safe and showed me how I could totally control a boat, as long as I respected the sea and the wind. Once I figured that out, I loved it. Not just knowing I was in control, but the speed and the excitement and the challenge.

"I signed up for my first race that spring, and I made a decent showing." I laugh, remembering the regatta with about two dozen, tiny, one-handed sailboats cruising about Saltend Harbor. "I wasn't the youngest one racing, but I was the youngest one who placed in the top ten. I was hooked after that. Have a seat." I lift my hands from the tiller and the sheet, turning them over to Ashton, who looks very nervous.

"I got a ribbon for a school footrace one time." Brian leans on the transom near the defunct motor, enjoying the shade of our tarp that I have tried to make into a makeshift bimini shelter. The blue edge flaps in the wind near his forehead. "I cut through the woods and ended up coming in second."

I frown. "So you cheated but still didn't win? I'm not sure

that's worth bragging about." Then, to Ashton, I say, "Okay, remember, tiller toward sail."

Ashton nods. "Farris and I never did much beyond the basics in school. There was no reason. Sometimes, we'd have tutors like Fly, or one of our thralls would…" He looks at me, and my eyes narrow. "Okay, I mean, servants…." A slight pause, then he finished, "…prepare to tack."

I respond to his "prepare" command. "Ready." But follow it with "*Enslaved* is the word, Abernathy." I say his name with a sneer. "And it's an ugly one." I glare at him for a moment and return my eyes to first the compass, then to *Noĕlani*'s course.

"Listen, the thralls were part of the household from my first memories, Shima." He approximates my tone. "Some of them were the only friends my sister and I had." He pauses, and his next words contain a bite. "Sorry if I didn't start on a childhood crusade. Maybe I should have run away and joined the pirates. Would that be enough for you?" He turns the tiller and calls, "Tacking."

Noĕlani turns in a starboard tack as I press my lips together, shifting to the right side as Ashton does the same, then ducking the boom and considering my response, which I intend to be filled with indignant anger. What comes out instead is: "That was a really good tack. Now, do the same to port." Both of us pause at this, and I hear him laugh very softly.

"Thanks. You're a good teacher." Ashton turns the tiller starboard and adjusts the sail with the mainsheet. "Prepare to tack," he repeats.

"Ready," I call.

"Tack," he calls back, ducking and shifting.

I duck as well and settle next to him port side. I smile. "You know, it's not too late. You could always become a pirate."

"Not sure they'd take me," he says with a tilt of his head.

Then Brian comments from his lounging position aft, "Count me out. Sounds like way too much work." Ashton and I look at each other and laugh.

A breeze gusted, and Ashton glanced again at the northwestern sky. There were more clouds now, and they seemed to be getting taller. The island off to the northeast loomed up in the distance, growing larger by the minute. He had been at the helm for some time. After his tacking lessons ended, Grey had leaned against the hull, eyes blinking as she scooted lower and lower. Her head bobbed to the side as she was asleep. Brian had gone back to sleep as well, so there were only the sounds of the waves, the wind, and the wake, along with the soft clink of the mainsheet. It was peaceful, and Ashton entertained himself by humming some of the tunes he had learned that morning and imagining himself to be the captain of a great sailing ship from the Old Days. He was so delighted by the notion of reaching land that he hadn't thought anything about the clouds the first time he saw them, but now, the wind seemed to be picking up in gusts.

Grey had been up most of the night and he didn't want to wake her, but he was getting worried.

Nudging her with his foot, he called softly, "Grey, I think you need to take over."

She jerked awake and sat up at attention. "Huh? Oh, no. Was I asleep?" Her face was curved in worry.

"You needed some rest," Ashton reassured her. "I was fine, but the wind is changing, and those clouds look different than..."

Her head pivoted in the direction Ashton indicated. "That's

a squall line." Grey's voice had a note of concern in it. "Hey, Brian. Wake up. We need to fasten everything down."

Brian shook his head as he woke. "Umm. Like what?" His voice was a slow drawl, especially in comparison to Grey's brisk orders.

"Take the tarp down and stow it," Grey indicated as she opened a compartment and pulled out the thing she had made with the rope and bucket. "Are you okay at the helm for now, Ash?"

Ashton nodded. "I'm good." He focused on his task. He was, however, surprised to hear her use the short form of his name. Typically, only his friends called him that, and while their open hostilities had ceased, he wasn't sure the girl would ever think of him as a friend. But now was not the time to contemplate that. He watched as Grey tossed the bucket-on-a-rope thing out into the waters in the front of the boat this time and tied it down securely.

She tossed a life vest to Brian and directed him to put it on and fasten a few other things. After she slipped her own vest on and stowed everything else possible in compartments, Grey came over to Ashton, holding the bilge pump and a third life vest. She pointed at the line of clouds. They were closer, with a dark, flat base, and there was obvious rain coming from them. "I don't want to take the mast off, but I'm going to reef the sail. The storm is coming fast, so I don't think we can outsail it." He watched as she manipulated the sail and tied it down until just a very small portion of it remained to catch the wind.

"Can we get to the island beforehand?" Brian asked from his place in the stern.

"Definitely not. In fact, we should turn eastward. We don't want to be too close to land during the blow. It could push us aground."

Ashton asked, "Isn't that what we want?"

Grey shook her head vigorously. "We want to go ashore in control of the boat. The storm would push us onto rocks and splinter *Noëlani*." Her hair blew first one way and then the other as she sat next to Ashton and put her hands on the tiller and mainsheet.

He stood and slipped on his vest, then held up the pump. "I'm guessing I need to pump any water that comes in?"

"You both are on bailing duty. Bailer, bucket, and pump. Whatever it takes."

Brian whined, "But I get seasick."

"It better not keep you from bailing, if you want to stay afloat," Grey stated, and Brian quieted but kept his sulky look.

The winds begin to whip from every direction, and as the dark clouds blot out the sun, the gentle, blue swells we have become accustomed to now darken and become tumultuous, growing in height and ferocity, becoming walls of water that spill in on our little *Noëlani*. The sea anchor I fashioned is somewhat effective in keeping us directed into the waves, and I am attempting to maintain our position as well. Ashton is bailing with both the bailer and the bucket as Brian sits on the side and operates the pump. A crack of thunder rocks the air as the sky brightens with a lightning flash. Okay, truth time: I'm scared. We have come this far. I don't want to die out here, so far from home. I squash these emotions down and focus on the task. The wind is pushing us toward the island, and while I want to go ashore, I will not let *Noëlani* be broken on the rocks.

The rain begins, at first with just a handful of drops, but then it comes down in sheets. I can't even see the bow of the boat. Lightning and thunder continue, and while the wind drops a bit, the waves are still tossing us about. I look to port and see a monster of a wave coming straight for us. It's going to knock us down. "Hold fast!" I holler out to my crew as *Noëlani* lurches fully onto her side, mast in the ocean, as the rogue wave washes over us, carrying hundreds of kilos of water with it.

I hear a scream, and then Ashton yells, "Brian!" I can see nothing but water flowing past me as I grip the tiller and the thwart hard. Then, as fast as the knockdown occurred, *Noëlani* rolls back upright, mast intact.

"Ash? Brian?" I call as I squint through the rain.

A dark form is at the starboard side, leaning precariously toward the sea. "Brian went overboard," Ashton bellows. "Can you give me a hand?"

My hands swiftly tie off the mainsheet and tiller, and I leap over to the side. Ashton holds Brian by the wrist, but the swells are still intense. I lean and grab the handle on his life vest and yell, "Pull." And we pull together, dragging the man up and over the side. His eyes are open, and his face holds a terrified expression, but he's alive.

There is a creaking, and I turn my head to see the boom swing toward us. I duck and Ashton puts up his left arm to block it as he, too, ducks. It smashes into his forearm with a sickening crack, and he howls with pain, pulling the arm to his chest. I move toward him. I can't ask if he is okay because he clearly is not. "As soon as the storm blows past, I'll take a look," I say loudly near his ear. He nods, and I see his mouth set in a grim line.

Grasping the mainsheet, I return to the helm. I feel miserable. My lashing of the boom was hurried and poor, and now, one of my crew has a major injury. I regain control of *Noëlani* and look again to port, fearful of another wave. Instead, what I see is more terrifying: rocks, really big rocks.

The sun shines gently down now, having had its face thoroughly scrubbed by the squall that moved along as quickly as it arrived. We are hove to, and I have moved the sea anchor back to the stern as a drogue. *Noĕlani* is bobbing a fair distance from the rocks that I had to negotiate at the close of the squall. Fortunately, the ones I saw were the farthest out in the sea, and I was able to turn our brave little boat directly away from them. If the storm had lasted much longer, I don't doubt that we would have been crushed on them or on the dozens of even larger ones that jut up, making a pathway to the green, tropical island they protect.

"So, when are we going to get onto land?" Brian's question sounds more like a demand. "I'm sick of this stupid boat." He has a few scrapes on him from his tumble overboard, but he seems to have taken the fall personally. When I was wrapping Ashton's arm with his robe tie and making a sling from the robe, Brian looked petulant and angry at the same time. "I notice neither of you went in the water. It was terrifying."

I wanted to remind him of my deep sea dive a few nights ago, compliments of him, but held my tongue.

"I don't want to try to sail among those rocks." I point to the jagged outcroppings that seem to be occupied only by seabirds. "We'll sail around them and find a decent place to come ashore."

"When?" He shoots the question at me.

Ashton turns. "Knock off the attitude, Brian." He shakes his head. "Maybe you could be a little grateful we fished you out." His face is a bit gray, his features tense. I know he is in pain, but he can kinda move his fingers, and the arm isn't deformed, so it must not be too bad. But what do I know? Mama M and Dr. Dalton are always the ones who take care of me, Kik, and Mac whenever we get hurt. I only know basic first aid.

When I open one of the forward compartments to pull out the last water bottle, I have to remove Ashton's backpack.

He exclaims, "You saved the backpack. Excellent." I hand it to him, and I'm glad to see color on his face as he checks the pockets and smiles. "Nice and dry. Amazing!"

I take a sip from the bottle, then pass it to Brian, who takes a deep drink, and then to Ashton, who takes a swallow and hands it back to me. I'm stashing it back in the hold when a sound reaches my ears. My head pops up, and the men are on alert as well. A rhythmic cross between a whine and growl is getting louder and louder. I know that sound.

We all stare at each other. I feel hope and excitement grow in my chest. The noise continues, getting even louder. We each start to turn our heads to find it, and then Ashton looks out toward the island and points. "A boat."

FIFTEEN

The Pirates

"Here! Over here! This way!" Two of the people aboard *Noĕlani* waved both their arms and yelled. Ashton waved his uninjured one and felt like dancing at the idea of being on dry land.

The motorboat turned slightly in their direction, and he saw their wave returned.

"They see us!" He couldn't contain his glee as he reached out, grasped Grey's shoulder, and gave it a little shake and squeeze. She was bouncing in place like a little kid and laughing.

Brian had moved to the stern closest to the approaching boat and was continuing to wave and yell. "We are saved! Come get us!"

As the boat approached, Ashton noticed it was painted black and looked well used. There were four men aboard, each holding... "They have guns," Ashton said in a low voice to Grey.

She glanced up at him, and her brow furrowed. "Well, that's okay, I guess. They probably have them in case they run into trouble." Though she voiced that as a statement, there was a definite question in her voice.

Brian moved back with them. "We are going home!" He was grinning from ear to ear.

"Well, we are a step closer," Ashton said. "How about I do the talking? I'm not good at much, but I can maneuver a conversation."

"Sure." Brian was now back to his friendly bro-self after his earlier anger at going overboard.

Grey gave Ashton a quizzical look but also nodded her agreement.

The boat slowed as it approached, with three of the men shifting their automatic rifles to their shoulders and pointing them at the crew of the *Noēlani*. While he had never actually fired a gun, Ashton had been a weapons aficionado back several years ago and recognized them as Chinese QBZs, or "cubes" for short. He raised his good hand up, opened the hand tied to his chest to show his palm, and stood tall, with his face pleasant and relaxed. Standing just in front of the other two, he quietly said, "Do what I do, and only speak if you have to." Brian and Grey followed suit and put their hands up, smiling.

As the boat swung around and cut its motor, Ashton looked at the men. All four were dressed in dark-colored, long pants and dark, loose, long-sleeved tunics that belted at the waist. The belts showed different colors. Two of the younger men wore black belts, the boat's driver wore a green belt, and the remaining man had a belt of deep maroon. Each had a bandolier of ammunition worn across their chest, and he could see at least two wicked-looking, curved blades tucked into the belts. They were all dark-haired and dark-eyed, with facial features of the Western Continent. The two younger-looking men sported some hair above their lips while the older men were clean-shaven. None of them smiled. The driver of the boat spoke to his crew in what sounded like some dialect of

Chinese. One of the black-belted, younger men answered and then moved forward.

"Who are you?" he called in standard FA, looking at Ashton. His weapon wasn't exactly pointed at him, but it certainly was pointed in his general direction.

Ashton willed his face to stay relaxed. "I'm Ash. This is my friend Brian and my sister, Grey." He could feel Grey's eyes on him as he said this but was pleased when she said nothing. "Our boat got wrecked several nights ago outside of Moku-o-keawe during a storm. We are glad to see people again, finally." What he said this time was true, but he carefully left out the word *yacht* as these men struck him as not unlike the types of men who had worked for his father years before. If he was right, they would be opportunistic and greedy as well as potentially violent.

The younger man reported the information back in his own language and received a short order from his captain.

"We will toss you a line and take you to shore. If you have any weapons, drop them in the sea now." He gesticulated with his rifle.

Ashton shook his head. "We have no weapons. My little sister has a small knife she uses to whittle. I ask that she be allowed to keep it as her mother gave it to her on her deathbed." He glanced at Grey, who glanced back, withdrew her knife from her pocket, and unfolded the smallest blade, carefully using her thumb to camouflage the long blade she had used on the fish.

She looked up at the man in the black boat and then quickly looked back at the knife, holding it more awkwardly than Ashton ever had seen. She then said, "Please, don't take Mama's gift," followed by a small, swallowed sob. Ashton was impressed with the theatrics and gave it a rousing applause in his mind.

The younger man repeated the request, and the driver leaned over, peered at her, and began to laugh. The other three men took up the laughter, and Green Belt waved and commented.

Black Belt Number One translated with a grin. "He says that is not a weapon, it is a child's toy. She may keep it."

Grey bobbed her head and slowly closed the knife and pocketed it. The man tossed Ashton a line with a large knot at the end, which Ashton fumbled with as he moved to tie it off. Grey stepped closer to "her brother" and said low, "Don't tie that one off—keep pulling." Ashton did as she said without acknowledgment. He pulled and saw the other end connected to a line that had three ropes, each tied securely to three large, heavy clips. As the ropes and clips came aboard, Grey moved to attach each onto the front of *Noĕlani*: one on either side and a shorter one just over the center front. Grey looked at Ashton, who nodded as if in approval, though he had no idea why there needed to be three.

The younger man on the boat yelled, "Okay?"

Grey gave a shadow of a nod, and Ashton yelled, "Okay." At her side, Grey put her thumb up and Ashton lifted his good arm and made a thumbs-up gesture. The black boat turned around and slowly began to motor away, the young man aboard letting more and more line out until both men and boat were close to two boat lengths away. With a wave, the black boat picked up speed, the line pulled taut, and *Noĕlani* was on the move to land.

"What was all that about?" Brian asks as we bounce along between the wake our towboat creates. I have taken down the sail and folded the boom up and made it fast. So now, we three can sit in the center of *Noĕlani* under the tarp tent and try to figure out what happens next.

"I am wondering the same thing, and why am I suddenly your sister?" I ask.

Ashton shrugs. "I'm not sure, but with those rifles, and the way they acted… Those guys seem like they could be… You know…"

"What?" Brian looks confused, and I am right there with him.

"Traders," Ashton answers with a glance forward to the black boat. "Traffickers. There's lots in the Southeast part of the Western Continent."

I am stunned into silence by this statement, something that does not happen frequently.

Brian leans forward and says in a hushed voice, "Do you really think so, Ash? Cause that'd be sort of awesome to say we hung out with traders."

"No, Brian. No, it would not be awesome. Traders are ruthless." Ashton pounds his good fist on the sole slightly. "And really dangerous." He looks at me. "I want to be careful, so I figured if they consider you my sister, they might not…" He moves his head from side to side as if that tells me anything.

Again, I'm fourteen, but I'm not naive. I've been listening to Mama's anti-trafficking stories for years. Of course, she tidies them up when we kids are around, but I've heard plenty of uncensored tales through the stair vent and the window to the back porch from her, Matt, and the unit. Traffickers buy and sell people—men, women, and kids. They steal them and treat them really bad. Even Mama was enslaved at one point, but she escaped, and she and the BPF have been working hard to stop traders, which is just another name for traffickers, and they've been real successful. Which makes me proud of Mama because owning another person is wrong. And hurting them the way some enslaved are hurt is super-wrong.

"Are you going to tell them you are an Abernathy?" His father was a big deal in trafficking. His being gone has been bad for the traders, according to Mama and Matt. If Ashton tells them his name, it might really help us get away—or it might make them hate us.

"No, not unless I have to. And you are definitely not to tell them you are from Bosch or who your mother is. As far as they are concerned, we have the same father but different mothers." Ashton frowns but is firm as he says this.

I make a disgusted face. "I don't want to be his kid."

"Yeah, well, join the club. At least you only have to be until we get home," Ashton says shortly.

Brian asks, "So, how come I don't get to be your brother?"

"Because you are an adult, Brian. Sort of," Ashton growls.

I start to open my mouth to argue about being some "little sister" who needs caring for, but I stop when I see Ash's face as he looks toward the towboat and its men and their weapons. He looks seriously worried. Instead, I say, "Listen, Ash, I'll be whoever you think I should be if it'll get us home. Thanks."

He doesn't answer, just nods, but I see the hint of a smile relax his features.

"I count five boats: our towboat and one more like it and then three fast boats. All with multiple motors. Handy if you have to get away really quick. There's a space between a couple of the fast boats, so there's probably another one out some-where," Grey mumbled low to Ashton as they were pulled into the small harbor that had a floating dock off to the left.

Ashton nodded. "I think you're right. What is that dock?" It did not have pilings underneath it but rested directly on the crystal-clear blue water of the cove, extending over the rough volcanic rocks to the white sand of the beach. The cove seemed to be shoved onto the foot of a mountain that rose precipitously like a green pyramid.

"It's one of those temporary ones. See? There's a stabilizing anchor at the end." Grey pointed to indicate the dock anchor. "A great idea, but I've heard they are super expensive—like, Abernathy-expensive." She cut her eyes over to Ashton and snickered as he rolled his eyes at the jab.

"Abernathy-expensive. That's a good one, Grey." Brian chortled as well at Ashton's expense.

Grey didn't acknowledge Brian's comment; instead, her face shifted into a thoughtful expression. "I'm pretty sure these guys don't live here full-time, but the camp is awfully big for just a stop-off."

"They've got nice tents, though." Brian pointed at the line of over a dozen, solid-looking canvas structures that had been constructed close to the edge of the green trees, undergrowth, and thick lianas that marked the start of the rainforest that ran to the mountainside. Two or three more permanent-looking shanties were just behind the stretch of tents.

People, mostly men as far as Ashton could tell, were all over the beach area and around the tents. Some moved purposefully, ferrying objects from place to place, while others roamed casually or even rested in hammocks. A fire pit was dug in the center, above the high tide line, and a tripod hung over it held a large, black pot. Ashton was sure he could smell something delicious, and his mouth watered, causing him to swallow. All in all, it seemed to him to be a pretty idyllic spot. "So, they don't live here, but they seem pretty settled in." He brushed a dirty lock of hair out of his face. "Wonder why they are here?"

Grey shrugged. "We'll find out soon enough, I imagine." The tow boat had cut its engines and tied up to the dock; three of the men were pulling *Noĕlani* toward them to dock her. Grey waited at the bow until they were close and then tossed the mooring line she had tied on the dinghy to one of them. They pulled *Noĕlani* alongside the dock, securing her, and Grey hopped off the boat, extending a hand to Ashton and Brian. "Careful," she warned as they each stepped onto the dock. "Even though the dock is on the water, your legs and your head may feel weird after being on the boat."

Ashton had noticed only a moment or two of wobbliness when he first disembarked in Moku-o-keawe from the *Abundance*, so he was unconcerned. His worry shifted when he found he could barely stand on the dock. His legs felt weak, and he had the unpleasant sensation that the dock was rolling under his feet.

Brian dispensed with any pretense and collapsed onto the dock after attempting a step or two. "My head is spinning, and my legs can't go," he whined.

The people on the dock who might be traders, but were definitely their rescuers, began to laugh until the one who had driven the towboat spoke to another man, who then walked over and offered Brian his hand. Brian accepted, thanking the darkly dressed man effusively as he leaned heavily into him, and was half-carried toward the beach.

The older man then motioned for Ashton and Grey to follow them. Grey wore a disgusted expression as she watched Brian limp away, then she looked up at Ashton and held out her hand. "So, dear brother, Ash, do you need some help as well?"

Ashton barked a laugh. "Thanks, little sister. I think my

legs can manage, though it does feel like the whole island is in motion."

"That's normal," Grey replied. "It's because you've been on a boat for so long, your body has gotten used to the motion of the sea. It'll pass soon."

"Good to know." Ashton took slow breaths as he moved down the dock, taking his time to be sure his feet landed where he was aiming. "There's a lot of people here. I wonder if they have someone who can set my arm."

"They do. I heard them talking about sending you to their physician." Grey's remark was off-handed as they reached the end of the dock.

Ashton grasped her arm. "Wait, can you understand them?" He used a low voice.

Her eyebrows went up and down as she nodded. "Some. It isn't exactly the dialect I learned, but it's close, so if I listen carefully and really think, I can make out the general idea of what they are talking about."

"Well, let's keep that little ability to ourselves until we figure out who these people are and what they want from us."

"Agreed. I will be playing the part of the scared, quiet little sister." She grinned up at him. "But don't get used to it, big brother, because it's only for a little while."

Ashton kept his face perfectly neutral. "Not to worry—the shooting pains in my knee will help me keep your true self in mind."

At that, Grey began to giggle so hard, she had to slap a hand over her mouth as she and Ashton descended the steps and trudged through the sand, following the man with the green sash.

"Hey, pretty girl, come dance with me!" Brian runs up to me and tries to pull me up from the sand, where I have settled after a brilliant meal of a fish and vegetable stew over rice. I even had a dessert of sliced bananas swimming in sweetened coconut milk, so I am very full.

I wrench my hand away. "No, thanks. You go dance for both of us." I wave him off. He laughs and stumbles away, weaving in and out of the circle of light the fire provides, swaying to the guitar music of one of the Si Hai Bang men. I turn to Ash, who sits near me in the sand watching the fire flicker against the dark of the night. "You both had one beer with dinner. Why aren't you acting so ridiculous?"

Ash points at me with the forefinger of his broken arm, which now sports a lattice-like, deep-brown, printed cast that encircles his lower arm and part of his hand. "One, because I am not Brian. And two, because I had a beer. Brian had a beer and a side of Glitter."

"Aha." I nod. *Again, with the Glitter.* "So, he finally got what he was craving."

Ash gives a snort of a laugh. "They offered me some, but I begged off, pointing at my arm." He shrugs. "I figured I should stay sober until I know we all are safe."

Nodding, I consider if there actually *is* any danger. I mean, I get his worry, but thus far, these Si Hai Bang people seem pretty harmless. Si Hai Bang means Four Seas People, and something about the name rings familiar in my head, but I can't quite place it. It will come to me.

Shortly after we arrived, Ashton was taken to see their physician in one of the bigger huts. When he came back close to a bell later, slightly flushed with a grin, he described the inside of the hut as "slick and high tech. There were computers, medical equipment, even 3-D printers." He pointed to his arm, which sported a newly printed, custom cast. "The physician was quite nice." He wiggled his fingers and looked pleased.

Once together, all three of us were taken to a magnificent waterfall that tumbled into a decent-sized swimming hole surrounded by tropical vegetation and flowers. The man who escorted us told us we could bathe, and they would take our clothes to wash and leave us with clean items to wear. I really didn't want to give up my GBW, but they were pretty gross, so I let him take them but kept my jacket and underwear. Ashton had insisted that I swim first, moving Brian and the Si Hai Bang man far back with him. I chuckled because even though he is tall and slender, he reminds me a little of Riki, my nanny/bodyguard on Bosch. Of course, Riki is shorter but has huge arms and legs and an immense chest and neck. But both men seem to fret about me the same way.

I tried to be polite, thinking I should speed through my swim and wash, but it was so luxurious to dip and dive into water that had no sharks, especially since my bleeding was still present. I lathered with the sweet soap provided and rinsed in the spray of a waterfall so clean that I could drink from it freely. When I swam back to the edge, I found an actual towel to dry with, and one of the tunics, with some engineering, became a decent dress that felt crisp and clean on me.

The men swam and washed after me, laughing and splashing. Ashton required me to stay in his view but to also turn around as they undressed and slipped into the cool water. He repeated the request as they came back to the side to dry and dress.

Each of them now had on a pair of the dark, loose pants and one of the tunics the gang wore. The Si Hai Bang were not kind in their remarks about the way the men were originally dressed. I made out words that, roughly translated, described them as toffs, fools, and idiots. I decided that they didn't need to know about that conversation, especially since I had the same impression initially.

Brian asked them if this island was cursed, and after discussion among four or five of the Si Hai Bang men, and my explanation of the word *cursed*, they began to laugh. One said in broken FA, "Best gift ever. No one comes to cursed island. All for us!"

Now, we are lounging in the sand on a starlit night around a warm fire on a tropical beach after washing in fresh water and eating our fill of delicious food. Ashton has told them that we need to contact our families as soon as possible, and they have said we shall before sleep. I try to imagine the delight in Mama's voice when I comm her. She does drive me up a wall at times, but really, I can't wait to tell her all the things that happened.

I lift the can of lemonade the cook gave me and take a swallow of the warm and sweet but also sour liquid—so good. I finally answer Ash. "I'm glad you didn't have any, but the Si Hai Bang seem okay. I mean, they are fixing for us to comm home soon after all."

Ash looks at me and nods, but his face shows me he is clearly unconvinced. I shrug. Nothing I can do about that.

Two songs later, I am almost asleep in the sand, my feet warm by the fire, when Ashton shakes me awake. The Si Hai Bang men are rising from their places and heading to the line of tents. One of the black-belted men walks over with Brian and a torch, beckoning us in standard FA. "I am Kuan-yin. Come, I will show you your beds."

"What about us comming our families?" Ash asks.

Kuan-yin pauses, tips his head, then smiles, revealing several teeth missing. "Yes. You can do comming from your hut. Come."

So, we stand and follow him. The dry sand is heavy to

flounder through initially, but the ground firms up as we walk toward the canvas tents. We continue beyond the tents to one of the small cabins that sits elevated on a platform. The man directs us up the bamboo steps, and we open the door. The cabin is tidy and fairly large, at least twice the size of *Noëlani.* It is constructed of bamboo poles and rough boards with a thatched roof of what appear to be palm fronds. There are two windows, one near the door and one on the far wall, but both are currently shuttered. Near the door is a table and four chairs, with an unlit lantern in the center. Shelves run along the left side wall, with a small cupboard on the right. In the back are two beds on the left and one on the right. A blanket is strung from the ceiling to create two rooms.

Kuan-yin says to Brian, "That is yours." He points to the single bed. Then he turns to Ashton. "Those are for you and sister." Ashton nods his appreciation. I look down to maintain the ruse of being scared of the world.

Kuan-yin nods back. "Go to bed now." It sounds like an order, so we each walk to the beds indicated. Then, our black-belted escort steps out with the torch and closes the door, leaving us in total darkness as we hear the loud clatter and clink of a chain and lock being pulled over the door we had just entered.

PART IV

Sailing In Bosch, Lesson Four

The Destination May Not Be the Point

On a land or air vehicle, our destination is our reason for taking the trip. While there may be things we see out the auto or the vessel window that are pleasing, we are typically eager for the kilometers to disappear behind us so we can reach our destination.

Not so with sailing. Sailing itself is a destination, and it will teach you things about yourself and your crew you could never learn from the safety of a vehicle on the road or a vessel in the sky.

While you have a course, heading, and bearing, you must also contend with the vagaries of wind and water. At times, to reach your intended port, you must sail away from it, turning back toward it as the circumstances of weather and wind allow. There is no direct path when sailing.

Don't neglect what seems to be small things. A good knot, clear tack, and balanced trim all can make or break a sailing expedition. Be certain of your skills, check and double-check before you set sail, and don't be afraid to ask a more experienced sailor for assistance.

Communication is key, even if you are solo sailing. Listen carefully to your crew or yourself and speak clearly for a successful sail. Anger has no place in sailing as the sea is unforgiving. Keep a cool head when making decisions, no matter what the circumstances.

SIXTEEN

Suo and the Bluies

"You. Get over here now," Kuan-yin calls to me as I return from the forested plateau to the beach camp, my basket filled with mangoes. "Chief Suo has returned and requires your presence."

I make my way down along the overgrown path thick with ferns; flowering bushes, some fire-red with tiny white centers; and low trees with small, five-petaled flowers in yellows and pinks, so beautiful and sweet-smelling but so unfamiliar to me. I heard the roaring of a fast boat as I hiked up the hill this morning, so it is unsurprising we are being called to learn our fate.

He waits for me to get in front of him, then hustles me with small shoves to my shoulder along with a few grunts that I guess mean *Hurry up*. He swats at the flying insects that pester him and gripes and complains about being an "errand boy." I ignore him, watching a few butterflies flit about until we reach the elephant grass clumps that then give way to the beach. Growling and cursing, Kuan-yin gestures over to where Ash is standing in the late afternoon sun. In front of Ash is a small canopy set with three chairs. There are people in the chairs, but I cannot make them out from my distance.

"Where's Brian? Isn't his presence also required?" I know my voice is insolent, but I don't care. I can't stand this man who has locked us up in our cabin each night and threatens us with beatings or worse if we disobey him.

He grabs my arm hard and takes my basket. "I'll take those mangoes." Then he leans into my face so close I can see the pores and pits on his nose and cheeks. His breath is far more unpleasant than even Darvin's as he hisses, "Don't question me, girl, or I'll make you sorry." The fingers of one hand dig into my arm while he curves his other forefinger under my chin, then strokes my jawline with the back of it. I've had enough. I keep my chin up and stare back at him, sending my anger through my eyes. I refuse to be the scared little sister around him any longer. I give him a swift kick in the knee, and he backs away, swearing. I quickly move to the red earth path back to the beach and hear him come limping behind me, still swearing, and describing what he will do to me when he has the chance.

Kuan-yin was at the door just after sunrise on the first morning, rattling the chain as he slipped it off the door and then walking into the hut to order us up. He no longer felt the need to force a smile as he explained that we were intruders and, as such, our fate was to be determined by the leader of the Si Hai Bang, Chief Suo, who was currently away. Until her return, we could wander the island through the day but must be back in camp by sunset. There was a laundry list of don'ts, of course: Don't go near the dock, don't attack or challenge any member of Si Hai Bang, don't try to make or steal a weapon, don't enter any hut other than our own, don't go into the cave that sat a kilometer or so behind the camp… All were followed up with, "Or you will be beaten, shot, or locked up in a cage as I desire." He leered at me with that last word, and I felt my face flush. I shifted closer to Ash and even to Brian.

Since then, we have essentially been ignored by anyone other than Kuan-yin. He checks on each of us several times throughout the day. I have spent my time exploring the island, disappearing after breakfast and returning before sunset.

Ashton was worried at first. "You could get lost out there. Or fall and hurt yourself."

I waved him off. "I'm careful. And I have a compass." I held up my trusty guide piece and showed it to him. "And you should see the views from the mountains. You can see the ocean on both sides. I have been able to study the cove and the area outside of it. I even saw some whales! And I saw an island off to the east and flashed in its direction with my mirror. I think it's too far away, though. It's also amazing how much the plants change as I move up and down in elevation. There are parts that are dry and brown and even have cacti."

The first day, I brought back several dragon fruit that I'd plucked off a tree-like cactus whose branches were more like vines that looked like someone's messy green hairstyle. On the second day, I found a bunch of round, red berries that tasted a bit like musky, juicy strawberries with a nice, tart bite at the end.

"Okay, fine," he relented as he ate his tenth berry, slurping the juice and giving an involuntary twitch of his face as the tartness hit. "You keep exploring. These are delicious."

Besides what I find, the Si Hai Bang provides us with plenty of water and food, and they welcome us to sit by the fire at night before bedtime—when we are locked back into our hut. They even still share their beer and Glitter with Brian, though Ash has declined both since the first night.

That first night was terrifying and miserable. With the windows closed and locked, and the three of us jammed into that small space, the hut quickly became steamy and oppressive. We could hear the gentle sound of the surf on the beach and the distant sound of frogs from the forest behind us, as well as the scritching and scratching of the rats as they began their night patrol, but we could see nothing. The cabin was so dark that when the men tried moving through the unfamiliar space to try the door and windows, they stubbed their toes and cracked their shins amid curses. I didn't even bother to try to move; instead, I fell onto my assigned bed on top of the covers, sweat pouring from my body and tears silently streaming down my face. I finally pretended I was Beverlee when the deep-sea merfolk tied her to a rock to keep her from returning to the marshes. I imagined her escape, both how the author related it and in several different ways of my own until I fell into a restless sleep.

Now on this, our third day in our paradisal prison of this beautiful, wild island, I walk barefoot through the sand to where Ash stands, Kuan-yin stumbling behind me, trying to stay at my heels. As we get closer, he raises his weapon enough to nudge the tip into my lower back. *Trying to look big and brave for your boss, Kuan-yin? Using a gun to get one fourteen-year-old to walk where she was going anyway doesn't look strong. Idiot.* I take my place at Ash's right.

"This is your sister, Mr. Castellanos?" A woman whom I assume is Chief Suo says in perfect FA from her seat in a woven reed chair. She is in her forties or fifties, with dark hair pulled back from a broad face that is deeply tan from the summer sun. Her dark eyebrows curve over dark eyes. Her nose turns up slightly, and her cheeks are a little jowly. Instead of a plain tunic, hers is a peacock-blue one with swirls that remind me of the sea. It is fastened across her stout midsection with a black tie shot through with gold threads. She wears heavy gold earrings and a long, gold chain with several shark teeth attached to it and sits in the relaxed way of someone who is used to being in charge.

The occupants of the other two chairs catch my eye, and I have to work to keep my face neutral. Seated on either side of Chief Suo are men with pale skin, light-colored eyes, and the facial shape of the people of Eternia. Both are dressed in robes, each a different shade of blue. They are the Bluest, or Bluies for short, from the Federal Alliance, a radical religious group always showing up on the New Earth news. Why are they here? Mama and Matt say the group is dangerous, though the times I have seen them on the Obi, they have just stood around in large groups, chanting or giving speeches about what the Federal Alliance should look like. I shrug inwardly; New Earth politics is not something I pay attention to, though it is very peculiar that they are so far from home. *I wonder if they would help us get back.* I am willing to grab onto any hope.

"Yes, this is Grey." Ashton puts a brotherly hand on my shoulders, and I nod in response to the chief.

"And what is your last name, Grey?" The chief looks directly at me.

I have to pause for a tiny moment to remember. I'm pretty sure it is the name Ashton and Brian called their other friends by. "Castellanos, ma'am, after my father."

She blinks and looks from Ash to me. "You don't look like siblings."

I jump in; I have prepped this story. "My mother was from the village of Kiharu in Edo. She met my father when he traveled to attend the Winter Festival one year. They fell in love. Mother didn't realize Father had another family until I was two, and then they had a big fight. But when she was dying, she arranged for me to be sent to stay with him after she passed. That was when I met Ashton. He is a very kind brother." I venture a small smile to test the waters.

'Well, that would explain your difference in appearance." She nods but does not return my smile. "And your story is quite interesting." She stands, and Kuan-yin and the men standing guard near the canopy step back and fold their hands as they look to the ground. She walks up to Ash and me. "Your other friend—Brian, I believe his name is—also tells an interesting story. He tells me that you..." She pokes a thick finger into Ash's chest. "...are the son of Rob Abernathy. And my guests..." Now, she gestures to the Bluies. "...assure me you look just like him, though not as blond, and you have that mess of hair on your face." She gestures at the week-old stubble he has finally ceased complaining about. Ashton looks at her and says nothing, but I see his body tension increase.

"And you, my dear..." She turns to me and grasps my chin gently between her thumb and forefinger, her eyes crafty and cunning as she studies my face. "...are Grey Shima, the daughter of the master commander of Bosch, Kat Wallace."

I hold my tongue, but I can't help but look at Ashton, whose expression is unreadable.

"My intent was to take all three of you to the thrall market when our business here is concluded. You are all young and healthy and would bring an excellent price. But Brian... Well,the story he tells is so intriguing. If he is correct, then the two of you could bring me far more markers in ransom than you could at the market." She tips her head and looks at us as if calculating our worth. "I could even get multiple parties involved in a bidding war. And your talkative friend, Brian, who seems to have a penchant for Glitter? Well, he can serve me as well. Isn't that right, gentlemen?" Chief Suo turns to her blue guests, and they chuckle and nod.

Ashton speaks up. "You are correct, Brian has a Glitter problem. And he cannot be trusted with the truth. Of course, we all know Abernathy's son, Nick, and I agree, as does my father, that I look like Rob Abernathy, but that is an issue between my father and my mother. However, Chief Suo, this *is* my sister." His hand goes even more firmly around my shoulder.

Chief Suo gives a hearty laugh that is taken up by her underlings and guests. "How charming and noble. Certainly, that would set you apart from being Abernathy's son if the stories I have heard about him are true." She returns to her seat. "We will verify the story. Kuan-yin, get their images and submit them to the processor."

"Yes, ma'am." He turns and half-runs to the cabin that Ashton had said was the physician's office.

Chief Suo picks up a tall drink from the table near her chair and takes a swallow. "The Bosch fancy themselves pirates, isn't that so, Grey Shima?"

Her question shakes loose the memory about the Si Hai Bang that had eluded me. At different times, both Papa and Uncle Kenichi (who is definitely not Papa's brother but Mama's yakuza friend) brought up the name when speaking of raids committed on some of the southern island ships of Edo. Not wanting to reveal my hand regarding Bosch, I choose my words carefully. "I have heard they do."

Again, she laughs. "Pirates who are soft and live on land and fly in fancy airships." She points at me. "Now, we, the Si Hai Bang, we are real pirates. We are at home on the ocean and are unafraid of anything. And we will do what is necessary to get what we want." Her finger now crosses her throat as if drawing a knife blade as she grins maniacally.

Papa cleaned up his stories about them when he knew I was listening, but Uncle Kenichi described the Si Hai Bang as brutal aggressors and gave a few gruesome details to under-line his point. All sorts of responses well up in me, most of them angry and confrontational as I really want to defend the

Bosch, but I beat them back. Even though Brian has traded our identities and our safety for who knows what, I need to maintain our deception for as long as possible. But I will certainly thank dear Brian later, with an elbow to the ear as Flossie taught me. For now, I simply shrug, but then realize there is something I want before this conversation ends. "Chief Suo?"

She looks a bit surprised that I have addressed her. "Yes, girl?"

"I want my mangoes back. I picked them." I gesture at the basket of fruit that sits in the sand near where Kuan-Yin had been standing.

The chief nods. "If you gathered them, then you may have them."

"Excellent." I dash over and pick up the basket, slipping it over my arm, intentionally not thanking her.

Kuan-yin returns with a camera and takes our pictures, capturing our images: Ashton's expression, which is annoyed and angry; mine, a bit triumphant as Kuan-Yi scowls at my mango reclamation. He then nods to the chief and returns with the camera to the physician's cabin. Chief Suo stands and beckons to her two blue-clad guests. They walk away from the beach, accompanied by the guards, past the cabins and into the brush following the path toward the cave we have been warned to avoid. My island brother and I are left standing in the sand. I feel oddly exposed.

We look at each other. Ashton announces, "I'm going to kill Brian."

I eat and drink during dinner only because I have to—for strength, not enjoyment. Ash and I avoid the after-meal fire tonight, instead returning to the hut as the sun sets. We discovered after the first night that we can open the windows a small amount to let the sea breeze circulate, a delightful change that has made sleeping far more comfortable.

We also figured out the lantern in the cabin, so we have light at night now. When we first got back to the hut, we both ranted about Brian's selfish stupidity and what it could cost us. After about a half-bell of that, we ran out of steam, with Ash saying, "Well, there's nothing to do but wait, as long as we aren't in imminent danger."

"But we need to figure a way for the three of us to get out of here before anything bad really happens."

"Agreed." Ashton nods. "We'll figure that out after Brian gets here."

Now, a bell or so later (as close as I can estimate), we sit at the small table, each intent on our own projects, a bowl of sliced mango in the center.

"I am going to need to find sandpaper eventually," I declare idly as I continue to shape my dragon, taking off bits of non-dragon-looking pieces of wood with my knife.

Ash sits at the table as well, sketching. He peers over. "It's taking shape. Is it going to have horns on its head?"

"He. And yes, he is going to have horns." I'm not sure how I know it's a he; I just do. He has a long-ish neck and sits crouched. "I still need to shape his wings, and then I'll refine the horns on his head." I look intently at the creature emerging from the wood. "So, you were right. They are traders."

"Mm-hmm. And pirates. Good job not jumping on the chief for her comments."

I give a shrug. "Honestly, if she tries to tangle with Mama and the BPF, and all that the Force can bring, I don't think she'll be pirating for much longer."

"I don't doubt it."

"How's your drawing coming?" I glance over to see what he is working on.

It was interesting to discover that Ashton Abernathy likes to draw and has an aptitude for it. He showed me the sketch he drew on the champagne label of me with my back to him on the bow of *Noĕlani*; it was really very good. I mean, I don't know much about art, but I liked it. Now, he has a stubby pencil and a few sheets of paper the physician gave him when he went to have her check his cast.

"It's coming—slowly." He looks at my work. "So, this dragon, does he have a name? You seem to like naming things."

I grin and hold up my almost-dragon. "Not yet. I think I need to get him closer to finished before his name will reveal itself." Ashton chuckles at my fancy. Then I ask, indicating his newest drawing, "Who are they?"

He tilts his head and looks at the paper appraisingly. "It's supposed to be my sister, Farris, and me. I've been thinking about her, now that I have a new sister." He grins at me. "I wanted a picture of the two of us together as adults." He sighs. "But I'm having trouble really remembering what she looks like. It's been years since I've seen her." He frowns as he looks at the paper. "I have family pictures with her in it back home…" He erases her nose and starts to resketch it.

I lean over. "It looks good to me." Odd. The picture stirs the same niggle of memory that the Si Hai Bang name did. It nudges my brain, but it is no more than a nudge. I smile. "It reminds me of something or someone, but I'm not sure what or who…"

Before he can respond, the door opens, and a very wobbly Brian comes in.

Ashton is up and out of his seat in a moment. He grabs Brian's shirt with his good arm and shoves him up against the wall, swearing in loud and creative ways. Kuan-yin comes in and yells, "You! Stop that!" He shakes Ash off Brian. Ashton releases Betrayer Brian but still swings his good arm threateningly and curses the whole time.

Brian slumps to the floor and looks up, his eyes unfocused. "Hey, man. Sorry, but it was too good an offer. They said I could have unlimited Glitter." He closes his eyes and leans back on the wall he is sitting in front of. "You should see the bricks they have, Ash. All stacked up and wrapped in burlap. It's amazing. I just had to lean in and breathe in the smell before I got a chunk." He smiles dreamily. "It was awesome."

"No fighting!" Kuan-yin points an accusatory finger at Ash, who holds up his hands as if in surrender. Then the Si Hai Bang man backs out the door, slamming it. We hear the familiar clinking of the chain and the click of the lock.

Ashton pauses and looks over at Brian, who is moving his head and shoulders back and forth against the wall in time to a song only he can hear and grinning. "Hey," Ash says, "no hard feelings?"

Brian gives him a sloppy thumbs-up.

"Let's get you into bed then." Ashton reaches around Brian's chest and waist and lifts him to his feet, half-dragging him to bed. He helps him undress to his underwear and pulls the covers over him. "All set?"

"Yeah, man. Thanks for not being pissed," Brian slurs.

"Oh, I'm pissed," Ash says without shifting out of his calm tone. Then he reaches back and punches Brian in the face hard with his uncasted hand. Brian's head falls limply to the side, and I stare, concerned.

Ashton takes Brian's face in his hand and checks his breathing and pulse. Then he comes back to the table, working the fingers of his punching hand, and resumes drawing.

I raise my eyebrows. "Don't break your drawing hand, Ash."

He grins, and we return to focus on our art.

There is rain when we awake the next morning, the first bit of weather since the squall. It smells clean and fresh, though it will add to the humidity as the day progresses. I stretch in my bed and do my body survey. There are some random sore spots and bruises, but my body feels fit. I am particularly delighted at the absence of pelvic cramping, knowing that it means my bleeding is finished.

Ash and I have developed a routine. We both wake when the lock opens and the chain is pulled off, but I stay in bed as he gets up, pees in the night pot they have provided, and then dresses. After that, he carries the pot outside and dumps it in the designated spot. Then he returns inside, sets it back, steps to the other side of the blanket, and announces, "Your turn." And that is how the day starts for us.

Brian, on the other hand, wakes slowly this morning with a moan. He pats his left cheek and eye with his fingertips. I watch as he discovers the swelling by the eye and the cut on the curve of his cheek. "What happened to my face?"

Ash glances over from the open door, where he stands gazing out at the rain. "You were flying pretty high last night, and it was dark when you came back to the hut. Maybe you ran into something."

Brian sits up, still feeling his injury. "Yeah. I bet that's it."

"We have a guard this morning. And here comes Mariko—I mean, the physician—and someone else." Ash points, and I move to the door to see an unfamiliar, dark-haired woman striding in our direction. At her side is a young man holding an umbrella over her head as he hustles to keep pace with her. They stop and say something to Kuan-yin, whose placement, in a guard stance several meters away from our steps, is also a new development. Typically, he unlocks the door, and we are free to move about the island. I'm guessing the events of yesterday have changed this. The woman Ash has identified as the physician comes up the steps, stopping on the second from the top, her umbrella boy one step below, standing on his tiptoes as he strains to keep the rain off of her.

"Good morning. I am Dr. Mariko A-Jian, the physician of the Si Hai Bang, and this is my assistant, Zhiwei." Her voice is both brisk and formal.

Ashton has just a hint of a smile as he says, "Yes, Mariko. I know who you are." There is a tease in his voice.

The physician glances at Ashton, and her eyes stay on him for a fraction of a second longer than they did on me. A very small smile plays at the edges of her mouth, but then she glances at her assistant. "Why, yes, Ashton. I will assess your arm in due time. For now, I need you both to move away from the door, so we may come in." She points toward the back of the hut. We shift back a bit, enough so she can easily get under cover, but she wrinkles her brow. "Farther." We move a meter or so back and then another meter as she continues to push the air in front of her with her hands. Finally, we have apparently satisfied her because they come in. However, before they do, they pause to put on surgical masks and goggles. Which is just weird and unsettling.

She shakes her coat and hangs it on the edge of the open door, directing Zhiwei to do the same. Then she shifts a dark green bag she had slung over her shoulder to her front. Plundering inside it, she removes some medical gloves that she and the assistant pull on; a small, black, zippered case; and a clipboard with a pen, which she hands to Zhiwei. "You will need to take notes."

Brian sits on the edge of his bed, oblivious to our visitors as he shakes his head and squints. He opens just his right eye and then the left as he tries to make sense of the light streaming in from the door. Dr. A-Jian goes to his bedside, with Zhiwei quietly moving with her. "How are you feeling, Mr. Walsh?" She gives his new wounds a cursory examination and says something to Zhiwei that he nods to and jots down.

"Umm, kinda crappy. My eye hurts. And my cheek. I need some more Glitter." He finally opens both eyes, and when he sees the physician, he tips his head and rubs the scruff on his face. "You have real pretty eyes and soft hands. We could have the Glitter together." He grins at her.

Dr. A-Jian sighs, ignoring his clumsy attempt at flirtation. "We will get you some brought in with your meals." She removes a thermometer from her bag and swipes it across his forehead, reporting its reading to Zhiwei. She then attaches a small wristband to his left wrist and pushes a button. "Sit quietly, please." Remarkably, Brian cooperates but still offers a wanton grin.

Ash and I look at each other, and his face wears the same perplexed expression that I feel. "What's going on?" I finally ask, unable to keep my curiosity at bay.

Her voice is still brisk as she says, "I'll be evaluating you both in one minute. Please be patient."

"Evaluating us for what, Mariko?" Ashton stands with his arms across his chest, his eyes narrowed.

The wristband on Brian beeps, and after Dr. A-Jian reads some numbers aloud to the assistant, who notes them on the clipboard, she removes it. "You three will be confined to your cabin and the immediate area around it. You will be allowed a section of the beach and will have supervised bathing times as your health allows." She pats Brian on the shoulder. "You should rest. I will send medicine for your cut." Brian obediently lies back and then pats the bed next to him, giving a shrug as the doctor shakes her head in a clear "absolutely not" motion.

Now, Ashton approaches Dr. A-Jian. "Mariko, what are you talking about?" Zhiwei steps in front of the physician, blocking Ash's approach. The physician says something to her assistant, and he steps aside, but I can see him still eyeing Ashton.

She moves over to Ashton and gestures to one of the chairs at the table. They walk over, and he sits as she carefully checks his cast, holding his injured hand in hers as she gently pokes and prods with her other hand. "There is no swelling. The arm seems to be healing well." She wipes the thermometer off with a small, disposable pad and takes his temperature.

"We feel just fine, Mariko. Why are we confined?" Ashton's face is serious. "What's going on?"

Dr. A-Jian speaks to Zhiwei. A conversation develops between them that is just a hair away from being an argument. The best I can make out is, she wants him to go back and get something from the office cabin, but he doesn't want to leave her alone with the…ouch. I know that word. It isn't a nice one. It gets used in Edo in a slightly different form to refer to foreigners. It is definitely a word that is on the list of ones that Papa and even Mama don't want me to use. Finally, the doctor says something akin to "And that's final." Zhiwei looks sullen, gathers his coat, and heads out the door.

As soon as he is gone, Dr. A-Jian turns to Ash, her entire face and body softening. She reaches out and touches his cheek in a decidedly un-doctor-like fashion. My eyes start to get big, but I take a breath and will my face to relax. I am so asking Ash for the story about her after she leaves. I survey her. She is pretty, with petite features and a jawline that comes into a V-shape, with full lips and dark eyes. She is about my height and, while almost as slender, has far more womanly curves in her breasts and hips than me. I mean, after all, she *is* a grown woman—a doctor.

She squats near the chair Ash is in and now takes his good hand, clasping it between both of hers. "Your friend was… exposed to a disease yesterday. We will be monitoring him for signs of it, and you and your sister as well." Apparently, no one has caught her up on the change in Ash and my familial relationship.

"What disease?" Ash asks as she stands and begins to take his vitals as well, jotting the data on the clipboard.

"I cannot say." Her lips are tightly pressed into a thin line.

Ash's eyebrows go up. "Can't or won't?"

"I am kept here by the Si Hai Bang. I must follow their directives." She gives him an apologetic smile, but her eyes radiate affection. *And the plot thickens!* Her brow wrinkles, and then she looks toward the door. "But there is something I can do. Take off your tunic." Now, my eyes do pop open. She digs into her bag and brings out a small vial and two even smaller packets. Ashton undoes his tunic, letting it drop behind him where he sits. Dr. A-Jian glances at me. "You, too, girl." My eyes connect with Ashton, who shrugs, so I turn and undo my tunic, tucking it around my not-a-grown-up-doctor's breasts, leaving my shoulders bare, and then turn back.

The physician has a small needle in her hand. She dips it into the vial, then proceeds to jab it into Ashton's upper arm with firm, regular movements. I relax. While I don't love them, I'm used to immunizations. We get them every year on Bosch. Dr. A-Jian moves to me after putting a dressing on Ash's arm. And as she prepares to jab my arm, she pauses. "You have a scar already."

I peer at the arm she holds and nod. "Oh, probably. We get

lots of shots and stuff on Bos…" I freeze the word in my mouth. She frowns and seems deep in thought. Without warning, she jabs the needle over and over on a tiny section of the surface of my skin. I flinch, but it is over quickly. She puts on a dressing and puts her finger to her lips. "I did nothing. Understand?" I nod as does Ash.

I turn and slip my tunic-dress back over my shoulders. I feel like I should know what that jab was for. It is different from most shots I've gotten. I know I got something similar a few years back, but I don't recall what it was meant to protect me from. Because the Bosch travel so extensively, we all get multiple immunizations each year. Mama says, by getting the shots, we are doing our part to keep away the Old Earth pandemics that killed so many millions upon millions, part of the past.

Dr. A-Jian gathers her materials and puts them away as Ashton re-ties his tunic. The two of them look at each other for several seconds before she moves to the door, pulls her coat from the corner, and slips it on. She tells him, "I'll be back later today," and then leaves without looking back.

SEVENTEEN

What Can We Do?

Ashton stood and made the door in two strides. He watched as Mariko walked with purpose away from the cabin, her dark hair flowing behind her. His hand went to his arm, where the small wound she gave him stung. Why hadn't she given one to Brian? Why just to him and Grey? Grey. Shit. He turned and saw the girl now sitting on one of the chairs, her right foot on her left knee and her hands clasped in front of her. Her face was expectant as she grinned at him.

"Are you going to make me ask? Or are you just going to spill it?" She tipped her head, clearly keen to hear Ashton's story.

Ashton stuck his tongue out at her. "I don't kiss and tell."

At this, she whooped and then slapped a hand over her mouth, looking at Brian, who was snoring in his bed. "That says it all, then."

Ashton grinned as he felt a slight warmth in his face. He and the physician had definitely taken to each other from the moment he stepped into her office. He made sure to "stop in" daily to have her evaluate his casted arm. And she seemed delighted whenever he appeared. He loved how her fingers felt so soft yet so expert as she ran them along his injured arm. Her eyes were dark, intelligent, and intense; he felt like he could lose himself in their depths. They had talked each day, sometimes for hours, Ashton sitting in one of her office chairs as she went about her work. They had even shared a small, sweet kiss yesterday before all the crap went down with Chief Suo. But now…

He decided to refocus the conversation. "What disease would Brian have gotten exposed to that would make her act that way? And from where? And what the hell were those jabs?"

"I feel like I should know. I am sure I've had something almost identical. That's why I have a scar." She pulled her sleeve up and showed her arm to Ashton, pointing out the small, circular divot near her left shoulder just to the side of where Dr. A-Jian had placed the dressing.

Ashton shook his head. "I don't have anything like that."

"You will now," Grey asserted. "How come Brian didn't get one if he was exposed?"

Ashton's face folded into worried wrinkles. "That's a damn good question, Grey. And I don't think there is a good answer to it." He looked over to where Brian lay snoring slightly on his bed.

"I don't get why we can't go out," Brian repeated for the sixth time since lunch. "It's bad enough we get locked in at night. And that doctor lady promised I could have some Glitter. I'm just going to go. I know where it is." He stood and headed out the door. Ashton, who sat at the small table, was still angry with the younger man and didn't bother to argue with him, focusing on his new drawing instead.

Minutes later, Brian was back inside, loudly grousing about how their new captivity was "totally unfair and not cool, man."

Behind him several paces, Kuan-Yin, now outfitted with a mask and gloves, held his weapon up. He used it to gesture at Brian as he spoke. "You must stay here until Dr. A-Jian says otherwise."

Grey commented from her seat nearest the front window, "Well, how convenient. Here she comes." She looked over at Ashton and gave him a simpering smile, followed by a kissing face before chuckling as she returned her focus to the dragon she was whittling. Ashton rolled his eyes but felt his heart beat a bit faster. *The kid's not wrong, Ash. You definitely fancy Mariko.* It was hardly the time to pursue romance, though.

Mariko came in—masked, gloved, and goggled—and dismissed Kuan-Yin with a wave of her hand. Her eyebrows went up as she looked at Brian, who was standing in the middle of the cabin. "You received the medicine I sent?"

"For my eye and my cheek, yeah. But what about my Glitter? I was promised all I wanted."

Ashton thought it was interesting that Brian's usual pursuit of any attractive person seemed to be pushed aside by his desire for more Glitter. *He's got the Glitterhead thing real bad.* He wondered why he hadn't noticed that about Brian before.

Mariko held up a small bag. "I have brought some. It should be enough…"

Brian practically grabbed the sack from her hand. "Thanks." He scrabbled in the bag, pulling out a brown chunk shot through with golden and green sparkles. It looked a bit like an overcooked chocolate cookie, dark and crumbly. He popped it into his mouth, chewed, and sighed. Then he went to his bed and tucked the bag under his pillow. He looked over toward Ashton and the girl. "That's mine, okay?"

Ashton waved to him. "Not to worry, Brian. We're good here." Mariko was taking his temperature and then Grey's. She pulled down her mask and paused to look at his sketch; a smile crept over her lips. "Do you like it?" Ashton asked.

She nodded and looked shyly at him. "I like it quite well."

"It would be better if you sat for it," he remarked as he surveyed the likeness of her he had drawn.

Mariko glanced toward the door. "That would be a bad idea for both of us." She leaned in and whispered in his ear, "But I will come back." Then, as he smiled, she pulled up her mask and walked over to Brian.

"You are feeling well?" She took his temperature.

Brian shrugged. "I had a little headache, but now that I have my Glitter, I am feeling good." He stretched his arms above his head. "Another few minutes and I'll be fantastic."

Mariko looked at her timepiece and murmured something.

"What did you say?" Brian asked.

"Just noting the twenty-four-hour mark." She jotted down a note.

"Ash said I may have some disease. But I feel okay."

The physician looked from Brian to Ashton and then to Grey, who sat whittling but glanced up. Ashton wanted answers but wouldn't press Mariko. He watched as she walked to the door and shut it. She motioned Brian toward the table as she approached.

Dr. Mariko A-Jian crouched next to the table and said in a low voice, "Listen carefully. The disease is in the burlap wrap of the Glitter. It is the reason the Si Hai Bang are here. They were commissioned by the blue men. The wrap has been impregnated with a special pox virus."

"Pox?!" Ashton heard the touch of panic in his voice.

"Yes," Mariko continued, "pox. The blue-dressed people wish to disrupt the status quo and create chaos. They have commissioned this to be done and delivered the pox to the suppliers of Glitter, the Bosch." She looked meaningfully at Grey, whose eyes grew large as Mariko spoke. "The Bosch will travel throughout New Earth making deliveries. They will spread the disease. They will be blamed, as will the current president of the FA, for the coming pandemic since they are allies, and both will be destroyed for their part in it."

There was a long silence following these words.

It was Brian who broke the tense quiet with a laugh. "Yeah, right. You expect me to believe that? I bet you were told to say that so I wouldn't go back to the Glitter storage shed." He began to giggle. "But I don't need to. I have your pretty behind..." He gave a quick slap to the physician's rump. "...to deliver it to me." He stood, swaying slightly, seemingly unaware of the shock on Mariko's face or the anger on Ashton's. "I'm going to lie down and enjoy my Glitter ride." And with that, he meandered to his bed and stretched out, eyes shut and a broad smile on his face.

"Why can't you immunize him?" Ashton said in a low voice as he watched Brian go.

Mariko looked pained. "He is the test case for the blue people to watch the progress." She sighed. "If I immunize him, and he does not get ill, then they will withhold their final payment and request refunds of the earlier markers. Chief Sou will blame me. And she will see to it that my family in Formosa suffers for my betrayal." She touched Ashton's knee. "I am so sorry. I cannot."

Grey asked, "What can we do to help him?"

Ashton looked at her with surprise.

She shrugged. "I don't like Brian. But pox is awful. I read about it in history this past year." She paused and her brows came together. "But Dr. A-Jain, the Bosch are immunized against pox, so they probably won't get sick."

Mariko nodded. "Yes, that is true. But I have heard the talk. The Blue ones will place the blame on the Bosch and make New Earth afraid of them. They have an ally in the FA military who will remove the president. Then the new FA government and other allies will bring military force to destroy the entire island of Bosch and everyone on it."

Ashton watched as first shock and then anguish appeared on Grey's face. "What?! That's my home. What about the people there? What about my family? You can't mean they'd kill everyone. My sister is only two, and there's my brothers, my friends. Matt. Riki. They can't kill Mama…" She looked at Ashton desperately. "Can they?" Her voice broke as she began to cry. "No. They can't do that." She buried her face in her hands, letting her knife and the small dragon that still had no horns fall to the table.

Ashton reached over and put his arms around Grey, and she sobbed into his shoulder. "You should go, Mariko," he said, his voice chill but shaking with fury.

Mariko looked at Ashton once more, but he did not look toward her. Instead, his eyes were studiously focused away from her as he gazed out the window, patting the girl who cried in his arms. Mariko stood, collected her things, and left.

We stroll with Brian to the section of the beach set apart for us. The Si Hai Bang stay well back, with guards stationed thirty meters or so away, weapons trained on us. They have the same harsh expressions as before, but now, there is a tinge of fear in them. There is food and a fire set up, and Ash and I force ourselves to eat bites of the simple meal of grilled fish, some kind of roasted, deep-orange squash, and roasted mango. Brian gobbles the food, moaning ecstatically over each bite and giggling in between. After dinner, he lies on the sand, talking to the clouds and the curved-beaked, sandy-colored birds that run back and forth on the beach, dodging the gentle surf.

Ash and I watch the sunset and discuss what is to be done. "How are we going to keep them from destroying Bosch?" My voice still shakes as the pictures of what could be dance in my head, but I push them aside to try to think of a plan.

"We have to get out of here and warn your mama and everyone else," Ash declares as he draws shapes in the sand, then angrily wipes them away.

"But how are we supposed to do that? We can't take Brian until the pox runs its course. That could be, like, a week or more, if I remember right from class," I argue. "And how do we get away anyhow? Those boats of theirs are fast. Even if we steal one, they have more of them to come after us with. And they have guns."

"You aren't wrong." Ash sighs a deep sigh. Then he says with a note of hope, "We could get guns from them and use them."

I consider this at length and then say, "Ash, I know how to shoot. After the Awful July, my friend Flossie taught me how with all different kinds of guns, even more than Mama knew about. And I'm pretty good now. I can shoot far and straight." I look right into his eyes. "But I don't think I could just shoot another person, not unless I thought they were about to kill me." I look away. "And maybe not even then..."

Ashton is about to reply when we both hear a moan in the twilight. Brian has his legs drawn up to his belly and a hand on his head. We crawl over to him. I put a hand on his arm. "Brian, what's wrong?"

He whimpers, "My gut hurts. Maybe I ate too fast, and my headache is back."

My hand moves to his forehead. "Ash," I whisper, "he's burning up."

"Let's get him back to the cabin. We'll get him some water and put him to bed." Ashton reaches down and pulls Brian to his feet, but after one step, Brian's knees collapse under him, and Ashton scoops him up like a child and trudges through the sand to get him to the hut.

"Should I go for the doctor?" I ask at the top of the stairs.

"Why?" Ash practically spits his answer. "She already said she won't do anything to help him."

I don't reply, just move in to turn down Brian's sheets. Ashton lays him down and proceeds to strip off his clothes. The skin on his chest is a dusky red color—almost bruised— and small red dots are scattered over his arms and legs. As I move to see his face, he opens his eyes, and the whites are bloody as if he had been in a fight. "Ash," I whisper, "look. Is that from when you…?"

"No. That's new." He breathes out. "Shit."

With eleven-year-old brothers and a two-year-old sister who mimic everything I do, I generally don't swear. But now I sit back on my heels. "Shit."

Ashton went out the door as Kuan-Yin was coming up to lock them in. Instead of shoving him into the cabin, the guard backed down the stairs. "Don't come too close." He held up one hand, then seemed to realize he had a gun and raised that.

"We need water," Ashton told him. "Our friend is sick."

"You are all sick," Kuan-Yin sneered, but his face held fear. "We should burn the cabin with you all in it."

Ashton had no time for this type of nonsense. "Is that right? And what would Chief Suo have to say about that?" He saw Kuan-Yin's eyes dart back and forth uncertainly. "Go get us four jugs of fresh water. Now. Or… I'll… I'll cough on you."

This statement made the Si Hai Bang man straighten up and look at Ashton in terror. "No. Do not do that. I will fetch the water. You stay in your cabin."

Ashton returned inside. Grey sat at Brian's bedside, holding his hand and dabbing him with a damp cloth. Brian moaned in pain. Grey turned her head. "His skin looks bruised. Even more than when we put him to bed."

"Kuan-Yin went to get water." Ashton kneeled near Brian and Grey. "We'll take turns with him tonight. That damn, useless doctor will be by tomorrow. There's nothing else to do."

On my second turn of the night with Brian, I hear a crunching sound as I go to plump his pillow. I pull out the small brown bag that holds his Glitter.

Brian is writhing on the bed. "Grey, my head," he moans piteously. "My belly." As he talks, I see a little bloody spittle drain from the corner of his mouth.

I reach into the bag, break off a small piece, pull it out, and look at it. It's the first time I've held or seen any so up close. I mean, I know what it is, of course. It is the main export of Bosch and comes from the peat bogs near the clay pits in District Five. Glitter was discovered over a century ago when the early settlers were digging clay to make bricks. Those early Bosch discovered that this peat was unique. It had a fungus that grew through it that made people relax their inhibitions and their bodies if they ate it. Honestly, I've never been sure what possessed the first person to actually put it into their mouth. The fungus that makes people high also gives the cut peat a glittery, gold appearance, with hints of purple, blue, and green. Hence, the name Glitter. "Here, Brian. Eat this."

He pushes my hand aside and turns his face away, but I lean in and coax him in a soft voice, "It's Glitter."

"Glitter?" His own voice is barely audible, but his face turns back to me, and he opens his mouth to reveal blood around the base of his teeth.

I pop the bit in, then pull off another bit and give it to him for good measure. I've never heard of anyone dying from too much Glitter, so I feel okay doing so.

Holding his hand, I spin stories about fairies, elves, trolls, heroes, and villains. His body slowly relaxes, and he falls asleep. I panic for a moment. "Please, still be breathing," I plead and touch his chest. It feels like there is a fire beneath the skin, but I also feel it moving steadily up and down. "Thank you," I whisper to him, mopping his brow, wrists, and elbows with a cool, damp cloth. Then I lean my head on the bedside and doze fitfully, dreaming that my mouth is bleeding glittery blood and my teeth are falling out one after the other.

This morning's visit by the physician included the two Bluies. They stood just inside the door and waited. The physician's movements were stilted, and her voice quivered slightly. Ashton didn't care. He could barely stand to look at her now.

"When did he start showing symptoms?" Dr. A-Jain asked as she took Brian's temperature and his vital signs.

"We need you to give him something for the pain. He keeps complaining that his head and his stomach are in agony. That's the word he used—*agony*." Ashton underlined the word with his voice.

"He started feeling bad a bit after sunset last night. Then he just got worse." Grey sounded exhausted. She had spent much of the night sitting with Brian. When Ashton had woken and roused her to return to bed, she shook her head. "He seems to like holding my hand. It's the least I can do." So, Ashton had brought her mattress, pillow, and blanket over to the floor next to Brian's bed and settled Grey there. He doubted she slept too much, though. He resolved to send her to sleep as soon as the physician left.

The Blue men were speaking to each other. They used hushed voices and hid their words behind their hands, but their excitement with the progress of the disease they had purchased was evident. One pointed to Brian and grinned. Ashton had enough and rushed at them, roaring, "Get out!"

The men were not as tall nor as fit as Ashton. One of them seemed to squeak in terror, and both turned immediately and ran down the stairs of the hut. They continued moving rapidly away, toward the beach. Ashton shut the door as hard as he could, though the construction didn't allow for a satisfying slam.

"Thank you," the physician said. "They are horrible." She wore a look that implored him to talk to her.

"I didn't do it for you." Ashton's voice could have frosted the summer sea. "Just get him some painkillers."

The day is drawing to an end. It's the first day on this island that I haven't left the cabin. After we ate breakfast, Ashton insisted I get some sleep, and when I started toward the bed near Brian, I felt his hand on my shoulder. "No, Grey. You get into my bed. I'll sit with Brian. You have got to sleep." His voice was firm, but kind.

I wanted to object, but I was so tired. I told Ash about using the Glitter for Brian, which he said was a smart idea, then I walked to the bed and collapsed. I didn't wake until the sun was past its zenith. Ash had saved lunch for me. It appeared that our meals were now being delivered to our door. I ate what I could. Now, I go over and sit with Ash as we tend to Brian.

Brian looks awful. His face is puffy and streaked with red splotches that run along his eyebrows, nose, and cheeks, obliterating his freckles. *His sunburn had just disappeared, and now, look at him,* I think. Below both of his eyes, reddish-purple bruises have developed, and his lips are always crusted with dried blood from his mouth, no matter how often we moisten and blot them. His sandy-brown hair is dark and slicked back with sweat and water.

He seems to have some type of mild rash developing on his chest, but there are red splotches as well on his arms and legs. Ash removed his underwear and put down some towels as he is unable to stand or even talk much.

"I gave him some of the pain relievers that damn doctor sent over and some more Glitter." Ash's mouth is tight, and he moves his head from side to side. He reaches up, scratches at the dressing on his arm, then looks at me seriously. "Grey, I don't know if Brian is going to get better. He seems to get worse by the minute."

"But maybe if he sleeps well tonight...," I start, not wanting to think about the other possibility.

"Maybe," he allows, "but either way, we can't let them spread this around the world. We have to stop them."

I stare at him, astounded by the suggestion. "*We* have to? You and me? A formerly ridiculously wealthy son and scion of the most horrible man to have lived and a fourteen-year-old whose best skills are whittling little animals and sailing?" I shake my head. "I don't think we are the hero types."

Ash knits his brow and purses his lips. "You might be right, kid. But we are all we got."

~

Ashton's head felt like it was about to split in half, and the muscle aches that had started earlier had run up his spine, giving birth to a generalized pain that made even the hair on his head hurt. He knew the sensations heralded a growing fever. His appetite at dinner was nonexistent, and he picked at the food that had been brought in. The one consolation he had was that he was able to avoid revealing his malaise and developing illness to Grey as she was focused on keeping Brian comfortable.

The physician had been over three times since this morning's visit with the Bluies. She came alone each time and wisely so. He had committed himself to tearing the arms off those blue bastards if they came within reach. He had never felt so much anger before. And this was real anger, not the kind he had to work up to get into bar fights when he was younger. This was anger directed at the inhumanity of those men and all like them who saw nothing wrong with dispensing cruelty and anguish if it advanced their ambition for power.

Now, on her last visit, before the door was chained for the night, he watched as the physician observed her patient and talked with Grey, taking her vitals as well as Brian's. When she came over to Ashton… "No." His voice was flat.

She looked perplexed. "Ashton, I just need your temperature."

"No." He folded his arms across his chest. "What difference does it make? You aren't a doctor, trying to heal anyone. You're a scholarly ghoul, recording the details of how we all are going to die." His voice grew louder with each word. "Won't that be a comfort to you when the world is perishing yet again? You can think, 'Hey I did nothing to stop this, but I've got great notes.'" With that, he reached out, pulled the clipboard out of her hand, ripped the paper on it, and threw the board to the back of the hut.

Ashton stared defiantly at her and watched her eyes dilate. He wasn't sure if they grew so black from fear or anger. He knew he was feeling both at that moment. He also was furious with himself for still finding those eyes beautiful. He was about to yell again when he heard a soft voice. "Ash. Don't. It won't help." He looked over and saw Grey sitting at his dying on-again/off-again friend's bedside and shaking her head.

He sighed. "I guess not." His voice was normal again. "But you don't get my data for your little paper." He turned his back on her but could still hear her shaky breath and small snuffles as she went about collecting the torn papers and the pitched clipboard.

"I'll be back in the morning." The statement was addressed to the room.

Grey answered, "See you then."

The physician took a step toward Ashton's back. "Ash..." Then she gathered her things and left. Ashton heard the chain and lock fall into place and felt a tear on his cheek. He couldn't remember the last time he had actually cried.

Ashton woke up from a fevered dream where he had been walking along a road in the rain, but it was hot. And it kept getting hotter until he realized the rain was boiling and burning his skin everywhere it touched him. But there was only the road, and he had to walk on it, helpless to prevent himself from being cooked alive by the storm until he heard his name being called. That's what finally allowed him to open his eyes.

"Ash? Ashton?" It was Grey, and she sounded… *Oh, no, please, no…* She sounded like she was holding hysteria at bay.

"I'm awake, Grey." He tried to scramble out of bed to get to her, but his body hurt so that he felt he was moving through thick mud. He finally got to the bedside, where he found Grey kneeling at the edge, her ear pressed to Brian's chest, humming a tuneless song. No sound or movement came from the younger man. "Oh, Grey, when…?"

She looked at him with shocked eyes. He should have stayed awake with her. *Dammit.* "I was singing to him and holding his hands, then he started breathing weirdly. All raspy. I kept singing to him, and then he stopped breathing for a moment and then started again. That kept happening until…" She inhaled a shaking breath. "…it didn't start again. I kept listening for it to start again, but it didn't, Ash. It didn't."

Grey began to cry in earnest, and Ashton knelt next to her and gathered her into his chest, holding her close and rubbing her back for comfort. A moment later, she drew back, reaching up to touch his face. Her face shifted from bereft to horrified. "You… No… You have a fever." She stood up and backed away. "I can't… I can't…"

"Listen, I'm okay for now," Ashton lied. "It's probably because I haven't slept well."

Grey just shook her head and looked wildly about the small cabin. She ran to the back window, wrenched the screen from it, gave the shutter a tremendous push, hopped up, and slithered out before Ashton knew what was happening. He rushed to the window. "No, Grey, don't go into the forest. Come back…." But all he heard were footsteps fading rapidly away to leave him with the sounds of night birds and frogs.

I run and run along the edge of the trees until I am well out of sight of the cabin. I stop and feel my stomach coming up on me, so I lean over and vomit, though not much is there. Brian is dead, and now Ashton… Is he going to die as well? I lean onto a tree and feel my tears start fresh and my throat grow thick. I gaze into the murky gloom of the forest and know I can't go any deeper in. It is so dark; I'll break my leg for sure. *You can't just stand here, Grey*, I scold myself. I'll check out the camp. I could explore the parts I have been warned against. There are probably very few guards to stop me this late.

The camp is still and shadowy. There is no moon, so I have to stand and let my eyes gather the starlight so I can see a bit. I move along the edges of the encampment using all the stealth I have learned playing hide-and-seek with my brothers and Mama over the years. My destination is the cave where we have been instructed never to go. And there it is. Squinting, I see no movement around it. I am surprised it is unguarded, but when I get close enough, I feel a decently made barrier across it, tightly chained. A bit farther toward the beach, two guards walk back and forth near the Glitter shed, but otherwise, the remaining Si Hai Bang are all blissfully asleep. Just asleep. Not dead. A sudden loathing wells up in me. I hate them all. I envision tearing the virus-laden burlap from around the Glitter and rubbing it on all these horrible pirates' faces, then laughing as they first bleed into their skin and mouths, then fade and die.

I gasp in shock and dismay at my gruesome vision. *I don't wish anything that awful on anyone. Focus on something good, Grey.* Dr. A-Jian had said it was good that Brian had someone to sit with him, so he wouldn't feel alone. Remembering this makes me suddenly ashamed that I have left Ashton alone now that he is sick. I berate myself for being selfish and scared, and before I know it, my feet are running back to the cabin. The window is up high, easier to drop from than climb to. I stop and take two long breaths, remembering when Pheidon had to get into a high castle window. So, secure in the knowledge that it must be possible, I boost myself from the ground to the platform, pulling hard with my arms and pushing my feet off the larger chunks of wood that support it. I have a moment when I think I may fall backward but regain my balance and shimmy along the platform until I can stick my hands in under the window and haul myself up. It takes three huge heaves to get my head and shoulders in, and it's a bit of a trick to wiggle the rest of the way. My landing is awkward and creates a reasonable-sized *thump* as I hit the floor, but I did it. I stand, feeling victorious.

That glorious feeling drains from me as I survey the scene. The small lantern is lit and sits on the table next to the head of Brian's bed. Its beams stream out and create a tiny, safe space on this awful night. Ashton has drawn the linens up over Brian's body and covered his once-handsome face. The sheets are smooth and carefully tucked around his head, body, and feet. He obviously took his time to get it just right.

Ash now lies on the mattress near our dead boatmate and crew member—I leave out some of the other things Brian proved to be from my description. Instead, I move to Ash and touch his forehead with the back of my hand. I feel my brow fold in worry. His fever is even higher than before. *Oh, no....* Using the lantern, I inspect his face and arms. No bloody spots or deep bruising color is visible. That's something good, at least.

I try a pep talk. "It's going to be okay, Grey," I say to myself in a voice quieter than a whisper. "You won't be left here alone with two dead men. It will be fine." I do a quick body check—

no sign of illness for me, though I have some scratches on my arms and legs from my crawl in and out of the window.

With all the resolve I can muster, I walk over to the table, gather another cloth and bowl and my whittling, and turn to care for the living patient. Sitting down crossed-legged next to him, I dip the new cloth into some fresh, cool water, carefully wring it out, and then, with soft, slow movements, place it on his head.

"You're back. And safe," Ashton murmurs as his eyelids flutter open. He gives me a small smile, though his voice is weak.

"Of course I'm back. Friends don't desert each other. Now just sleep." I pat his arm.

Ash closes his eyes and whispers, "Thanks, friend." Then he sinks into sleep. Turning to my task, I begin to carefully sand the now-horned dragon who has finally told me his name: Iyashi, the Dragon of Healing. *Don't you dare die, Ashton Abernathy. I'm making him for you. Don't die.*

EIGHTEEN

Anger Herbs

"Grey?" A soft voice repeats my name. "Grey, wake up." I feel a gentle hand shake my shoulder.

My eyes pop open. "Ash?" There's desperation in my voice that even I hear. "Oh, Ash... Please..." He is still here; one of my hands is on his chest, and the other is holding his un-casted hand. His body is still hot, and his face flushed with fever, but he is breathing steadily.

"Grey, what happened?" The soft voice again.

Cutting my eyes upward, I see Dr. A-Jian's face peering at me, wearing a soft expression of sympathy. The night's events flood back to me. *Brian. Brian's dead.* "What do you think happened?" I pull my knees up under me and shift my stiff body from where I lie sprawled on the hard floor. Lifting my head from the edge of the floor mattress, my gaze travels over Ash and up to the bed where Brian's body is wrapped and still. "Brian's gone, and now Ash is..." I feel tears starting but refuse their delivery. I have responsibilities. I have to take care of him.

Dr. A-Jian kneels next to Ash and takes his temperature and vitals. Her face is grim as she pulls the sheet down and looks at his chest, then goes to his arm and removes the dressing. The wound she gave him is red and inflamed. It looks like it has developed into a large blister. I reach over and touch the dressing on my arm. It is sore as well, and I can feel a bump underneath. Dr-Jian breathes out what sounds like a sigh and smiles as she looks at the wound on Ash. "It's okay, Grey. This is a vaccine reaction. A very robust one. He's not sick."

My brain is slow and sluggish as I try to process what she is saying. "So, he's not going to die like Brian?"

"There's no sign of disease, only reaction. He should recover in a day or two." She is fussing with the covers on him, shaking them out. She goes to flip his pillow. "What's this?" She points to the strip of sheeting with a knot in it that now hangs around Ash's neck like an amulet.

"The dragon I carved is called Iyashi. He's a dragon of healing. I made it for Ash and put it on him last night." As I say this, I realize how childish and fanciful I must sound to a doctor who has spent years learning the whys and hows of the human body. *She must think I am a ridiculous baby.*

She gently loosens the knot on the amulet that holds Iyashi, then lifts him from his spot in the notch of Ash's collarbone. "Thank you, Iyashi," she says and brings him to her lips for a small kiss. "Thank you for keeping Ashton safe." She replaces him and tightens the knot that holds him next to my friend. Then she puts an arm around my shoulders and gives me a squeeze. "Thank you, Grey, for creating Iyashi and for being such a fine friend." She says it with so much warmth that I can't help but start to cry. As I snuffle, Dr. A-Jian wraps me in a hug, making soft, shushing noises. I close my eyes as she does this and imagine it's Mama holding me. I don't try to stop the tears that flow.

After several minutes, we release our hug, and the physician slips on gloves, a mask, and goggles, then goes to Brian and gently lifts the sheet. Her face is sorrowful, and I watch the goggles steam slightly as her eyes fill with tears. She tucks the sheet carefully back around him and moves away toward my escape window, her back to me.

Finally, she turns back, pulls her gloves off, and wipes her eyes, which are now red and puffy. "I will have the guards come and take Brian for burial. It should be done today. But I will tell them to mark the place so you and Ash can visit it." She picks up the screen from the floor and reattaches it to the window without comment.

"I want to pick some flowers for Brian," I hear myself say. "Will you stay with them both?" I don't know why I trust her. But I do.

"Absolutely." She nods vigorously. "You run and get the flowers. I will tidy the cabin and then, when you return, I will get broth and some of my grandmother's healing herbs for him." She looks at Ashton with affection.

I am reluctant to leave Ash, but Brian deserves some beauty to take with him to…I don't know…wherever it is we go. Matt's mom, I call her Mama Mae, says we go to heaven. Mama says she doesn't know, but she hopes there is a lovely place for those who were kind and brave. She said her Grandma Rina spoke of Valhalla, Folkvangr, and Hel. I shake my head. There's no time to contemplate such things. Another day…

Dr. A-Jain goes to have a word with Kuan-Yin, and I am able to slip out with my basket as they talk. I run to the foothills and gather piles of the sweetest-smelling, brightest-colored flowers in pinks, reds, and oranges as quickly as I can, loading my basket full. I am back in less than a bell, and when I return to the cabin, Kuan-Yin has gone, and Ashton is on his bed. Mine has been pushed close to Ash's and is made up with fresh sheets. Dr. A-Jain sits at his other side in a chair pulled over from the table. Food has been brought in, and there is bread, honey, and fruit.

Setting my basket down, I go check on Ash. He is resting quietly, though his face still feels on fire. This worries me, and I look at Mariko.

"The fever is his body's way of developing immunity. It is not so high as to be dangerous." Her voice is matter-of-fact, but I hear tenderness in it.

"I don't have a fever. Does that mean I could get sick?" I hadn't realized I was worried about this, but now, as I say it, I feel a stab of alarm.

Mariko pauses. "I... I don't think so. Let me see your arm." I pull the tunic sleeve up, and she loosens the tape and lifts the dressing. "There is a reaction. It is small, but present. Likely, you have antibodies circulating from your first immunization. That is probably why you do not feel ill." She frowns. "I'm sorry. So very few people are still vaccinated for the original pox, and this vaccine is so new, as is the pox strain, that I have not had experience with a patient receiving both jabs."

I look at her. She sits holding Ash's hand, her fingers tracing it in soft strokes, but her face looks as though she is in deep pain. It reminds me of Mama's face as she looked at me that last afternoon of the Awful July. "Who is your family in Formosa?"

A shocked expression crosses her face now, but then she smiles, and her eyes stare off into the distance. "I have a daughter. Not too much younger than you, though she has not seen ten years yet and is still very much a child, unlike the young woman you are. She lives with An-ma, my grandmother, in Puli. I send them all my markers, and the Si Hai Bang in Formosa look out for them. Her father was one of them before he was killed. They said I must work for them to pay the debt of their protection. That was four years ago. The

Si Hai Bang do not tolerate betrayal. If my actions ever came to light, they would kill An-ma and sell Akemi as a thrall." She closes her eyes, and a tear slides down her cheek.

"That's not right. You should not have to do the things you do to keep your family safe."

"Ah, Grey." Her face shifts into a thoughtful expression, eyes looking up, mouth curved in a soft smile. "Once that infant comes into your arms, you will do whatever it takes to help them grow and keep them safe. I will endure whatever pain—even the scorn and loneliness…" She looks at Ash and puts a fresh cloth on his brow, her fingers trailing along his heavily-stubbled jaw. "The world delivers to me if it means Akemi and her cho-ma are safe. I'm sure your mother feels the same about you and your siblings."

I frown. "Yes…," I say slowly. Of course, Mama wants us to be safe. But I never really thought about the things she has endured to keep us that way.

Mariko rises. "Let us prepare Brian with his flowers. Then, you should eat and sleep. While you do, I will fetch broth and An-ma's herbs for Ash and return to watch over you both."

"I'm hungry." Ash's deep voice wakes me. The sun is slanting in through the front window, indicating that it is close to setting. Ashton is half-sitting in his bed, pushed up on his good arm, looking around as if trying to orient himself. I stare at him, first in delight that he seems stronger and then in confusion…. Something is very different about him. What…? It's his beard. It's gone.

Mariko's voice comes from the front of the cabin beyond the blanket. "I am bringing food."

Ash frowns and starts to say something, but I stop him

with a hand on his arm. "Don't be angry with her anymore," I whisper. "She had good reason for what she did. I'll explain later."

He looks at me, his face a mix of curiosity and skepticism, but he nods and whispers back, "Okay, but only because *you* say so."

I grin. "Feel your face."

His casted hand reaches up, his fingers trace his jaw, and he grins widely. "Did you?"

I shake my head, and Mariko comes around the blanket with a tray filled with bowls and cups. She smiles at Ash. "You are awake." She sets the tray down and feels his brow, then his pillow. "Excellent, your fever has broken. Your pillow is quite damp with sweat. Let me change it." She reaches for it, but Ash grabs her wrist.

"Did you shave me?" he asks.

Mariko nods. "Yes. You had told me once you did not like the feel of a beard. Plus, you were so feverish, and I wanted to assess for lesions."

Ash releases her wrist and returns the hand to his face. "You did a good job. I like being able to feel my skin. Thank you." His voice is not warm, but cordial. I guess it's a start.

After a quick body scan, I swing my feet out of bed and go to survey the tray. I wolf down a slice of mango and then walk over and pick up the pot. "I need to..." Then my eye catches the empty bed on the other side of the blanket. My breath leaves me in a whoosh. I reach up and jerk the blanket down, piling it and the pot on the floor. "I'll just go outside." And I beeline for the door before anyone can say anything.

When I return, the blanket has been folded into a neat square and placed on the foot of the empty bed that now holds a bare mattress. Ash is up and out of bed, sitting with Mariko at the table talking. I come over and peer at the bowl of soup in front of Ash. "Smells good. What is it?"

Mariko smiles. "Broth with miso and fish, mushrooms, and greens. I also put in an herbal mix to help with his liver because he is often so angry."

Ash snorts a laugh and takes a bite. "It's good. You may want to make a bowl of anger soup for this one." He gestures to me with his thumb. "She gets mad a lot too."

"Well, like sister, like brother," Mariko says coolly.

We look at each other and then at her. I say, "You know, we aren't really…"

Mariko waves off the statement. "Family is not always about blood, but about heart." She stands. "I must go. There are many questions I must answer." She heads toward the door.

"Mariko, wait." Ash stands and follows her. I turn away to give them some privacy as they draw close, and I hear the murmur of soft words between them. Moments later, she has walked down the stairs into the dark, and Ashton has shut the door.

He returns to the table and looks at me. "Thank you for gathering flowers for Brian. And for taking care of me. And for Iyashi." He lifts a small, red, leather pouch on a black cord. "Mariko got the pouch for me after I found him."

I blink back tears. "You're welcome. Thank you for not dying."

He gives a small laugh in response. "My pleasure."

We shift the conversation from the island and its specter of death, discussing instead what we will do when we get home, ignoring the very real chance that neither of us will ever see home again.

NINETEEN

Resurrection

Ashton and Grey walked through camp the next day after breakfast. They had been surprised to find no sign of the chain for their door when they left the cabin that morning; usually, it hung to the side in preparation to lock them in at night. There was also no sign of Kuan-Yin as a guard, and no one challenged them as they moved beyond their section of the beach.

Ashton still felt tired and a bit sore from his bout with the fever, but he was definitely on the mend. He had another serving of the soup Mariko had made him this morning. Yesterday, she had told him about her daughter, and he wanted to kick himself for his callous behavior toward her. So, today, he had asked Grey to show him where some of the best flowers were. He figured it might help as he apologized again to his physician.

The Sai Hi Bang were not giving them the same large quarter as when they thought they carried the disease; instead, they glanced at the two captives and whispered. Ashton contemplated what had changed, besides Brian dying. He still was in shock about that, although he had seen it approaching.

"Hey," Grey said low to him, "heads up. Look who's coming toward us."

He looked up to see Chief Suo and the nasty Bluies. He licked his lips and tasted the bitter herbs from the soup. *Hope two doses will keep me from mauling them.*

It was the taller of the Bluies that addressed him. "Mr. Abernathy, I am Deacon Christian Peterson, and this is Elder Dennis Edwards. We are part of the Blue Alliance Committee and are very interested in speaking with you." The man cast a disparaging glance at Grey as he added to Ashton, "Alone."

An unruffled grin spread over Grey's face. "Well, *Mr.* Abernathy. I will do some exploring. Meet me near the waterfall when your 'business' is concluded. Whistle a line of 'Spanish Ladies,' and I'll come get you for our outing." She turned to the blue-draped men, her expression dour. "My mother doesn't think much of you and your group. I'm beginning to see why." With that, she marched off, and Ashton worked to keep from laughing at the outraged expressions on the two men's faces.

Now, Elder Edwards spoke, and his voice was on the high-pitched side. Ashton guessed it was him who had emitted the squeak the other day. "Well, if that doesn't go to show you the dangers of allowing women to be in charge beyond their abilities... Between the unacceptable and unqualified President Alyssa Russell in the FA and that Wallace woman in Bosch, our mission to restore leadership to the men of New Earth is clearly needed."

Chief Suo cleared her throat and narrowed her eyes so that her gaze was sharp as he said this.

"Well... I...er..." The elder refocused on his compatriot. "Deacon, shall we walk with Mr. Abernathy?"

The taller man nodded. "Yes, Dennis. Shall we, Mr. Abernathy?"

The deacon indicated a path on the beach and stepped to Ashton's right side, the elder flanking him on his left.

Ashton looked from side to side and waited, then lifted his foot and stepped. The Bluies began their steps just behind him. *Interesting*, Ashton thought.

The deacon lost no time setting forth his proposal. "Mr. Abernathy, as you may know, we, The Chosen of New Earth, or the Bluest as we are known to the masses, heavily supported your father in his ascent toward the presidency. It is unfortunate that circumstances developed to prevent him from gaining the office. But you have now demonstrated that you are a worthy candidate for us to back."

Elder Edwards piped up, "Indeed, you have thrown off the shroud of death and risen anew! Nothing short of miraculous!"

"We have power over the masses, Mr. Abernathy. They will move in the direction we indicate." The deacon's voice was lush with appetite. "With your name and our backing, we can restore the Abernathy fortune and name, and together, we will rise in power. We will smooth the way for our kind to take their rightful place on the planet and will care for the lesser peoples, allowing them to work for the good of the Chosen and retain our protection."

The deacon's voice was reaching a crescendo when Ashton put up his hand with one forefinger extended to the sky. Both Bluies went silent. Ashton stood and closed his eyes, images of his childhood, of that July, of the past three years, and of the past week spinning in his mind. "So, you are offering me a chance to return to my old life."

"Yes," squeaked the Elder.

"With even more power," the deacon's voice practically sang.

Ashton moved his right leg in the way he knew would

provoke a stab at his knee. He felt it run up through his leg and nail itself into his spine, causing his shoulders to twitch just a bit. Then he put his casted left hand to the amulet around his neck. "Well, Elder Edwards, you are correct. I have... How did you so poetically say it? 'Thrown off the shroud of death and risen anew'?" Ashton saw the smaller man, who was looking more and more like a rat, nod in approval. "But where you are wrong is in assuming I wish to follow in my father's footsteps. Thank you both, though, for helping me crystalize a thought I have been rolling about for some time. Your offer and the constant use of the name have assisted me in making my decision. I no longer want to be an Abernathy." Ashton put his hand to his forehead as if tipping a hat. "Good day, gentlemen. I have another appointment."

I hear the strains of "Spanish Ladies" and slide off the rock I have been relaxing on while fanning myself with a large leaf to keep the flying insects at bay. I take a few steps down the path and then greet my companion. "Hey, Ash. How was your meeting with those ridiculous Bluies?"

His face folds into an expression of someone who has just smelled or tasted something off. "They are awful. And more than that, they are a threat to all of New Earth." He spreads his hands and barks a low laugh. "And they want me to lead with them."

I can't imagine the Ash I know now taking up with such horrible people, but the old Ashton Abernathy... I raise my eyebrows. "And...?"

"And...it has caused me to recommit to the idea that the virus must be destroyed here, never to leave this island, and these people must be stopped."

I am motionless for a few moments, considering what this might require of us. Of me. "Ash, I'm not my mama. I can't just go in, guns blazing, riding a motorcycle. It's not who I am."

Ashton's lips are pressed together, and his jaw is set. "Grey, I'm not my father. I cannot sit by while good people are killed for power and control."

I take in a deep breath and let it out as a sigh. "They might kill us, Ash."

His face grows even more serious as he turns and looks me in the eye. "Listen to me, Grey. I need you to get off this island and get home, to grow and change the world from Bosch. So, if you wish to willingly offer your help in doing this thing with me, I will take it. But while I am ready to die to stop this disaster from happening, I forbid you to."

His intensity is almost overwhelming, so I grin to shift the mood. "Wow, you have been promoted to choosing who lives and who dies?"

He snorts a laugh, and I see his shoulders relax. "Yes," he confirms as he lifts the red pouch around his neck. "Iyashi has branched out from healing."

The idea of something happening to Ash causes me a pain I can't explain, and I want to cry out for him to run and hide. But clearly, he has a goal. I make my decision. "Let's go get the flowers for your girlfriend, and we can discuss what my mama calls: the details of a mission."

TWENTY

Plans Change

The sun set hours ago, and we have heard no clink of lock and chain. I mentally cross off the need to crawl out the back window and search for a bolt cutter. That'll save time.

Ashton is rocking back and forth ever so slightly, his right leg bouncing, signaling the nervousness he has denied about twelve times.

I am, however, as Mama M would say, as nervous as a long-tailed cat in a room full of rocking chairs. When I was very small, I got my finger caught under her rocker while my brothers and I were rough-housing. She held me in her lap in the same rocker as she wrapped a soft bandage around the bruised digit and told me that people have used that expression for centuries. I think about a cat with soft fur, golden eyes, and a long tail. Mama never had an animal in the house when she grew up, and neither did Papa; so, we kids never did either. I make a resolution—if I get home mostly in one piece, I'm getting a kitten. Or a puppy. Nope. I'm getting both.

My technique to stave off my long-tail-cat nerves is to imagine I am going on one of the pretend missions my brothers and I would embark upon in the backyard, and later, in the woods on the way home from school. Mama would talk with her unit about initial planning, gathering details, revising, and having a backup—or contingency—plan, and we kids always eavesdropped and implemented the lessons learned. Tonight, Ash and I have everything but a backup. But there is no more time to plan. Chief Suo has decided to break camp and leave the island tomorrow, and Ashton and I will be taken to Formosa to be ransomed to the highest bidder. Ash says it is most dangerous to me because the person who probably hates him the most is Mama, which would likely work in our favor if we were together. But the chief has made it clear that we will be separated, and Ash is firm that this is not going to happen.

I look out the window. The crescent moon has set, and the night is as dark as it is going to get.

"It's time. Are you ready?"

He stands up and swallows. "As ready as I'm going to get." He slips his arms into his backpack.

I spit in my hand and hold it out. He wrinkles his brow with disgust like the old Ashton, then laughs, spits in his, and we shake.

I have on my GBWs and slip on my coat inside out so the yellow doesn't show. My pockets are full on either side, heavy with ammo I collected earlier. We open the door a crack. No guard.

"Are you sure they are all asleep?" I hiss to Ash.

"They are all drunk and passed out. Believe me, if there's one thing I know…," Ash says quietly but firmly.

When we delivered the flowers to Mariko this afternoon, she glowed with pleasure. I wandered outside for a bit, only coming in when Ash opened the door, looking a bit flushed but very pleased. Mariko had on a similar expression, and it took all I had in me not to sing the kissing rhyme at them. We sat and visited a bit, mentioning to her a little of our plan and the strange way we had been treated today. She explained to us that the Sai Hi Bang are very superstitious people. It turns out that since Ashton beat death by surviving the unsurvivable virus, he is now viewed as some sort of demigod. That title made me almost fall off my chair laughing. Ash kicked at me and told me to respect my elders and my demigods, which made me laugh even more.

As we were laughing and kicking at each other, Mariko went to the closet, whispering, "I have a secret weapon that may be even better than being a demigod." She then pulled out a box with a dozen bottles of alcohol in it. Ashton looked at each one, and for several of them, he exclaimed and whistled. Thus was born the section of the plan in which the demigod drinks with his new worshippers, making my job a whole lot easier.

Now, as we stand at the top of the stairs before embarking on Project Viral Destruction, I ask in a hushed tone, "So, how come you aren't drunk, if they all are?"

"Because I'm a demigod, of course." His voice is quiet but definite.

"What?"

He grins. "No, I drank from two bottles. One with rum that I took an occasional sip from, and one with tea that I guzzled."

"Very well-thought-out, your demigod-ness," I grin back as I whisper.

He shoves my shoulder. "Enough. Let's go."

We head down the stairs and make our way to the beach. It is deserted; the soft rush of the waves is all we can hear. We proceed to the firepit and gather up some ashes, smudging them on our faces as camouflage. Ashton balks initially, but I insist. "We have to. Mama always used to when she ran extractions, and besides, if *Ash* and *Grey* are going to pull off this caper, we might as well live up to our names."

That makes him smile, and we smear ash all over the parts of ourselves where our bare skin shows.

This is the part of the mission where we must split up to accomplish all the tasks. My job is the boats. Slipping quietly onto the docks, I board the closest fast boat. It is sleek and powerful. As I run my hands along it, I toy with the idea of using one of these to escape but then remember how far away I could hear the engine. Drunk or not, they'd hear us, and we'd be shot at. Besides, we agreed that *Noĕlani* deserves to take us home.

These boats each have three, big, dual-powered engines, capable of using both biodiesel and solar. Solar is easy—I take a page from Ash and Brian and simply pull off the charging covers. I use my knife to sever any connectors and toss the cover into the cove. Then, I pull a rock from my pocket and smash the matching connectors on each of the motors. The next step is to pry up the casing and cut some random wires. My last job is to take a bottle of sand I gathered and pour a measure of it into each of the biodiesel tanks. These motors will not be moving anyone anywhere, at least not fast. I pause before moving on to the next boat and then drop to my belly and pull the drain stopper. That'll do it.

By the time I have finished with the second fast boat, I have my system down to about five minutes, or what seems to be that amount of time. A quick calculation tells me I will finish with my sabotage in a bell and a half. While I am trying to be as quiet as possible, a few unavoidable bangs and rattles emerge. So, after each engine is destroyed, I pop my head up like a ground squirrel looking for hawks, or in my case, nasty pirates who would be happy to shoot me. Seeing none and being thankful for the effects of the drinking Ash supervised, I return to my business until I am on the last boat—the one that towed us in. This one and its mate each have two smaller outboards, so the process goes faster. I consider the last engine. It isn't that big… I make a last-moment decision and disconnect it from the transom. I consider hauling it to the dock, but it turns out, it weighs a bit more than me.

Okay, Grey, think. I could just let it drop into the cove, but I want it. I grab two life vests, fasten both onto the motor, and rig a rope to guide it from its original home to *Noĕlani*. It takes about a quarter-bell to do so, but I saved time earlier, so I'm good. I release the motor onto the rope guide, and to my joy, the vests keep it afloat. A quick dash over to *Noĕlani* with a whispered "Hello" to her, and I pull the motor to me. I settle it in place, tipping it up so we can use the rudder as we sail, and just like that, we have a working motor.

I start to leave and then pause. These boats are packed to travel tomorrow. Advantage Team Viral Destruction. I climb back into the chief's boat and check the stowed gear, dragging out a real sea anchor, a case of bottled water, and a box of high-calorie bars. I also grab one of the solar floodlights, checking to be sure the battery is charged. My haul of booty is stowed on *Noĕlani*, and I feel very much like the pirate I was born to be.

Now, to wait for Ash's signal.

Ashton moved toward the Glitter shed as soon as Grey split off for the docks. His job was to clear the guards near the shed and set fire to it. He quietly moved up the beach and headed toward the left. As he moved into the tree line, he thought about what Mariko had brought up when they summarized their plan.

"What about the cave?" she asked.

Ashton had frowned. "What about it? What's in there?"

"I don't really know, but once, I heard the chief refer to it as 'the lab.' I don't have access to it." Mariko shrugged.

Ashton and Grey had looked at each other. Grey bit her lip and then asked, "Contingency? Deal with it if we have time?"

Ashton nodded. "Do you suppose they grow the virus there?"

"They do keep it locked up." Grey's face reflected her concern.

Now, he surveyed the area around the Glitter shed. Grey had reported two guards the night before. With no moon and trees blocking the starlight, Ashton felt like he was gazing into a deep, black well. He could only just make out the shape of the shed. He paused to see if he could detect movement, opening his eyes wide to do as Grey said and, "Collect the starlight." A sound caught his attention, low and rhythmic. He laughed silently as he realized its source—a snore. He circled toward the back of the shed, where two lumps, both emitting snores, appeared. The last night on the island and plenty of liquor had certainly put those two at ease. He glanced toward the cave. He had time.

The cave mouth was exposed, and the gate Grey had mentioned was illuminated from within by rays of faint light leaking through the bamboo structure. It was chained and locked. What now? He looked back to where the snoring guards lay. It would make sense that they would have the keys. *Okay, Ash, let's see how drunk they actually are. Deep breath —and go.*

Crawling near the men, who smelled strongly of tequila, he put one hand on the nearest guard's shoulder as a test. The man snored deeply from the back of his throat and rolled toward Ashton, who shifted backward a few centimeters and held his breath.

There was no jingle when he rolled, Ashton reasoned. *Check the other one first.* Initially, he thought to lean over the first guard but rethought the strategy and crept around the shed to come up on the other side. As he knelt, his knee bumped something. *That's not a rock.* His hands felt the ground and the object. It was one of the guards' automatic weapons. *Demigod beginner's luck.* He put the strap over himself, but it seemed stuck. The backpack… He removed the weapon and the pack, replaced the weapon, and shifted it to where he could reach it. Then, finally, he replaced his backpack. But he still needed the keys. Moving his hand a few centimeters a minute, he carefully felt at the nearest man's belt and was rewarded by the feel of keys. *This is going well*, he thought with excitement. And in the back of his head, he heard Grey: "Rule One: Keep calm and don't be overconfident."

A breath in. He found the keys, but how to get them loose? Belt…okay. His good hand manipulated the man's belt buckle and wiggled it open. He stopped three times as the man stirred. He now had a real weapon. *But collecting and using are two very different things, Ashton.* Would he know how to use it if the man woke? Could he? He worried about this question as he inched the belt out of the loops on the guard's pants. And then the keys were in his hand. He scooted back on his butt, stood, and took them to the gate.

It was the fourth key that gave a reassuring click, opening the lock. Ashton eased it off the chain and took off his backpack. He pulled out the robe he had been wearing on the *Abundance* the night it all began. *I don't think I'm even the same man I was that night*, he pondered. No time for philosophy. He wrapped the silk around the chain as he inched it from the gate, muffling the clinking of the links. He opened the gate and stepped inside.

As he anticipated, small lights were attached every few meters along the wall. Two modified shipping containers sat in the cave. Nearest the entrance was a smaller square one, about six by six meters. A bit farther back sat a larger, rectangular one. Ashton chose at random and went to the larger. A regular door had been put in, which Ashton opened. He stepped into the dark container. Light. There must be a switch. His hands ran lightly along the walls near the door until he found one. He shut his eyes and flipped it. Brilliant light flooded all around him, and he had to stand for several minutes, slowly opening first one eye and then the other to acclimate to the brightness.

As he did, he saw flashes of what was definitely a lab. White walls and cabinets lined the room, with light-gray countertops holding a variety of scientific equipment, some of which he recognized, but much, he did not. He was smart enough to understand one thing: They made that damn virus here.

He started to raise the butt of the rifle to smash the equipment when something caught his eye.

On the floor was a flower, wilted but still a brilliant red. His eye followed it and saw another, this one pink, and then another, all of them leading to a medical-style trash bin by a wall that held several very large drawers sitting at waist height. As if in a dream, he wandered to the bin and stepped on the opening mechanism with his foot. Inside were more flowers, their fragrance still strong. They had been stuffed into the bin and wrapped in a sheet. He pulled the sheet out, then threw it to the ground. He looked at the wall directly above where the bin sat and grasped the handle of the unusually large drawer. He pulled; nothing happened. Frowning, he shifted, then leaned in and gave a strong tug as the drawer rolled toward him a centimeter or so. Another tug, and chill air poured from the opening as a large slab appeared. He looked down and saw Brian's disfigured face with its bloody lips and eyes. Were they keeping him here to study? To use to make more of the virus? He would not accept that fate for Brian.

As his anger grew, he thought about how agonizing Brian's illness and death had been. And he imagined that same scenario playing out hundreds upon thousands, maybe even millions, of times over as the virus spread throughout New Earth. No. Not if he could help it. He would blow this damned island up if he had to and give Brian the sendoff he deserved.

First, he gathered all the flowers that Grey had collected from the bin and heaped them onto Brian, covering his face with delicate blossoms. Then, systematically, he walked from bench to bench to counter, turning the gas on fully for the burners that were not lit. His eyes searched the room and fell on the canisters on the wall marked O2 for oxygen and N for nitrogen; he turned them on as well. He paused at a cabinet marked *Variola1977 Variety S.H.-2367 Vaccine*. He gathered a dozen vials and stuffed them into his backpack. If he lived, he'd pass those on. He walked out of the lab and shut the door. His plan was to check the small container and then light the shed on fire before returning to toss a match into the large one.

The door to the small container opened easily. He found the switch, flicked it on, and was surprised when three people, two women and a man, sat up in their small bunks. One man's eyes went big, and he moved toward a wall comm.

Ashton pointed the weapon at him. "Don't move, or you're dead." It was a line he had heard many times in movies he had watched. To his surprise and delight, it worked. "Get out of here." He gestured with the gun. "The lab is going to blow up."

The three pajamaed people who Ashton guessed were scientists looked at each other and hustled for the door, with Ashton right behind. Outside of the cave, they were blanketed in darkness. One of the scientists said, "Please don't shoot us."

I can't even see you, Ashton thought. But he said, "You just stay still and quiet, and everything will be fine." *Yes, that sounded like I know what I'm doing.* He walked over to the small shed, reached into his pocket, and drew out two matches. He put on a mask and opened the door.

"Hey, what are you doing?" a voice yelled. "Get away from there!"

Another voice added, "Where's my weapon?"

Ashton lit the matches against each other, then tossed them onto the pile in the center. Then he pivoted and grabbed the weapon, feeling for the trigger. He pointed it to the ground and yelled in his deepest voice, "Stay back." A spark from the fire beginning to grow in the shed, fed by the dry leaves on the ground, sprang out and hit his arm. "Ouch!" He unintentionally squeezed the trigger, and the weapon discharged a burst of five rounds, striking the ground and creating havoc. The scientists screamed and scrambled for cover; the guards yelled, and the one with a weapon raised it.

Ashton threw himself to the left of the shed with a plan to crawl to the back. He heard the guard's weapon discharge and felt something hot against his shoulder. The flames were now growing as they consumed the peat and the burlap that the Glitter was wrapped in. More shouts came from the beach. *Just go, Grey, get away!* He could see the guard raise his weapon and point it at him. Ashton realized he was now clearly visible. He had planned to dodge behind the shed, but his feet were frozen in place. All he could do was stare at the barrel that meant his destruction.

Then the guard fell to the ground.

I am on the dock, waiting for the signal that Ashton is on his way, and I can release *Noĕlani* so we can leave this cursed island. *Brian was right about that.*

Gunshots!

My head turns to where *Noĕlani* bobs in her mooring. "I don't think that's the signal," I murmur. Ash and I had agreed that if there was trouble, I was to just set sail without him. *Sorry, Ash. I guess I lied,* I think as I take off in the direction of the noise.

At the speed I am running, I make it to the shed in a matter of moments, but as I do, all around me, I can hear the camp waking up. We don't have much time. If any. At the tree line, three people in pajamas run past, their mouths in wide O's with no sound coming from them, like a silent scream. There. The shed. *Well done, Ash!* I see flames flickering and growing larger by the moment as the Glitter and the awful virus it holds are destroyed. Ashton is standing frozen to one side. A couple of meters in front of me, a guard is raising a weapon at him. I reach into my pocket and draw out my ammo, a large, black, volcanic stone. I aim, hold my breath, and throw. The guard drops like a stone.

I run to Ashton. "Let's get out of here."

He looks at me, and his face shifts from shock to anger to what looks like despair. "What are you doing here? Go! Get sail. Get safe."

"Not without you." I grab his hand and pull.

"No, I have to destroy the lab. Brian is there. And the virus." He glances toward the cave. "Look, I'm taking you to the boat, and you will leave. I have to finish this."

My mind whirls as I try to think of a way to convince him to set sail with me and forget the cave.

"Let's go." He lifts the weapon he has slung on his shoulder, and we take off for the dock.

"Do you even know how to shoot that thing?" I yell as we run.

"No. But I did anyway."

I will have to ask for an explanation of that statement later.

Out of nowhere, a person appears in front of me, and we collide. It's Mariko. She looks up. "Get out of here," she urges, scrambling to her feet and retrieving her small medical bag.

Now Ashton grasps her by the arms. "Go with Grey. Get to safety."

She shakes her head. "I can't. My daughter…"

The camp is fully awake now. Behind Mariko, I see the chief marching in the sand toward us. "Heads up. Chief on the move."

Mariko casts a fearful glance over her shoulder to where Chief Suo trudges. "Hit me. Hard," she demands.

Yes, good idea. "Ash, hit her."

"No, I can't…"

"Ash, they'll kill her otherwise."

Ashton looks as stricken as I have ever seen him, but he raises his good hand to slap her.

"No. With the back of your cast. Leave a mark," Mariko begs.

"Do it!" I intone.

It happens in a moment; Ashton lets his arm fly and strikes this woman who has been so good to us. She falls to the sand with a sob. Ashton pushes me toward the dock and turns to leave.

Then hell opens its doors as an explosion rocks the beach and sends smoke and light billowing upward.

TWENTY-ONE

Return to the Sea

We both are knocked to the ground but manage to get to our hands and knees and scramble to the dock. Ash looks behind him, where Mariko lies on the sand, weeping, and starts to turn back.

I don't know much, but Mama taught me about recognizing opportunity. "No!" I shout in his ear. "She has to stay. But this is our chance."

He looks at me with pain in his eyes and nods, crawling, then crouching, then running with me to *Noēlani.*

We push off, and since there is no stealth necessary now, I drop the motor into the water and turn it on. I hold my breath as it gives a small grumble and then it roars to life, and we speed toward the mouth of the cove. I have been studying the cove at high and low tide and have mapped the rock pattern in my head. I set a course for south-southeast and increase our speed.

"Ash," I call, "there's a floodlight in the bow. Use it to sweep for rocks."

There is no answer, but I hear movement, and the light comes on. "All clear." The voice is choked with emotion.

I pause and consider what I should say. There's nothing that will make him feel any better. But maybe that's not the point. "You saved her life, Ash. And her daughter's." I pause. "I'm sorry it sucks so bad."

I hear a sad laugh. "I don't want to be a demigod anymore," my friend says.

"Nope. I imagine you don't."

We motor along for close to half a bell. I have heard no gunshots from the island since we left, which bolsters my hopes for Mariko. But now, we are too far away to hear anything but the ocean.

"Port clear. Starboard clear," Ashton calls, and I am impressed by his language, though I know any compliment won't land just now.

"Shifting east," I call. "Next stop, Moku-o-keawe."

Noĕlani turns and I look to port. A large cloud billows upward from the island, blotting out the stars.

Ashton sits down near me and says, "I think I loved her."

"I know. I think she loved you back."

"I'll never see her again."

"Maybe not. But you never know."

After a long pause, I laugh a bit. "You know, I went on the Great Sea Race partly to show Mama that I didn't need her to tell me what to do. That I could take care of myself."

Ash gives a sad laugh. "Well, you have. And you took care of me. And Brian." He digs in his backpack and pulls out a bottle. "Here's to Brian." He raises it to the smoke plume that still rises into…the heavens, I guess. He takes a swig.

"Let me try that," I say, reaching for the bottle.

Ash pauses for a moment, then shrugs. "Sure, why not?" He passes me the heavy bottle.

I tip it to my lips and pour a healthy swallow into my mouth. At first, it is sweet like raisins, but after a moment, my lips begin to burn and then my tongue. I swallow heavily. I feel like one of those traveling fire-eaters who came to the city in Bosch to perform one summer. I give a cough and then breathe through my mouth, passing it back. In a croaking voice, I ask, "What do we call this?"

"Rum."

"And do we like rum?"

"This is a pretty excellent bottle of rum." Ashton tips it up and takes a long swallow.

"Okay, one more. I either kinda like it or really hate it." He returns the bottle to me, and I take a smaller sip this time. Now that I am prepared for the burn, I find I kind of like the taste. "If only they could make it so it didn't burn so much."

Ashton chuckles. "Grey. You don't need to drink rum. And you shouldn't with some strange man."

I smile. "Well, you are pretty strange. But you're no stranger." I pick up the bottle to toast, but I skip the swallow. "To friends made upon the sea. Especially ex-demigods."

Ashton takes the bottle and raises it. "To my new little sister-friend. I wouldn't want to be shipwrecked with anyone else." He takes his drink and then one more.

A soft whir high above us reaches our ears. The sound is so familiar, it could be considered a part of me. I look out to the south. A large spotlight sweeps the ocean from the sky. "Hey, Ash. Turn the flood to the sky, will you?"

He turns the flood on and sends the light toward the vessel that I can't yet see but I know will have a black hull with the etching of a pirate ship on it and will be flown by a mother who will never give up on me. "Ash, I'll tell Mama about Mariko. She'll figure out how to keep her and her family safe. Don't worry."

Ash swings the light around for another signal. "I'd like

that, Grey. Thanks." There is a pause. "Hey, let's sail the rest of the way. I need to practice my tacks."

"Great idea." I turn the motor off. "Let's unfurl the sails, Ash, and head for home."

"Aye-aye, Captain."

Epilogue

The late October rain soaked the artist as he trudged home from the Grayson Yang gallery, where he worked as an assistant to the gallery manager. His neighbor from 3-D, in the Sunset Yard section of Truvale, which housed a growing and vibrant artists' community, had helped him get the job, and he was intent on keeping it.

He came to his small, rented walk-up and marched up the three flights of stairs, whistling the melody of "Spanish Ladies" until he came to apartment 3-B. He unlocked the door, wiggling the key three times to the left and once to the right. "Thrice to port and once to starboard," he mumbled and stepped in. A sign above the front door read *Noĕlani II*, a nod to the cozy dimensions of his place. He collected the mail from the floor, tossing the lot on the small table. Then he stripped off his coat, took it to the washroom, and hung it on a hanger to drip in the tiny shower with its chipped tiles and brownish-black stains on the grout. Then he proceeded to dry his rain-soaked, shoulder-length, dark-blond hair and the beard that he had been growing for close to six weeks with the thin towel that hung on the door.

He moved to the wall that was his kitchen and turned the heat on under the kettle. Above the sink was a framed sketch of a pretty woman with long, dark hair and a soft smile. He put some dry noodles into a bowl to await the life-giving water and poured a glass of wine from the stoppered bottle on the counter. Flipping through the mail, he dropped the first three items into the recycling bin and then stopped and held up the fourth. It was from Bosch.

He still wasn't good with self-denial, but he made himself wait to open the letter until the water had boiled and he had poured it over his noodles and added the powdered broth and spices.

When his dinner was ready, he sat down, opened the envelope, and read it, eating noodles with one hand as he held the red leather pouch that hung from his neck with his other.

Hi, Ash!
Hope things are going well for you at the gallery, and
Ms. Odutola is able to see your talent and your skills.
School has been going, well, better than it ended, and
Leia and I have smoothed things out. She is very
involved with her new boyfriend, Carmen, but says it's
okay if I don't have one. (Gee, thanks!) I know she just
wants me to feel things like she does, so her comments
don't bother me so much (yes, as you can tell by that
sentence, I have gotten a new therapist. Her name is
Emily, and I love her).
Mama and I are still fighting sometimes, but we are also
laughing together more. She has told me some stories
about growing up and being my age, though I think
there is more to her stories than she lets on, and I have
told her a few stories about this past summer on the

water. That sounds very romantic to say it that way, doesn't it? As if we were out for a pleasant sail.

Oh, Darvin is finally out of the hospital. Someone who wishes to remain anonymous, but I am pretty sure has the initials AA (ahem), has paid for him to have the experimental bionic and stem cell therapy at the University of Haida. Darvin writes that he has now taken six steps on his own and can feel his little toe. Pretty impressive for someone who broke their back in two places.

I'm sure I'd love to tell AA thanks, if only I knew who it was. ;)

I have saved the best for last. Yesterday, three refugees from Formosa landed in Bosch—a mother, her daughter, and her grandmother. Can you possibly guess who they are? I told you Mama would fix it. She always does. Now, if you want to know more, you have to write me back, and I really think you should consider spending your winter holiday here if you can get the time off work. Otherwise, we might have to come to Truvale and invade the Noĕlani II, which I am sure does not have room for all of us.

Write soon and comm sooner,
Miss you,
xo
Cap'n Grey

"Grey, there's a big package down here for you," my brother, Kik, calls up the stairs.

I pull Jerome the Wanderer, my little black ball of fur, off my chest where he has settled, purring, as I read and tuck him next to Rum, who is not a puppy but a grown-up dog with red-brown fur who believes that her place is next to me at all times, especially in my bed. She lifts her head and eyes the kitten, but then relaxes. "I'll be right back, Rummy." I scratch her between her ears, then slide out the bed and head downstairs.

Kik and Mac are holding a rectangular package, maybe a meter by a half-meter. "Open it!" Mac says with excitement. Mama and Matt sit at the table, trying to get Rini to finish her dinner. It's her new thing—she wants dinner to last for over an hour.

"What do you think it is?" Mama asks, peering over.

I look at the return address and give a squeal. "It's a drawing! From Ash!"

"How nice," Mama says, but I know she doesn't mean it. She didn't spend much time at all trying to get to know Ash once we were back in Moku-o-keawe. But that's her issue. He's my friend.

I tear the brown paper off and unwrap the padding. "Oh," I sigh. In a simple frame is a pencil sketch of two people, a man and a girl, on a sailboat named *Noēlani*. The sail is in broad reach and full, and the sea is calm, with the hint of land in the distance. The drawing is titled *Unfurling the Sails*.

A note floats out of the wrap, and I bend to pick it up.

Grey,
This is the third of three sketches I have done from this
past summer but the first I felt was actually complete.
Ms. Odutola said I could try to sell it at the gallery, but I
told her it was spoken for.
I will bring the others when I visit during the winter
holiday. I certainly would love to have a chance to write
to Bosch's newest refugees before that time, so please,
forward me their address. (Now!)
Since you have all kinds of other relatives—dozens of
siblings and hundreds of aunts and uncles—you must
make it clear that on my salary, they will all have to
make do with any sketches I can create while I am there.
Thank you for teaching me that a boat will only move if
a sailor is willing to brave the wind and the sea. You
taught me what it means to be courageous in the face of
pain and fear.
Your friend and demigod,
Ash
P.S. What do you think of my new name? No more
Abernathy for me!

I finish reading the note and look back at the drawing. In the
lower right-hand corner the artist has signed his name in
black: Ash Grey.

Acknowledgments

I want to express my love and appreciation for all the readers of the *Pirates of New Earth* series who asked for a young adult book that they could share with their kids. I had always had Grey's story in my head as she grew in *Pirates* and I am delighted to present what I hope is the first of many Grey Shima adventures.

Thank you to Brittany, Judi, Iris, Melissa, Kate, Carey, Laura, Bea, Lia, Junie, Anna, Ramona, and Jude for being early readers and giving helpful guidance and feedback to make Grey's first adventure strong and relatable.

As always, thank you to the amazing Martha Bullen of Bullen Publishing Services for her support, guidance, friendship and for showing me Chanticleer Garden.

Thank you to my patient editors, Andrea Vanryken and David Aretha for keeping an eye on my em dashes and my tendency to go on at times.

Many thanks to the brilliant Ian Koviak and Alan Hebel of The Book Designers for listening closely and creating yet another knock-it-out-of-the-park cover.

I am awed and overflowing with appreciation for Joe Harrington's talent, ability to listen and willingness to "do just one more tweak" on the map of the Drowned Islands and the interior illustrations in *Unfurling*. His work is amazing which is why I have the Bosch Pirate Force logo he brought to life tattooed on my right shoulder

I send buckets of love and appreciation to my children and

their partners who are truly bonus kids for me, for their unwavering support and love.

Love to my grandsons, who now have a book their Monster wrote that they are allowed to read!

And, as always, all my love and gratitude to Rick, for always being in my corner, even when I'm not even in it. You are the best.

Sarah Branson, an award-winning author and experienced midwife, weaves thrilling tales of action and adventure with airborne pirates amidst a world transformed by fires, floods, and pandemics.

Sarah first started conjuring stories of pirates when her family hopped a freighter to Australia when she was seven. She has since grown up, traveling the globe, raising a family, and teaching science and history to middle school and high school students in the U.S., Brazil, and Japan. Her diverse life journey inspires her storytelling.

A Merry Life, her debut novel, received prestigious honors. It is the first book of her *Pirates of New Earth* series that has captivated readers. *Unfurling the Sails* is her first novel written for teen readers.

Sarah and her husband call Connecticut home. She firmly believes the strength and resiliency of the human spirit combined with the power of badass women will create a better world for all.

For more information and updates:

www.sarahbranson.com